# A YARN-OVER MURDER

# A YARN-OVER MURDER

## THE BAIT & STITCH COZY MYSTERY SERIES, BOOK 2

ANN YOST

Book and cover design by eBook Prep
www.ebookprep.com

July, 2020
ISBN: 978-1-64457-150-7

*ePublishing Works!*
644 Shrewsbury Commons Ave
Ste 249
Shrewsbury PA 17361
United States of America

www.epublishingworks.com
Phone: 866-846-5123

*For the Yosties: Adam, Cathy, Julian and Elliott*

# ONE

I t's easy to say I had a bad feeling about Liisa Pelonen from the first
time I saw her. I mean, hindsight is twenty-twenty, right?

The thing is I clearly remember telling my sister that someone that
lovely would stir up trouble.

"Don't be a drama queen, Hatti," Sofi had said. "Liisa's just a teen-
aged girl. No more, no less."

Which is about as ridiculous a thing as you can say, since teen-aged
girls are always more and never less.

Liisa came to Red Jacket to finish her final year of high school after
her home school closed. It was too far to commute from her father's
cabin near Ahmeek and Arvo Maki, our town's funeral director, de facto
mayor and all-around Grand Pooh-Bah invited her to stay at the
mortuary with himself and his wife, Pauline. It was a grand gesture and
widely approved, at least at the beginning.

Things go complicated when Arvo got a bee in his bonnet, as Pops
would say and he unilaterally named Liisa Pelonen to the coveted title
of St. Lucy for this year's festival and pageant. It was like heaving a
boulder into a still pond. The unfortunate decision ripped the fabric of
our tradition and infuriated the mother of the current St. Lucy hopeful,

which is something you can only appreciate if you know what the role means to the community.

Think Texas cheerleader. Think prom queen. Think Miss America.

St. Lucy is the gold standard in Red Jacket. Most of the girls enjoy dressing in the white robe tied with a blood-red sash and wearing an evergreen crown of candles on their heads. The real conflict is between the mothers, all of whom believe a stint as the thirteenth-century martyr is a status enhancer guaranteeing their offspring a successful and prosperous life, mainly because it will make them more likely to marry a high school grad, i.e. someone who is employable.

There was no guarantee that Astrid Laplander, a younger version of her short, squat, dark-haired mother, Ronja, up to and including a faint mustache, would get the part but it was likely. There's a pecking order and she was next in line when Liisa Pelonen turned up looking like every picture or poster of the Swedish St. Lucy and Arvo simply could not resist giving her the part.

I consider December sixth, a week before St. Lucy Day, as the moment the trouble that had been rumbling under the surface, came to full throttle. The sky darkened, the animals howled and the waters of Lake Superior churned. And now, seven days later, Liisa Pelonen was dead.

As I stared at the lithe body now curled into a fetal position on the wooden floor of the Maki's sauna, a phrase from an Agatha Christie novel came to me.

`Life is hard for a woman. Men will not be nice to you if you are not good looking, and women will not be nice to you if you are.`

I saw Liisa for the first time last summer at Perk Up, a student-run coffee shop across from my own shop, Bait and Stitch, on Main Street. I'd entered the shop with Arvo and another middle-aged man, and all three of us froze as the slender girl in the green polo shirt and khaki shorts looked up with a smile.

She was just that beautiful. Her thick, silver-blond hair was caught in a loose braid and her widely spaced, long-lashed eyes were the color of the sky reflected in Lake in the Clouds, up in the Porcupine Mountains.

Her lips were generous and her teeth white but I could not put my finger on how her smile seemed to have the full force of the summer sun behind it.

There was, I remembered thinking, some kind of alchemical magic to make a blond-blue-eyed girl stand out like that in a community where you can't swing a dead cat without hitting someone of Nordic or Scandinavian descent.

The magic, I later learned, did not affect everyone to the same extent, but Arvo was truly, madly, deeply under the spell.

It came to me that I wasn't surprised that such a girl was loved too much or that she'd been murdered.

The term slashed through my thoughts. *Murdered?* We do not run to violent crime here on the Keweenaw, a witch's finger of land that crooks into frigid Lake Superior. For one thing, we don't have the weather for it. With more than two hundred inches of snowfall each year, it's hard to make a quick getaway.

And then there's a diminishing population. We have more elk than moose and more moose than people. We can't afford to kill any of them —people, I mean, not moose—off.

Mostly, though, we are all Evangelical Lutherans which means we've been fed Luther's Small Catechism almost since birth and we are all experts in the Ten Commandments.

Liisa's death had to have been an accident.

A harsh sob brought me back to the moment and I glanced at Arvo who was sitting on the lower *lavat* or bench of the sauna, his broad back bent, his face in his big hands. My gaze lifted to meet Pauline's eye. She stood next to him, tall, spare and strong, her narrow face pale, her lips twisted in anguish and her hand resting on his back. It was a perfect snapshot of their twenty-five year marriage.

My heart went out to them both.

"How? Why?" Arvo's sobs finally turned into words.

Pauline shook her head even though he couldn't see her.

"She must have tripped over something and hit her head."

It was a plausible explanation since there was an ugly glob of congealed blood near one fair temple. I forced myself to draw nearer to the body and peer at the wound. It looked deep, too deep for a collision with a wooden floor.

Pauline Maki seemed to read my mind.

"Maybe she hit a sauna stone when she fell," she suggested. I scanned the area but could see no stone or any object that could have caused the wound. There was nothing in the sauna but a dry wooden bucket with a matching scoop, the electric sauna stove with a grill over the top of the stones and a fresh *vihta* or birch stick hanging on a hook on the wall.

Arvo shook his head but didn't look up.

"There is no stone. No weapon. Someone hit her."

"She may have slipped on the floor," Pauline said, in a calm, soothing voice.

But there was no indication that the floor had been wet. And Liisa was fully clothed in a pink parka over a rhinestone-studded sweatshirt, a pair of jeans and fur-lined snow boots, which meant she had not been in the midst of taking a sauna when she died.

"Maybe she had a heart condition," I said, recalling an event that had happened to someone else out at the Painted Rock Lighthouse last summer. "If her heartbeat tended to be irregular, she could have suffered from syncope."

Two sets of eyes looked up at me. Both were filled with tears.

"She did," Pauline said. "She told me when she first got here. She has a history of fainting due to syncope. That's when the heartbeat gets erratic and too far apart, blood pressure drops and the person faints."

"Oh, yes," Arvo said. "Now I remember about that. You asked me to find out whether there was any way to prevent the fainting and I talked to someone down at the hospital. But there wasn't. Ah, Pauly. You were such a good, caring mother."

Tears sprouted in Pauline's eyes.

"If only we could have kept her safe."

"We should have done so," Arvo said, pulling himself together and sitting up. "We were her in loco parentis, you know. Her *aiti* (mother) and her *isa* (father)."

I thought that was going too far but going too far characterized everything about Arvo's relationship with the visitor. Suddenly he groaned.

"She was only seventeen."

"Eighteen." Pauline corrected him. "Today was her birthday."

For some reason, that revelation hit me hard. Liisa Pelonen had, presumably, awoken today ready to celebrate the start of adulthood only to find death.

"I'll call 911," I said.

"*Voi kauhia!*" Arvo jumped to his feet to utter the strongest curse in the Finnish-American handbook. "Over my dead body! We are not going to turn our girl over to that cretin, that butcher. Clump will throw her into the vault and go down to the diner for *pannukakku*. (The vault is a square brick structure that houses the bodies of those who die when the ground is too frozen for burial and pannukakku is an oven pancake, very popular in Michigan's Upper Peninsula, particularly when served with butter and lingonberry syrup.)

Arvo finally got to his feet and announced a decision.

"No Clump. Liisa will stay here with us, Pauly and me. Meanwhile you, Henrikki (my real name) will investigate to find out what happened here."

"Me?" The word emerged as a squeak.

"Who else? You have done it before."

That was an exaggeration based on the fact that I fell backwards into a murder investigation last summer only because I was on the premises.

"Besides," Pauline put in, supporting her husband, as always, "you went to law school."

"One year," I reminded her. "We only got as far as torts."

"But you were married to a lawyer," Arvo reminded me, as if I'd absorbed his knowledge through some kind of married osmosis. "And, don't forget. You are our police chief."

"Temporary," I said. "Acting. I just agreed to help out while Pops is up at the Mayo."

"Exactly," Arvo said.

I glared at him. "You told me I'd have to do nothing worse than pry quarters out of the frozen parking meters on Main Street."

He looked at me then and I was humbled by the expression of guilt and loss in his blue eyes.

"I would give anything for this not to have happened, Henrikki. Anything."

Guilt sluiced through me. The Makis, best friends of my folks and our next door neighbors all my life, had been gobsmacked by tragedy. They needed my help. And I couldn't blame them for not turning to Sheriff Clump, with his reputation for tightfistedness and laziness and his well-known animosity to Arvo and Pops, who is Red Jacket's sole police officer.

"Of course, I'll look into it," I muttered.

Arvo stepped closer so he could hug me.

"Tomorrow, *tytto*," he said. "Go home now and get some sleep."

---

I closed my eyes and caught a picture of Liisa as she had looked that afternoon in the parade. She'd stood on the back of Ollie Rahkunen's rickety sleigh behind Claude, his gaseous reindeer, and held her candle high while all the children of the village, wearing cone-shaped hats, waved star-topped wands as they danced alongside.

I remembered thinking she looked cold.

I hadn't realized I'd spoken aloud until Arvo spoke.

"She was cold, isn't that right, Pauline? She was late for the parade and did not have time to put on the longjohns."

Of course. I'd been St. Lucy once in my not-very misspent youth and now I remembered the tradition of wearing long underwear underneath the white robe.

"Why was she late?"

The color had still not returned to Pauline's face. She shrugged her lean shoulders and held her hands out to the sides.

"Liisa told me she had gone down to the Frostbite Mall to buy a dress for the Snowball Dance last night," she said. "She went with a friend who had car trouble on the way back and they got here just before the parade began."

"She should have worn her parka," Arvo said. It was as close to a criticism of Pauline as I'd ever heard and I knew she took it that way because of her quick intake of breath.

"I know. I thought it would ruin the line of the costume." She sniffed and Arvo patted her arm, awkwardly, as if he knew there was no point now in crying over spilled milk.

"After the parade, when we got home, she had a sore throat," Pauline said, in a wobbly voice. "I bundled her into the shower, then fed her some sweet tea and toast and rubbed Vicks on her chest and sent her to bed."

I almost smiled at that. There is a jar of Vicks Vaporub in every medicine cabinet in Red Jacket. It, along with the sauna and hot coffee, is believed to cure pretty much any ailment.

"I should have stayed home from the smorgasbord," Pauline said, berating herself. "But I had promised Elli I would bring a cranberry Jello mold and, well, a promise is a promise."

My cousin Elli owns and runs the Leaping Deer, a renovated bed and breakfast on the other side of my parents' house. Out-of-town guests always stay at Elli's and she provides a breakfast and supper smorgasbord for them and for most of the rest of us.

"When did you leave the house," I asked, somehow feeling the timing was important.

"Six fifteen. I came back a while later to get a few jars of cloudberry jam for the visitors from Lansing. I checked on her then and she was fast asleep."

"When was that?"

"Oh, I didn't look at my watch. Possibly six-forty five or so."

"So that was the last time either of you saw her until you came home around nine-fifteen," I said. They nodded and Arvo closed his eyes.

"She wasn't in her bed. We looked all through the house, even in the embalming room. That sauna was the last place. I still don't know why she was here."

Or why she was killed, I thought, but didn't say.

It's time I introduced myself.

My name is Henrikki Hiltunen Lehtinen Night Wind, but as two of those names belong to men who are no longer in my life, I just go by Hatti Lehtinen.

I'm about five feet, six or seven inches tall, with wheat-colored hair and blue eyes and a smattering of freckles across my nose. No one would call me fat. No one would call me thin, either. I guess I'm somewhere in between.

I grew up with my sister Sofi, who is six years older than I, several inches shorter and considerably more curvaceous and my cousin Elli, who is six months younger than I, and an elf. Our coloring is so similar that our friend Sonya Stillwater, a Navajo midwife, claims we resemble a set of Finnish nesting dolls, a description that was more accurate before I chopped off my waist-length hair and allowed my tresses to fall in short layers like the petals of a wilting chrysanthemum.

Our Northern Michigan town is small, insular and composed mostly of descendants of Finnish miners. Sofi married early but Elli and I spent summer evenings catching lightning bugs on the lawn and snow-bound winter afternoons in my parents' attic pretending to be castaways or princesses or Anne Frank.

In short, it was idyllic.

But the Keweenaw Peninsula, even more than the rest of the UP is dying. There are snowmobile paths where there used to be railroad tracks and silent, solitary mineshafts where there used to be industry and ghost towns where there used to be miners and merchants and their families. There are few jobs. The only thing we have in abundance are fields that were once full of leafy trees and are now littered with poor rock.

Some of us are content to stay and make a life surrounded by older generations and the peers we've known since we were little Lutherans. I wanted to see what else (and who else) there was in the world so I enrolled in a law school downstate. My mother refers to this as the time I ran away.

It went fairly well for a few months but in the spring, lightning struck when I fell violently in love, dropped out of school, married and moved to Washington, D.C. Six months later I was back in Red Jacket sleeping in my childhood bed with the glow-in-the-dark stars plastered on the ceiling and much the worse for wear.

But that was a year ago. Nowadays I run Bait and Stitch, a hybrid fishing-slash-knitting supply shop on Main Street and, like everyone else in our little town, I wear more than one hat. At the moment, I'm standing in for Pops, my stepdad, Carl Lehtinen, who was injured in a snowmobile hit-and-run collision in November, which is why Arvo wants me to investigate Liisa Pelonen's death.

"One other thing, Hatti," Pauline said. "I think we should agree not to tell anyone about this until the end of the weekend. All of us, including Liisa, worked hard on the festival. She wouldn't want to see it spoiled." She turned to her husband. "Do you agree, dear?"

He shook his leonine head with its mat of tight, blond curls.

"Our girl would not want the festival spoiled."

I braced myself as the thought brought tears to his eyes but suddenly they flew open.

"*Voi!* The pageant! Who will be St. Lucy?"

I caught a quick glimpse of Ronja Laplander's face when she got the call telling her the dream for Astrid had come true.

"I don't think," I said, "that will be a problem."

Half an hour later I'd slogged through the foot of snow that covered the lawns of the funeral home and my family's Queen Anne, changed clothes and dropped into bed.

"What a day," I complained to my companion. "What a conundrum! There appears to be no reason for anyone to have killed Liisa Pelonen and no way in which it could be done and yet the girl's dead. Geez Louise. The last thing we need on the Keweenaw is another murder."

Larry, an excellent listener, even for a basset hound, said nothing. He just draped himself over my stomach and allowed me to rub the soft skin behind his droopy ears.

It's an effective form of meditation and, in fact, beats out soft music, sleeping pills, and even warm milk.

# TWO

A cheery voice jerked me awake the next morning.

Betty Ann Pritula, the Keweenaw's answer to Martha Stewart, is the host of *The Finnish Line,* or as Pops likes to call it, *The Finnish-Me-Off Line.* The indefatigable woman comes across our airwaves at six o'clock every morning (including Sunday) with all the news that's fit (or unfit) to print, including births, deaths, potlucks, PTA meetings, traffic changes, weather, recipes and what she calls editorial opinion but which is, in reality, gossip.

A Keweenaw booster of the first water, Betty Ann's style is folksy, conversational, and friendly, but the bottom line is that she simply loves to tell people what to do.

"Roll up your sleeves," she commanded today, "and roll out your dough! We are going to make old-fashioned gingerbread houses and, never fear, I will guide you through every step!"

I pulled on a pair of bright red corduroy jeans and a light green sweatshirt emblazoned with the words, LONDON, PARIS, NEW YORK, ISHPEMING, while Betty Ann touted her own recipe for royal icing.

"This stuff sticks so good that if they'd used it at the battle of Jericho, those walls would not have come tumbling down," she bragged.

"I've found just the right combination of egg whites, lemon juice, almond flavoring, and meringue powder. You can't go wrong with my patented icing. Good gracious me, it's as reliable as Vicks."

*Vicks.* I froze, my fingers locked around the handle of my hairbrush. I'd been so focused on the irritating chirp of Betty Ann's voice that I'd almost forgotten about the corpse in the sauna and the fact that I'd been assigned to investigate Liisa Pelonen's untimely death.

"And be sure you stop by the first annual Finnish Christmas Pageant in Red Jacket today," Betty Ann continued. "It is called *Pikkujoulu*, or 'Little Christmas.' For those of you not in the know, 'Little Christmas' refers to the parties we hold in our homes during the early weeks of December. Finnish arts and crafts will be sold, as well as refreshments from Main Street Floral and Fudge and Patty's Pasties. Join us under the brand new tarp in the Copper County High School parking lot on the corner of Main and Church Streets. At two o'clock the action will move to St. Heikki's Finnish Lutheran Church—that's the one that looks like Quasimodo's summer home—up on Walnut Street where the young people of Red Jacket will perform a pageant in honor of St. Lucy, the martyr who chose blindness and death over marriage."

The cheeriness in her voice did not waver as she mentioned the tragic, if apocryphal, death of St. Lucy and it occurred to me that she was the female counterpart to Arvo. I knew they were fast friends.

"This year's St. Lucy is the lovely Liisa Pelonen, from Ahmeek," Betty Ann informed her listeners. "Liisa has a wonderful singing voice and intends to pursue a career in music."

Well. For once Arvo had not contacted his press agent. I wondered, with a pang, if he'd stayed up all night with Liisa's body.

I felt a little sick as I snapped off the radio and pattered down to the kitchen, fed Larry and let him out then started the coffee. Just as I poured my first cup, my cell phone rang. Well, rang is probably the wrong term. It chimed out the first bars of Meatloaf's *Bat Out of Hell.* It was half-past six and the sound jangled my nerves. I checked the caller I.D.

"Hey, Sofi," I said, unable to keep the accusatory note out of my voice. "What's up?"

"You. And me. It's the day of Arvo's stupid festival, remember? So

I'm at the shop mixing up a fresh batch of eggnog fudge. And don't make a face. People from out-of-town like something seasonal."

"Why can't you just do chocolate walnut and top it with sugar decorations, like holly and candy canes?"

"Is that really what you want to talk about at this hour?"

I didn't really want to be awake at this hour and I certainly didn't want to face the day ahead.

"What do you need?"

"You to come down here and help me shlep the fudge over to the festival. It's sure to be snowing and I want you to drop me at the door. About ten o'clock?"

"Sure," I said. "I need to stop at the B and B and then at the shop to check on Einar, anyway. But why are you calling me this early?"

"Because," she said, "there's something suspicious going on and I want to know what it is."

I sucked in a quick breath. Was it possible our oh-so-efficient grapevine had already broadcast the news of Liisa's death?

"What, uh, are you talking about? And why would I know anything about it?"

"Oh, little sister. Don't ever try to play poker. Your voice alone is a dead giveaway. I want to know why Astrid Laplander is substituting for Liisa Pelonen in the pageant this afternoon."

I stalled to give myself time to think.

"Where did you hear that?"

"Horse's mouth. Ronja, herself."

It was a pun and a cruel one. We had once upon a time observed that Ronja Laplander, for all her short stature, had a face like a horse. Unfortunately, we'd done it in front of our mother who promptly washed our mouths out with soap.

"C'mon, Hatti. You're the worst liar I know."

"I don't lie," I said, indignantly.

"You don't lie well, I'll say that. You can't even really prevaricate. I can always tell when you know something and don't want to give it up. Hell's bells, everybody can tell. What gives?"

"You're talking so fast," I said. "How much coffee have you had this morning?"

"I had to be up at three a.m. Does that answer your question? Now answer mine."

"What did, uh, Ronja say?"

"She was waiting outside the shop when I got here at four. She wants me to make a fresh evergreen wreath for Astrid in time for the pageant. She said Liisa's still sick with a sore throat and fever. But I know how much Arvo wants his guest to play St. Lucy and doubt whether he'd agree to the switch unless Liisa was dead."

The comment hit me hard and, for an instant, I didn't speak at all.

"I know you called Ronja last night about the St. Lucy thing," Sofi said, but her voice had gentled a little. "There's something wrong, isn't there? I mean, more than a sore throat."

I made a decision.

"I'll tell you what I know," I said, "but not now. Not on the phone. Later, after we get to the festival."

"Okay," Sofi said, but it seemed she wasn't ready to throw in the towel.

"There's something really wrong with Liisa, isn't there? What is it? Did Ronja break into the funeral home last night and break her legs?"

"No," I said, shocked at how close she was to the truth. "I'll pick you up at ten."

I disconnected the phone, poured a cup of coffee, and pondered. Sofi had unintentionally sparked an idea in my mind.

The day before the parade Pauline Maki had been shopping in Bait and Stitch. She'd just bought a skein of pearly pink washable wool to make a hat and mittens for Liisa and she'd started to tell me about her "brainstorm" for a project for our knitting circle, the Keweenawesome Knitters.

"Brace yourself," she'd said, with one of her pleasant smiles, "I'm thinking heirloom lace."

Heirloom lace is arguably the most sophisticated, complicated type of knitting there is, in part, because of the complex charts that have to be read and stitches that have to be counted and in part because delicate lace weight yarn, which is easily split, is not easy to work with.

"Contrary to popular thought," Pauline said, "lace is not just yarn-overs and knit two together. It is beautiful and mysterious and we are all going to learn its secrets while making our own Shetland Wedding Ring shawl. I've already ordered skeins of a very fine yarn spun from the chin hair of the musk ox on the Shetland Islands. The shawls we knit will be so delicate that each will be able to fit through the center of a wedding ring."

"Wedding ring?" the door had crashed open so hard the little bell I'd attached flew off its hinges and caromed across the wooden floor. "You are planning her wedding already? Who is she marrying? Someone else's boyfriend, then?"

The angry words had exploded from Ronja Laplander, owner, with her husband of the Copper Kettle, a souvenir gift shop. She steamed across the floor toward us, the heavy unibrow under her dark, Dutch-boy hairstyle contorted like a spastic caterpillar and her small fists dug into her wide hips. Ronja's default mood, unless she was speaking of her wares or her five daughters, was grumpy. For the past week, though, she'd behaved like a category four hurricane, spewing angry words like flotsam and jetsam at everything in her path. At the moment, she reminded me of a bottom-heavy Great Lakes barge steaming through the Soo Locks that connect the waters of Lake Superior with those of Lake Huron.

"I beg your pardon," Pauline had said, peering down at the other woman. She sounded bewildered, and no wonder. People in town did not speak like that to Pauline Maki but Ronja was beyond considering anything except her own sense of ill-use.

"Your husband is not a king. He is not a dictator. He is just a citizen, like everybody else and yet he took it upon himself to ruin our tradition. He should be arrested. Boiled in oil. He should be beheaded!"

I noticed Einar watching, out of the corner of my eye. His placid expression had turned grim, as if he expected Ronja to carry out her suggestions.

"I don't understand," Pauline said and I thought that was probably true. Although she had lived among us for twenty-five years and although, in carrying out Arvo's schemes, she probably did more good for the community than anyone else, I had always had the sense that she did not understand us. I felt a flicker of compassion for the woman.

Whether or not Arvo was king was debatable. But Pauline was, for all intents and purposes, the power behind the throne.

"This was Astrid's year to be St. Lucy."

Understanding registered in Pauline's fine brown eyes.

"Ah. Arvo gave the role to Liisa and that has upset you. I'm sorry for it. I know my husband can be a bit, well, high-handed."

I spotted a slight easing of the deep lines bracketing Ronja's mouth and knew that Pauline Maki had found the best thing to say. And then disaster struck.

"What if your daughter—Astrid, is it?—What if she is St. Lucy next year?"

I groaned, inwardly, as Ronja drew herself up to her full five-feet of height and blasted deadly words into the taller woman's face.

"Next year is for Valentina! And then Stella, then Olga, then Vesta. You understand nothing about St. Lucy. Nothing! But then, you do not have a daughter!"

The natural color drained out of Pauline's face leaving two bright spots of blush on her cheeks. For a moment, I thought she would faint. But she pulled herself together (Pauline always pulled herself together) and, at the same time, I grabbed Ronja's thick forearm and steered her toward my backroom.

"Let me get you a cup of coffee," I said, attempting to drown out her protests. I managed to keep her out of sight until Pauline, forgetting all about her newly purchased pink yarn, was gone.

"That wasn't fair, you know," I said to Ronja. "That St. Lucy pick was Arvo's fault. He's besotted with the girl."

Ronja had calmed down, somewhat, and she nodded.

"I know, Hatti. But I just wanted it for Astrid. I wanted it so much. And, anyway, it was wrong. If we don't have tradition, what do we have?"

As the incident came back to me I couldn't help wondering if the cosmos had been distressed by Arvo's altering of tradition and whether that had had anything to do with Liisa's death.

Nonsense, I told myself. But I, like other Finnish Americans, believe there are unseen forces at work and that there is a clear theme to our earthly life that can be summed up in our proverbs:

Do unto others as you would have them do unto you.
As ye sew, so shall ye reap.
Every stick has two ends.
What goes around comes around.

Was that what had happened to Liisa? Had she been felled by Karma? I shook my head. Only, I thought, if Karma had taken the form of a human being. Somebody had caused that gash on the girl's head.

Somebody had killed her.

# THREE

Most of the houses on the Keweenaw are typical of the UP, more than seventy-five years old, wooden, two-story affairs with steeply pitched rooflines to allow gravity to aid in snow removal and ground-floor windows set high off the ground to prevent drifts from blocking the light.

Calumet Street is a little different.

For one thing, it is the highest point in town and, from our second-floor windows and balconies, we have a great view of the town. No doubt it was the setting that prompted early copper barons to choose the street for building their homes. Most of the homes boast unattached garages that face onto an alley running behind the street which has allowed the front yards to blend together with no unsightly driveways.

Three houses in from the intersection of Tamarack and facing south is the Maki Funeral Home. Next to it is a Queen Anne Victorian, painted yellow with white gingerbread trim and a fish-scale covered witch's hat tower. My family has lived there for the past quarter of a century.

To our west is a large, rambling structure that was once a family home then became a rooming house, then a motor inn and finally, my aunt and uncle ran it as a kind of residential hotel. Several years ago they decided to retire to Lake Worth, Florida, one of the few Finnish-American communities located in the sunbelt and widely considered the third point in the Finnish golden triangle that also includes the Keweenaw and Helsinki.

Aunt and Uncle Risto bequeathed the shabby barn of a building to my cousin Elli, a tiny individual who looks like a fairy but who has the energy and drive of Hercules. Finnish Americans speak with respect about the quality of *Sisu* which is a combination of perseverance, determination, and endurance. *Sisu* is Elli's middle name. She spent three years arranging loans, hiring contractors to renovate the kitchen and bathrooms, doing carpentry work herself as well as scrubbing and polishing the scarred walnut of the grand staircase. She scoured the countryside for antiques and light fixtures, for carpets and stained glass panels similar to those used in the hotel's heyday, 1910. She even managed to find facsimiles of flowered draperies and awnings and her piece-de-resistance—the elephant hide wallpaper in the dining room.

Elli's renovated bed and breakfast gets five stars in the Michelin Guide, or it would if it were listed there, and is probably the best known hotel in the UP.

I was gone most of the time, out on my ill-fated adventure but in contact with Elli and I approved everything she did except for the name.

"The Leaping Deer? I don't know, El. I'm afraid it'll remind people of roadkill."

"Nonsense," she'd laughed. "Most of the folks will come in the summer and they'll be so preoccupied with blackflies, they won't even think about deer on the highway."

That was vintage Elli. Smart, funny and intent on her mission.

The bed and breakfast had become a gathering point in the community, as Elli could be counted on to provide plenty of food for breakfast, brunches and supper smorgasbords, and she never turned anyone away. When we held an event, like the St. Lucy Festival, others in the community contributed their specialties, including hotdishes, Jell-O molds, egg coffee and bars along with several Finnish specialties. Those volunteers who had been the engine of the church since its inception, had, for decades been referred to as Lutheran Church Basement Women. Nowadays they were called the Ladies Aid, and they wielded enormous power, none more so than their president, Mrs. Edna Moilanen.

I found Mrs. Moilanen, along with the pastor's wife, Sirpa Sorensen, laying out the food on Elli's long table. I spotted my favorite, a fresh oven pancake *pannukakku*, next to a jug of lingonberry syrup and a plate of sausages as well as freshly baked bread *pulla*, and fish cakes, a tray of squeaky cheese, herring salad, blueberry strata, made with the berries Mrs. Sorensen had frozen last summer and Edna's party dish, vinegar cabbage. The scent of coffee hovered above the rest and served to blend the other strong scents together. I heard the blue-ribbon committee guests from Lansing making appreciative sounds as they descended the walnut staircase and I didn't blame them. For once, though, I wasn't hungry.

"So, Henrikki," Mrs. Moilanen said, looking up at me over her granny glasses, "heirloom lace, hmm?"

I smiled at the short, stout woman with blue-rinsed curls and a habit of sewing fussy collars on her sweatshirts. It occurred to me that if Mrs. M. did not want to venture into heirloom lace, we might get out of it. With the exception of Arvo, the lady had more clout than anyone in town, including the mild-mannered Reverend Sorensen.

It's impossible to exaggerate the extent of Mrs. Moilanen's influence. It was due, not to the fact that she was the widow of a longtime assemblyman who was also a church deacon, but to her position as president of the Ladies Aid. No one seemed to remember how she had acquired the title, only that it was for life, like the Supreme Court, and it gave her decision-making power in choosing who would work set up and clean up for church potlucks, funeral suppers and so forth. She chose who would dust the piano, who would fold up the best (funeral) tablecloths, who would arrange flowers and who would get to wear the fancy, organdy half-aprons as opposed to the flour-sack coverings.

Mrs. M. was a tartar but, as my mother said, she was conscientious and held to high standards and the pick could have been worse.

"She means well," my mother said, "and she is efficient. Also, Henrikki, Edna is the kind of person who can be counted on to bring at least two dishes to every smorgasbord. And not just a Jell-O mold. Two hot dishes."

"Do you have a problem with the wedding ring shawl project," I asked, hopefully.

Mrs. Moilanen straightened her spine which resulted in a lift of several inches to her massive bosom.

"I feel it is my responsibility to make certain we are not embarking on it for the wrong reason."

I gazed at her, not understanding. "Wrong reason?"

Mrs. Moilanen sighed as if she despaired of my little gray cells.

"Pauline Maki is pushing this, then?"

"It's her idea. Yes."

"For the guest, Liisa Pelonen?"

"I believe she said she'd like to make a shawl for Liisa." A spasm of regret hit me as I remembered why Liisa would never get to use the wedding ring shawl and I missed Mrs. Moilanen's next words. "I'm sorry. What did you say?"

"Ah, Henrikki," she said, not critically but with a certain air of disappointment. "You are always gathering wool. Can you not put together the dots? If Liisa Pelonen is about to be married it can be for only one reason."

I finally got it. Mrs. M. was suggesting that Liisa was pregnant and facing a shotgun wedding. Nothing, I thought, could be further from the truth.

"There has been some hanky panky going on," Mrs. M. continued. "And, no wonder, then. That girl is too pretty for her own good."

The guests were filtering into the dining room and I knew it was time to cut off the topic of conversation.

"Nonsense," I said, trying to maintain respect in my denial. She was, after all, the Ladies Aid Czar. "I plan to make a shawl for Charlie for her hope chest. (FYI: Charlie would die to hear me use an old-fashioned term like that on top of which she was a raging feminist and had no intention of ever getting married.) Anyway, I doubt whether any of us will finish up the shawls. They are very difficult to knit, you know."

Mrs. Moilanen's faded blue eyes narrowed on me and I remembered, too late, that she prided herself on her competence in all domestic matters.

"You may not finish your shawl, Henrikki," she said, "but I will finish mine." She turned to one of the men from Lansing and gave him a bright, welcoming smile. "Good morning! Did you sleep well? Won't you try our eye-opener?" She pointed to the dish in front of her. "It's my very own vinegar cabbage."

I was so busy admiring the way she shifted gears on a dime, as Pops would say, that I didn't get out of earshot quickly enough and after the guest had moved on, Mrs. Moilanen lobbed a parting shot.

"You should be making a wedding ring shawl for yourself, girl. You are not a spring chicken any longer, then."

Technically, I am still married, but, all things considered, I decided not to point it out.

"Yes, ma'am," I said, meekly.

"By the way," Mrs. Moilanen added, "whatever is wrong with that Liisa Pelonen, anyway? I understand Astrid Laplander is to take her place. She sings like a frog, you know."

# FOUR

I managed to make my escape from the smorgasbord a short time later. Still, I couldn't stop thinking about what the Ladies Aid president had said about Liisa Pelonen.

"She's too pretty for her own good."

Was her exceptional beauty behind her death? If so, how? Was she killed out of jealousy? Did that mean I had to seriously consider Astrid and Ronja Laplander or Barb and Diane Hakala as suspects? Just thinking about the possibility started a surge of panic that had me gasping for breath. No. Never. If Liisa's death was, in fact, a homicide, the perp had to be an outsider.

Normally I like to take my time and enjoy the pristine look of my town after a snowfall.

Unlike other UP towns that resemble old-west outposts, Red Jacket has a historic downtown with several blocks of two-story buildings that include cupolas and pillars and little balconies on the second floor. Our library was a former union hall and it is large and spacious and built with rose-colored stone from the Jacobsville quarry. We have a gold-domed opera house, too. Most of all, we have a cathedral. The building that houses St. Heikki's Finnish Lutheran Church is tall and medieval-looking with flying buttresses and gargoyles. Sofi refers to it as Quasimodo's winter home. If this architecture looks out of place in the otherwise very rural Keweenaw Peninsula it is because it was built at a time the town's coffers were overflowing with the profits from mining and selling ninety-five percent of the world's pure copper.

When the copper gave out, so did the gravy train, and what we have left is a group of buildings that look a lot better with a cover of snow than without it.

But, like I said, I wasn't thinking about the weather. I found myself wishing I had someone to talk to about Liisa Pelonen. The idea of calling Jace and asking for his help flitted into my mind just long enough to practically give me a seizure. I was still breathing heavily when my cell phone sounded.

"Hey, Hatti," Sonya Stillwater said. "Did I wake you?"

That drew a choked laugh.

"No. I can safely say I've been up for eons, am fully caffeinated and parked in front of Bait and Stitch. Geez Louise I'm glad to talk to you."

Sonya, who is probably the only Navajo living on the Keweenaw Peninsula, arrived like Glinda, the Good Witch, several years ago. She is about my height with long, gleaming black hair usually worn in a thick braid that brushes against the denim overalls she wears all-year-round. In addition to taking care of pregnant women and delivering babies, she is an all-purpose healer and is always willing to help in any medical situation, whether it is an emergency or not. She has been a godsend to mothers who need to know whether their offspring are suffering from strep or a virus and she can take X-rays to determine whether a fall has resulted in a broken bone. She's always willing to listen to the story of a stubbed toe or a tummy ache, she is an expert at applying Paw Patrol Band-Aids and she administers injections for insulin and flu shots. Despite her avowed ignorance of needle arts, she's become a member of our knitting circle and a close friend.

"Me too, you. Have you talked to Einar? Did he tell you I was in yesterday?" She didn't wait for me to answer. "I had a few minutes and I wanted to get some reassurance on this lace project."

I groaned, knowing what would come next.

"Einar looked at you as if you'd just flown in from outer space and were speaking Klingon."

She laughed. "Pretty much."

"Well, listen, Sonya, there is no pressure on you to make the wedding ring shawl, okay? It's going to be tedious and time-consuming and stressful because once you've knitted the stitches, you can't tear them out. The threads of a fine yarn just shred when you do that. I'd advise calling in sick for the duration."

"Nonsense," she said, lightly. "Like I've told you before, H, I'm here for the whole Yooper experience and that includes learning to love pasties and *gloggi* (Finnish eggnog), rice pudding, snow, and ridiculously complex knitting projects."

"You forgot monosyllabic men."

"Oh, that's my favorite part. Nothing like a man who knows his place."

I laughed. "Well, don't worry about the project. Lace is just yarn-overs and knit two together. It's basically a series of holes. And, anyway, Pauline Maki is in charge of it and she won't let anyone fall behind. I believe she intends to run the circle like a bingo game where she calls out the next stitch, then waits until everyone has done it before moving on."

"Very thorough, our Pauline," Sonya said.

"Yes. Perfection wouldn't be too exalted a description."

"How's she doing with the guest? I imagine having a teenager in the house is quite an adjustment for a childless woman."

*OMG.* I'd forgotten about Liisa. A black cloud of anxiety seemed to envelop me like a winter fog on the Great Lake.

I found I was holding my breath.

"Hatti? There's something wrong, isn't there?"

In the split second that it took to decide to confide in her, I came up with what I thought was a brilliant idea.

"Liisa Pelonen is dead. Last night. The Makis found her in their sauna about nine-fifteen when they got home from the smorgasbord at the B and B. They want to keep it quiet until the end of the weekend and they want me to figure out what happened to her."

Sonya absorbed my rapid-fire delivery of the shocking news with her usual quickness.

"Where's the body?"

"Arvo has it. Probably in the embalming room."

"You want me to take a look?"

I exhaled as the weight of being the only one responsible slipped off my shoulders.

"Would you?"

"Unofficially, of course. I can't do a full autopsy but I can look her over, see what I can tell you."

"That would be wonderful. She seemed to have sustained a wound near her right temple but it didn't look that deep and we couldn't see any other reason for death."

She cut me off.

"Let me get my own first impressions, okay? I'll head over there as soon as I've delivered Mrs. Kaukola's baby."

"That shouldn't take long," I said, all keyed up now. "It's like her thirteenth, isn't it?"

"Ninth. And every baby is different. Besides, Mrs. Kaukola's getting a little long in the tooth. I'd have liked her to have this one in the hospital but she doesn't hold with that. Or so she told me."

"Mrs. K is old school. You're lucky she's not insisting on having it in the sauna."

"Didn't I tell you? She is. It's the only place she can get away from the hordes, she says, including her husband."

"Evidently."

Sonya chuckled. "Will the Makis mind if I stop by?"

"I'm sure not. They may be out though. Today's the *Pikkujoulu* Festival and St. Lucy pageant."

"I'd forgotten. Key in the milk chute?"

One of the things I loved about Sonya was that she'd taken the time to learn our traditions, including the custom of keeping an extra house key in the chutes that were as ubiquitous as saunas in our community. The story we told was that we were less afraid of theft than we were of freezing to death in our endless winter. The reality, though, was probably that our language of love was the giving and receiving of food and nobody wanted to miss a fresh huckleberry pie or a pot of fish-and-potato soup.

"Yep."

"Hatti, do you happen to know whether the girl had an arrhythmia?"

"You're talking about syncope, aren't you? I asked Pauline about that. She said Liisa did have a history of fainting."

There was a brief silence.

I grimaced. "Pauline decided on the heirloom lace because she wanted to make a shawl for Liisa."

"Kind of breaks your heart. What do you think we're looking at here? Some kind of an accident?"

I shivered. "I hope so."

"In other words, there's a chance it could be, what? Murder?"

I shivered, again, even though it wasn't a fresh thought.

"Is there any motive?"

My mind flashed to Ronja Laplander and I shook my head.

"Not really."

"Listen, if you need help in figuring this out, you might consider talking to Max Guthrie. I understand he was some kind of a cop in his former life."

"How do you know that? I didn't think you knew him at all?"

Max Guthrie, a man's man with a wicked sense of humor and the easy swagger of a man who knew everything there was to know about women and liked it, had arrived in Red Jacket a year earlier. He'd bought Namagok, an abandoned fishing camp and had revived its small cabins and lodge house. He and I had bonded on the subject of fish. Both of us, it seemed, preferred eating them to catching them.

"I guess I heard it somewhere. Never mind. Listen, I'm here. It's baby time."

"Thanks for the impromptu autopsy," I said, "and good luck with the sauna thing."

"Better to be born in one than to die there," she said, and rang off.

It seemed to me that as far as Finnish proverbs went, that was as good as it gets.

# FIVE

It occurred to me as I climbed out of the Jeep that I didn't have a quarter for the parking meter but that was all right. I could just add a quarter when I emptied the meter at the end of the week. Just a perk of my job as top cop.

I found it mildly reassuring to find my assistant in his usual spot behind the cash register, perched on a high stool and working on one of his intricate fishing flies.

I'd inherited Einar Eino, a short, rounded, bald-headed man who was a dead-ringer for a tonttu, which is a Finnish household gnome, when Pops let me take over the bait shop. He (Einar, that is) probably disapproved of my plan to stock yarn and knitting needles, but, if so, he never said and he even, on occasion, deigned to ring up a set of circular Addi-Turbos or several skeins of Cascade Superwash. Best of all, he knew everything there was to know about fishing in local lakes and rivers and he, uncomplainingly, handled all the live bait from red wigglers to mealworms.

Like many Finnish-American men of his generation, Einar normally economized on his words. Not today.

He'd looked up at the sound of the bell I'd attached to the door and his normally stolid face exploded into a scowl.

"Henrikki. You shouldn't wear box."

"Box?"

"For costume. Fellas want curve. You never get no husband."

I'd forgotten there was one theme that could jolt Einar into language and that was my deplorable love life. And Sofi's. I realized he was referring to the St. Lucy's Day parade the previous afternoon. Arvo had instructed all the shopkeepers to wear costumes depicting characters from the *Kalevala*, which is the Finnish creation myth. I used gold spray paint to turn an old Hotpoint box into the Magic Sampo, a mill that could turn grain into gold.

"Luckily," I reminded him, "I already have a husband."

Einar ignored that and continued his criticism.

"Sofi, too. Man don't want witch."

My sister had worn a bathrobe and a long purple wig intended to identify her as Louhi, a pivotal figure in the Kalevala. Louhi is sometimes good, sometimes bad, but she's always a witch.

"Duly noted," I said, eager to move on. "Did you go to the parade?"

I was ninety-nine-point-nine percent sure that he'd say no, he'd gone home to sauna. I was wrong. He nodded.

"Girl cold," he said, which I interpreted as his observation about Liisa Pelonen in her role as St. Lucy.

"She was cold. She got a sore throat and a fever."

I stopped, abruptly, suddenly realizing I was speaking about Liisa as if she were still alive.

"Scared, too," Einar said.

My heart jumped. It took a lot for Einar to offer an opinion. What had he noticed that I'd missed?

"You thought the St. Lucy girl looked scared?"

He didn't respond and I knew he wouldn't. Einar, as I kept forgetting, did not approve of repetition.

"Any phone calls?"

"*Joo*," he said, which means yes.

I waited for a minute then prompted him.

"Who called?"

He shrugged. It was really and truly time to get an answering machine.

"Okay. Thanks. I'm going over to the high school now, for the festival. You'll be okay here?"

This time Einar didn't even look up but we understood one another and it occurred to me that the world might be better off with fewer words.

Sofi was ready and we loaded her trays of fresh, uncut fudge into the back of my Jeep and drove the block-and-a-half to the parking lot of Copper County High School. It just happened to be most of the parade route and jogged my sister's memory.

"It's too bad it didn't happen in reverse," she said.

"What?"

"If we'd held the pageant first, Liisa would have been healthy enough to sing and Astrid Laplander would have gotten her chance to stand in the back of Ollie's sleigh and help prop the candles with snowballs at the old Finnish Cemetery."

I said nothing and she looked at me, suspicion in her sky-blue eyes.

"C'mon, Hatti. Let's have it. What's really going on with Liisa Pelonen?"

I made a face and wished my sister didn't know me so well.

"It's a little more complicated than Liisa having a sore throat," I said.

"Define complicated."

"Liisa's not sick. She's dead." I stared at the giant tarp set up on the high school parking lot. "That thing is big enough to cover Lake Erie."

The purchase of the tarpaulin had been a no brainer. I mean, you can hardly hold an outdoor event in the Upper Peninsula during the winter without some sort of protection from the weather, but the debate that raged for two entire sessions of the Keweenaw Chamber of Commerce was based not on cost (which would have swallowed our entire budget for the year) but on color and imprint.

Most of us wanted a generic dark gray tarpaulin that would last (we hoped) for years in the snow. One of us (Arvo Maki) wanted the tarp printed with a checkerboard of the blue-and-white Finnish flag interspersed with sprigs of holly and the larger-than-life words "WELCOME TO PIKKUJOULU!"

Even after Arvo offered to pay for the new tarp, there was consternation about buying something so impractical. Finns, like other Nordic and Scandinavian people, believe in something called *kalsarikanni*, which translated means drinking at home, alone, in your underwear. *Kalsarikanni* or *Pantsdrunk*, promotes the zen-like values of relaxation, lack of pretense and appreciation of minimalism. (A popular cross-stitch sampler in many of our homes reads: Use it up, wear it out, make it do, do without.)

In any case, the chamber (which consisted of Arvo, Sofi, me, Mrs. Moilanen and Arnold Hakala) finally agreed it was only fair to let Arvo choose the design for the tarp and I'd forgotten the whole issue.

I remembered it now as I gazed at the slate-gray fabric that covered the entire parking lot and noted the discreet red letters that read: The Maki Funeral Home, Red Jacket, Michigan, and knew that, once again, Pauline had prevailed on Arvo to do the sensible thing.

"Hatti!" Sofi was pounding my shoulder to get my attention. "What do you mean Liisa is dead?"

I turned to my sister.

"Dead. Like a doornail. Or a Dodo bird. Or roadkill. Arvo and Pauline found her last night in their sauna and Sonya's going to take a look at the body this afternoon. I've been tasked with finding out what happened and the Makis do not want everybody to know until after the festival."

Sofi listened to this terse recital in silence but all the color drained out of her face, her eyes were wide and when she spoke, it was in a whisper.

"Hatti. Do you think someone killed her?"

I sighed. "I sure as sugar hope not."

# SIX

I nside the tent, strategically placed space heaters cut the chill of the winter morning and, of course, the much-debated tarp protected us from the falling snow.

Music, piped in by the equipment borrowed from Arvo's chapel, included recorded versions of several holiday favorites, including: *Varpunen Joulaamuna* (The Sparrow on Christmas morning, which is the tale of a dead baby brother returning to wish Christmas greetings as a sparrow, *Heinilla Harkien Kaukalon,* (On the Hay, in the Bull's Trough) and the ever-popular, *Hanki, Hanki, Hanki!* (Snow, Snow, Snow!)

I helped Sofi set up the fudge in her booth then strolled through the honeycomb of stalls. I looked for and didn't see the trio of Burberry wearing dignitaries from Lansing, the ones from the Tourist Council that Arvo had invited as special guests, in the hope that they would vote to name our town as one of the stops on the proposed UP Snow Train.

Neither Arvo nor Pauline was present, either, which was unusual enough.

Patty Huhtasaari, owner and proprietor of *Patty's Pasties,* was selling her signature product along with the jellies and jams put up by an order of monks who live and work up in the cliffs near Eagle Harbor. A jar of thimbleberry jam caught my eye and tweaked my memory. Hadn't

Pauline said she'd gone back to the funeral home shortly after six-thirty last night to gather a few jars of jam? Was it possible she'd seen someone lurking in the shadows waiting to hit Liisa on the head? Unlikely. If Pauline had seen someone she'd have mentioned it.

Anyway, Patty is my mother's age and looks it but then, getting up every morning at two a.m. to make fresh pasties would age anyone.

"Looks like a good crowd," she said to me. I nodded and it struck me that we consider a good crowd to be somewhere in the double digits. "Think we'll be able to replace Frankenmuth as the go-to Christmas place?"

I hoped she was joking. Frankenmuth, Michigan, (or as it calls itself, Little Bavaria), is located in the middle of the mitten and is devoted year-round to the holiday. Among its attractions are an enormous Christmas shop, an all-you-can-eat, family-style fried chicken dinner, an Octoberfest, a snow fest and a fire muster, to say nothing of a tourist-friendly brewery. And Bavarian architecture and a covered bridge. The town is advertised as far away as the Pennsylvania Turnpike and draws more than three million visitors a year.

"I think your pasties alone would attract visitors," I said, loyally.

"Yeah," Patti said. "Too bad it takes an extra eight hours to drive up here. I remember when we had a railroad and working airports and a Greyhound Bus."

"The good old days," I murmured. I picked up a jar of jam. "I see you're selling products for the monastery."

"Why not? The jam's great and it's for a good cause."

"What's that?"

Patti's lips twisted into a half-grin. "Oh, you know. Support the monks. Something like that."

I laughed and looked more closely at the jam jar. It was Lingonberry, which, along with the cloudberry, grows almost exclusively in places north of the forty-seventh parallel. It is one of our signature items, along with pasties and *pulla*, and Trenary toast, a twice-baked rusk suitable for dunking in coffee.

"Save me a beef-and-onions pasty, will you? I'll be back," I said, moving toward the Copper Kettle's booth. I knew that Ronja and Armas Laplander, after buying Calumet Gifts and changing its name, had struggled with the erroneous perception that it was a fudge emporium. In fact, they sold everything else: Decorative rocks and chunks of copper, kitchen utensils, sweatshirts and calendars, and magnets and mugs. They even sold a tee-shirt with the word "Fudgie" printed on it, a reference to a tourist from below the Mackinac Bridge.

I noticed that Armas and the younger daughters were manning the booth today.

"*Hei,*" I said to Ronja's husband. He looked at me and blinked but I know Finnish men and didn't expect any actual words. I turned to Valentina. "Where's your mom today?"

"Mama's at the church," Olga piped up. "Astrid gets to be St. Lucy."

"Mama said it's a miracle," added Vesta.

A miracle based on a murder? Didn't that make it a curse? Of course, I didn't say that.

"That's nice for Astrid," I said, with what I hoped was a sincere-looking smile.

Armas shocked the heck out of me with a soft-spoken, totally ironic, rejoinder.

"And for Ronja."

Well, well, well, I thought as I waved goodbye and continued on my way. So Armas Laplander understood the craziness of Ronja's obsession. Did that mean anything? Was it possible that the short, determined woman had gotten frustrated enough to take matters into her own hands? I just couldn't believe it. Ronja was opinionated, stubborn, abrasive and a champion for her children. She was not a killer. Nobody in our community was a killer. Surely.

"Hey, Hatti," called out Diane Hakala. Diane, who is one of my mom's best pals, was setting out hand-milled soap in the Hakala Pharmacy's booth. She is tall and solidly built with a 1960s beehive hairstyle and a large wardrobe of sweat clothes. This morning she had on a Christmas red-collared sweatshirt embellished with a fabric Christmas tree draped in blinking lights.

"Are you plugged in somewhere," I teased her, pointing at the tree on her chest.

"Oh, no, dear. There's a little battery. Have you heard about Liisa

Pelonen? She was forced to drop out of the pageant because of her sore throat. Ronja gets to play St. Lucy, after all."

"You mean Astrid."

"Oh, yes. Of course."

It occurred to me that someone (my guess was Pauline) had done a masterful job of keeping the real news about Liisa off the grapevine.

"Ronja says it was divine intervention," Diane continued.

"What do you think?"

She looked at me for a long moment, her blue eyes guileless and direct.

"You know, Henrikki," she said, dropping her voice, "I don't think God really bothers with that sort of thing. I imagine it was just chance that gave Liisa a sore throat."

"Hmm," I said, noncommittally.

"But between you and me and the fencepost, it wouldn't surprise me to find out that Ronja resorted to blackmail."

My eyebrows shot up. That was the last thing I was expecting.

"Blackmail?"

Diane shrugged. "You know how it is. Everyone has secrets. I wonder if Ronja found out something Arvo doesn't want people to know and threatened to expose him."

"I think," I said, gently, "you've been watching too much Law and Order."

"Probably." Diane smiled and I was relieved to see she didn't really buy the blackmail supposition. "I think it's because of the girl's extraordinary looks. It's almost impossible for someone that pretty not to alienate other women, you know?"

"Liisa's just a girl," I pointed out.

"Exactly," Diane said. And a thought struck me.

"Did Barb want to be St. Lucy, too?"

She shot me an odd look. "Barb was St. Lucy last year, don't you remember?"

I didn't remember anything about last year. I'd arrived on the Keweenaw the day before the St. Lucy parade and I'd been too shell-shocked from the abrupt end of my marriage to have noticed anything.

"Barb was supposed to marry Matti Murso this summer." A note of bitterness had entered Diane's pleasant voice. "But Matti fell for Liisa, hook, line and sinker."

"Matti?"

"Tauno Murso's son. Down at the Gulp 'N Go."

I knew Tauno. Like Einar and Armas Laplander, Tauno Murso seldom spoke but his bicep revealed volumes. I never thought of him without picturing him in a white wifebeater tee shirt that exposed his upper arms and the tattoo that read: Born to Lose.

"Barb and Matti had been together since the first grade," Barb continued. "Now the wedding's off."

Teen-aged marriages are not uncommon in the UP. About half of each year's senior class marries the summer after graduation. I would have thought, though, that Arnold Hakala's daughter would have attended college.

"I'm sorry," I said.

Barb nodded. "Matti was a real catch," she said, regretfully. "Captain of the Muskrats hockey team and apprentice to his dad at the gas station. He's got a future. Barb's been heartbroken but what can you do? It's not really even his fault. No guy could resist that kind of beauty, you know?"

My heartbeat quickened.

"What do you mean?"

"You've seen her, Hatti. Barb says when she sashays down the hall at school all the men stop dead, you know, like they were playing freeze tag. Even the drama teacher, Mr. Horton."

"So Matti was one of the smitten?" She shook her head.

"Matti was more than smitten. He was slain. And the shame of it is that she's only been out with him once. Liisa went with him to the Harvest dance. The rumor is she only agreed to that because Pauline had made her dress and she didn't want to disappoint her hostess."

I ignored the part about the dress.

"So Matti and Liisa weren't, I mean, aren't dating?"

"Oh, no. But he and the other boys heard she was sickly last night and none of them showed up for the dance. It was me and Ronja and Mrs. Frankfurter from the library and eleven girls. We were all home by nine p.m."

I nodded, mentally registering the Hakalas alibi and Matti's lack of one.

"I guess the girls were disappointed last night," I said, disingenuously, but the silly question got the job done.

"Not Barb. She knew ahead of time. She stayed home with Arnold and watched re-runs of Freaks and Geeks in her room."

Bingo! Barb could have climbed out the window of the family home on Walnut Street without her father knowing, waded over to the mortuary, and smashed Liisa Pelonen in the head. No alibi for her then.

We were interrupted by a customer interested in the fragrant soaps so I moseyed on over to my own booth. My spirits lifted as I gazed at the rainbow display of yarns, sample Nordic sweaters, hats, and mittens, listened to the clicking of needles and soft chatter and basked in the welcoming smiles of the ladies wedged into folding lawn chairs, my great Aunt Ianthe Lehtinen and her lifelong best friend, Miss Irene Suutula.

Aunt Ianthe was working on a soft, sparkly, mohair scarf for Charlie, and Miss Irene appeared to be concentrating on a swatch of intricate lace. The choice of projects, I thought, went a long way to describe them. Pops's aunt is a substantially built extrovert of more than average height with a crop of blue-rinsed curls, bright blue eyes and the warmest heart of anyone I know, with the possible exception of Pops, himself. Of course she was making a crazy, over-the-top item (no doubt requested by Charlie) for her great-grandniece.

Miss Irene, Jeff to Ianthe's Mutt, is small and meticulous with her white-blond hair, arranged each day in neat braids coiled around her head. She, too, has blue eyes, although hers are beginning to fade. She, too, has a warm heart, and Sofi, Elli and I spent many hours of our combined childhoods at their home across Calumet Street, a Victorian fantasy of lacy curtains, antimacassar-covered furniture and a perennially full cookie jar. We were welcomed from the time we play Candyland through canasta and Mahjong and the aunts, not our mothers, taught us to love knitting.

The ladies always seemed so happy and serene and Elli and I had often half-joked about becoming Aunt Ianthe and Miss Irene in our dotage. They had grown up together, attended the local Finnish college together and they had chosen separate but similar careers in that Aunt Ianthe had taught primary school at Red Jacket Elementary and Miss Irene had become the community's piano teacher. They never seemed to argue, a fact that I had always marveled at and mentioned once to my mother.

"It hasn't been all beer and skittles," she'd said. "There was that time, you know."

"It's forgotten now," Pops had chimed in. "All's well that ends well."

Naturally his effort to gloss over 'the time' made it fascinating to me.

"What happened?"

"It was some twenty years ago," my mom said, not unwilling to share what must have been a juicy story. "Alma Poitsu and her husband decided to retire to Lake Worth and the church needed an organist. Both ladies wanted the position and each applied without telling the other."

"I don't understand," I interrupted. "Surely the job would go to Miss Irene. She's the musician."

"Henrikki," Pops said, in a kindly voice, "your great aunt studied the piano, too, as a child. She loved music but she loved Irene, too, and she gave up her dream of teaching the instrument and, instead, taught reading and writing."

I'd heard Aunt Ianthe play Christmas carols on the piano at the bed and breakfast and I found it hard to believe she'd been a serious musician but I just nodded.

"Anyway," my mother continued, "things were awkward in town. Everyone thinks a lot of Ianthe and it just seemed so obvious that she would have to defer another musical dream. They were as stuck by pride and history as the board of deacons that had to make the decision. Thank the good Lord for Pastor Rinne. He was a modern-day Solomon, you know."

Pops, who does not approve of gossip, became impatient and finished the story himself.

"Pastor Rinne offered a compromise. Ianthe is not fond of sharps and flats so she would be invited to play all the hymns in the key of C. Miss Irene gets all the rest of them."

"Which meant," my mother interrupted, "that Irene gets Be Still

My Soul." It was our best hymn, written by Finland's uber-hero Jean Sibelius.

"It's worked well for twenty years and I think it is time to forget the back story," Pops said. He'd returned to reading the newspaper, the Daily Mining Gazette.

---

"*Hei*, Hatti," Aunt Ianthe called out. "Happy St. Lucy Day!"

I grinned at the two of them and prepared to pass along a bit of good news.

"Sonya has gone to deliver Mrs. Kaukola's baby."

"Oh, land's sakes, dearie," Aunt Ianthe said, on a peel of laughter. "We know! Elise Sorensen visited her last night and reported that she was nesting. And we, ourselves, noticed the full moon so we knew that baby would come today. Why do you think Irene is already working on a layette?"

I gazed at the piece of knitting on Miss Irene's needles. It looked like a Brillo pad.

"Don't worry, dear. Lace is like a butterfly in a cocoon. It doesn't reveal it's beauty until it is blocked."

"Dressed," Miss Irene said, with a sunny smile. "In lace knitting it is called dressed."

"Oh, yes," Ianthe wagged her head up and down. "We looked that up on the Google, you know. And dressed is a much better term because when the butterfly emerges from the cocoon, you know, it is dressed so beautifully."

"Now Israel loved Joseph more than all his children because he was the son of his old age, and he made him a coat of many colors."

Some years earlier Miss Irene had begun to quote the Bible in the middle of a conversation. The random habit had morphed into a pattern of punctuating Aunt Ianthe's uttered thoughts and it only seemed natural to wait for a verse. This one, though, had been easy. Joseph's coat of many colors.

"Thank you both for taking on the booth," I said. "It makes my job as acting police chief so much easier."

Aunt Ianthe's blue eyes were shrewd.

"I would guess, Henrikki, that you cannot wait for your parents to get back from the Mayo. It is a great responsibility to be in charge of the law though, luckily, we have no crime in Red Jacket."

"Thou shalt not kill," Miss Irene said. For once, there was no smile on her face and my blood ran cold. Did my elderly relatives know about the death of Liisa Pelonen? But that was impossible. For one thing, Pauline Maki was in charge of the secret. And, for another, Aunt Ianthe would have mentioned it to me first thing.

"Oh, I almost forgot to show you what Irene and I found up in the attic." Aunt Ianthe said, struggling out of her lawn chair to retrieve something from a box. It was a doll, probably eighteen inches high, with bright blue eyes and thick blond braids. She was wearing the plain white shift, red sash and the crown of candles of St. Lucy.

"Doesn't she look like Liisa? I believe I made the outfit for Sofi many years ago but Irene and I thought we would give it to Arvo."

"Why Arvo?"

"To try to make up for his dear girl missing her chance to sing in the festival," Aunt Ianthe said. "You know, of course, that she is still sick and that Ronja Laplander's daughter is to take her place." I nodded and my great aunt sighed. "I'm afraid little Astrid does not have much of an ear."

"Or a voice," Miss Irene said. "But God works in mysterious ways."

"Yes," Aunt Ianthe said, thoughtfully, "but it is hard to imagine what He is thinking on this one."

"It's a consequence," Miss Irene said, somewhat unexpectedly. "Liisa had no time to put on the longjohns."

I couldn't help wondering whether the girl would still be alive today if she had bundled up before the parade and failed to catch a chill and a sore throat. Had she been murdered (if she'd been murdered) because she'd been unlucky enough to catch a cold? Or was there something more behind her death, a relentless killer who would have found an opportunity one way or the other?

"She was dreadfully pale in the sleigh," Aunt Ianthe said.

"And I looked, and behold a pale horse: And his name that sat on him was Death, and Hell followed with him."

The quotation took my breath away. It must have shaken Aunt Ianthe, too, because after a short pause she said, "be careful with Revelations, my dear. It is not popular in some quarters. And, I am certain, it would upset Pauline."

"What makes you say that?" The question was out before I thought.

The old ladies exchanged a pointed look.

"Pauline is very protective of Liisa," Miss Irene said.

"Very protective," Aunt Ianthe echoed her friend. "We don't believe we have ever seen her as happy as she has been this year. Motherhood is what she was missing."

"Pauline Maki isn't Liisa's mother," I said, with more heat than necessary.

"No, dear. Of course not. It is make-believe. But not, I think, to Pauline."

Miss Irene's next words struck a chord somewhere inside me.

"No more lies," she quoted, "no more pretense. Ephesians."

A pair of trim, middle-aged women, lift tags hanging from the zippers of their puffy ski jackets, stepped into our booth.

"What an exquisite sweater," said one of them, gazing at the reindeer prancing across my aunt's generous chest. "I had no idea there was such a strong Norwegian influence in the UP. Are the mittens for sale?"

There was a brief silence, and I knew Aunt Ianthe was trying to decide whether or not to point out that we were Finns not Norwegians, and Miss Irene was working on a suitable Bible verse about making mistakes. It seemed like an excellent time for me to move on, and I excused myself and stepped out onto the canvas-lined concourse. An instant later I felt a gentle hand at my elbow. I looked down into Miss Irene's concerned face.

"There is something wrong, isn't there, Henrikki? I can sense it."

Pops always jokes that Miss Irene has the Finnish Second Sight. She does seem to have the knack of reading between the lines and of probing below the surface.

"Something about Pauline and Arvo."

I found I couldn't lie to her.

"Yes. But, Miss Irene, I'm not supposed to talk about it."

She patted my arm.

"Of course, Henrikki," she said. "Please let me know if I can help."

A lump formed in my throat as I thought how much I loved the two old ladies. I found myself pitying the beautiful dead girl and taking comfort in the fact that she had spent her last months with a couple that loved her like a daughter. Family really was everything.

# SEVEN

There was a healthy turnout at the festival and Sofi's booth which offered coffee and fudge (even if the latter was eggnog-flavored) was the most popular spot. Despite the long line of customers, my sister turned the operation over to her daughter, grabbed my arm and hauled me over to one of the card-tables borrowed from St. Heikki's social hall.

"How dare you just tell me Liisa Pelonen's dead, then just leave me in the lurch."

"Ssh," I put my finger to my lips. "How did that leave you in the lurch?"

"Curiosity, silly. I want to know who, what, when, where and why." She paused. "And how."

"You already know who," I pointed out. "And when. I don't know yet how she died or why or whether it was an accident."

Sofi leaned so that her eyes were only a few inches from mine.

"But you don't think it was an accident, do you, little sister? This whole thing wouldn't be so hush-hush if there were an innocent explanation."

"That's not true." Sometimes I'm oppositional with Sofi just because she's my big sister. "Arvo didn't want to ruin the rest of the festival by making it public." I paused. "Or, maybe it was Pauline. Anyway, everybody worked hard on this and the Snow Train thing is riding on it."

Sofi sat back in her chair.

"Does anybody really believe folks are going to drive ten to twelve hours just to ride around the UP in a train that will probably get stuck in the snow?"

"It'll be like the Orient Express," I said.

"Yeah. Up to and including a killing."

"Hush! I mean it, Sofi. I promised discretion on this."

She didn't argue with me. Instead, she wiped her face with a tissue she had in her pocket and then fixed her eyes on the passersby.

"Have you come up with a motive?"

"Not really. I mean Ronja was upset about the St. Lucy thing and apparently Barb Hakala's boyfriend fell for Liisa hook, line, and sinker. Nothing else."

"She was extraordinarily beautiful," Sofi said. "You know, that kind of beauty carries a heavy mandate. All eyes are on you all the time and people are judging. I imagine that people like Princess Grace and Audrey Hepburn had to be diplomatic at all times. Admiration isn't far from envy and envy isn't far from hate."

I stared at my sister. I wasn't surprised at her insight but I was surprised that she expressed it.

"You sound like you've given this a lot of thought."

"I hadn't. Not until the insect."

Three years earlier Sofi's then-husband, Lars Teljo, had a one-night stand with a barmaid whose first name was Cricket. It seemed to me that the affair was the final straw in toppling a shaky marriage. Sofi's view was that Cricket, aka the insect, had destroyed a healthy union and a perfect family.

"Surely you don't think Liisa was killed because she was so beautiful."

"Why not? St. Lucy was."

That wasn't strictly true. St. Lucy (if, indeed, she existed) was martyred because she refused the hand of an Italian nobleman, preferring to stay pure in the name of Christ.

"You know, H, it's possible that, just like with St. Lucy, some guy wanted Liisa and she refused him so he killed her."

I thought about the hockey-stick wielding Matti Murso. Somehow, that didn't seem any more plausible than considering Ronja or Diane Hakala or either of their daughters.

"Maybe Sonya will say it's an accident."

"I wouldn't hold my breath." She frowned. "What is it they always say about killing women? That it is someone in the family circle? Some man." Horror flashed in those baby blue eyes. "You don't think that Arvo…" Her voice trailed off.

"Of course not. That's absurd."

Arvo and Pops have been best friends for many years and the funeral director has been an honorary uncle for Sofi, Elli and me. When we were younger he'd show up on Christmas Eve wearing the costume of *Joulupukki*, (literally, Yule Goat), which is our version of Santa Claus. Our relationships with the Makis were much like those with the aunts; they attended our celebrations, our recitals and school events, and we considered them family. The only difference was that we did not have the run of the mortuary but that never bothered me. I understand that it is Arvo's business and has always been his home but I've sometimes wondered how Pauline could bear to live just a floor above the corpses.

"It couldn't be Arvo," I repeated. "Not in a million years. Besides, he loved Liisa like a daughter."

"Speaking of daughters," Sofi said, "you really should talk to her actual-factual father."

"Jalmer Pelonen," I said. "You're right." I fished my cell out of my parka pocket. "I'll see if Arvo has located him yet."

Sofi went back to her booth. I found a quiet corner under the edge of the tarp and punched in a number. It wasn't until he'd answered that it occurred to me Arvo would normally have been all over the festival marketplace. Where was he?

"Where are you," I asked, before he could say hello.

"The Nugget."

The Nugget is the relatively new casino on the Copper Eagle Reservation some fifteen miles east of Red Jacket. Built after The 1988 Indian Gaming Regulatory Act, the casino was supposed to bring prosperity for all the residents of the rez. Needless to say, like everything else in the UP and on the Keweenaw, in particular, it was too far from the population centers to score much in the way of traffic.

"Why aren't you at the Christmas market? We've got a good turnout."

"The guys from Lansing didn't show a lot of enthusiasm for arts and crafts."

"What about fudge?"

"Heh." It was a tepid laugh, at best, for Arvo. "They had something a little stronger in mind."

He sounded discouraged and I tried to cheer him up.

"They'd probably had enough snow. I notice they all wore Burberries with scarves but no hats or gloves." The stylish outerwear had made them stand out among the Keweenaw natives who tended to wear heavy parkas, tan, ankle-height Wolverine boots, and the stormy kromer, a fur-lined cap with earflaps invented and sold in Iron Mountain.

"Any news on the Snow Train?"

"A shoo-in," Arvo said. "The detour to the casino clinched it. But I think we'd have gotten it anyway. There's plenty to see in Red Jacket, what with all our historical architecture and the remains of the railroad and the mine shaft."

"And, of course, the ethnic festivals you and Pauline have come up with. Who could pass up a chance for snow, smorgasbord and St. Lucy?"

There was a momentary silence and I bit my tongue. I hadn't intended to remind him of last night's tragedy.

"You know, Henrikki," he finally said, "it almost seems as if it didn't happen, you know? Like I imagined it. Like when Pauline and I go down to the church in a little while, she will be amongst the starboys and girls and she will be wearing the crown and carrying her candle."

The wobbliness in his voice nearly broke my heart.

"I'm so sorry, Arvo." After an awkward silence, I changed the subject. "Have you been able to get ahold of Jalmer Pelonen?"

"No. Einar says he is still ice fishing at Lake Gogebic."

"Einar? My Einar?"

"You did not know, Hatti-girl? Jalmer and Einar are old fishing buddies."

I tried to imagine Einar having a buddy of any kind.

"Jalmer goes every year for two weeks at the beginning of December. Like clockwork."

"So he should be back tomorrow, right? The fourteenth?"

I imagined the poor man coming home to the worst news a father could get and added, "poor guy."

"He will want to see her," Arvo said. "I have made her beautiful again, with makeup and the white dress Pauline made for her to wear to the Harvest Dance. She looks like an angel."

Even as my heart ached for Arvo, Pauline and for Jalmer Pelonen, I wondered how many laws we'd broken by moving the body. If there turned out to be any indication of foul play, the sauna would be designated a crime scene and it should be sealed off. The very fact that none of that had occurred to me nearly a day later revealed how unprepared I was to investigate this situation. My anxiety poured out in words.

"We really should call in the professionals."

"No, Henrikki. No. Not until tomorrow."

I suddenly remembered to tell him about Sonya's unofficial autopsy.

"That's all right with you, isn't it? And Pauline?"

Arvo took a moment to consider but eventually agreed.

"You do what you must do, Hatti-girl," he said, with a sigh. "We will see you later, at the church? Pauline is already there, in charge of the pageant. I married a worker bee, you know."

"Right. Uh, Arvo, can you think of anyone who might have wanted to harm Liisa Pelonen?"

"You asked me that before. The answer is still the same. No, no and no. She had no enemy. She was perfection."

"You don't think she was too perfect for her own good?"

"Would you ask the question about Jesus Christ? Or Sibelius?"

I refused to back down.

"Sometimes people who are extraordinarily good or beautiful incite jealousy in others."

"No one would want to kill Liisa," he said, in a low voice. "No one who knew her."

"What about you?"

"What!?"

"I mean, what if someone wanted to hurt you through Liisa."

"There is no one," he said, finally. "It must have been an accident."

After I disconnected I realized I had no interest in going back into the Christmas Market. I wasn't needed at the shop and the prospect of going home to change sheets and clean the place for my parents' return seemed like an uninspired choice. All I could think about was Liisa Pelonen and why she had died last night on the floor of the Makis sauna.

I left the key to the Jeep with Sofi and started the walk home. The snow was falling but it was a light, fresh, lacy snow. I caught a few flakes on my tongue and breathed in the fresh, cold air.

Jace and I had never experienced a snowfall together because we'd met in the spring in Ann Arbor then married and moved to Washington, D.C. Since I had grown up in Red Jacket and his grandfather lived on the Keweenaw, we'd talked a lot about the heavy Yooper snowfalls and we'd planned to build snowmen and have a snowball fight at the first opportunity.

Of course, there never was an opportunity. We hadn't been married long enough.

Three blocks of wading through a foot of snow was too long to dwell on the frustrations of my cracked marriage and, by the time I turned from Third Street onto Calumet, I was frantic to think about something else. And then it hit me. Arvo was at the Nugget and Pauline at church. This was the perfect time to revisit the scene of the crime. If there'd been a crime. I was beginning to think that there had.

# EIGHT

E ven though the funeral home was built during the same turn-of-the-century era as The Queen Anne and the inn, it bore no resemblance to the other two structures. There were no records left from that time, but most of us assumed that the architect must have been eccentric, or, as Mrs. Moilanen liked to say, a crackpot.

With its thick, ugly shingled roof curling over the upper story like a serpent, its dark brick façade, and the ground floor's slitted windows, the house resembled a medieval fortress.

I collected the key from the milk chute just inside the carport on the wall of the downstairs kitchen but I didn't let myself into the back. Instead, just in case I'd gotten my signals crossed and there was someone home, I circled back to the front door.

It was a double-door with two separate knockers and two matching plain evergreen wreaths intended to send the message that the Makis were aware of the Christmas season but that they intended to observe the holiday in a low-key, non-decorative way out of respect for any mourners. I picked up one of the knockers and banged it against the door and, while I waited for someone to answer, I felt the old sense of unease that I always felt around this house of death.

No one answered, of course. Not even a ghost.

As I unlocked the door and let myself in, the butterflies in my stomach turned into bats. I told myself I was being ridiculous. I'd lived next to the funeral home all my life and I'd been in here dozens of times for funerals. There was nothing to be scared of, nothing at all. Even so, the breath caught in my throat and I could feel my heart thumping against my ribs.

I slipped off my boots and walked down the shadowed, carpeted hallway in my stocking feet toward the downstairs kitchen at the end of the hall. The kitchen, too, was shadowed and I didn't turn on a light but the pale light filtering in from the window revealed the 1950s black-and-white linoleum on the floor and, in the corner, the Norge refrigerator with its humped shoulders.

The Maki money had been spent on the newest wing of the house which lay beyond the kitchen. It consisted of a corridor that connected a greenhouse and a modern, electric sauna.

As I gazed at the lacy, green-and-black shadows, the pinprick glow from the plant lights and the snow falling on the glassed-in roof, I thought of a snowglobe and the magic of the place drew me inside.

I opened the door very quietly, like a sneak thief, and drank in the scents of earth and peat and fertilizer and new life. Rows of potted plants lined up neatly in low tables and a soft, pleasant sound reached my ears. Mozart. Pauline's plants were listening to Mozart. I felt a curious sense of comfort and relaxation and I realized that this was, in every sense of the word, Pauline's sanctuary; this was where she came to get refreshed, renewed, recharged.

I wandered through the short rows of tables, each with a neat sign indicating, not their species but their age or stage of growth. "Seedling, Fledglings, Sprouts, Tweens, Mature, Late Bloomers, Silver Streakers. It was like an enormous, chlorophyll family and reminded me of the paper dolls Elli and I used to draw and clothe, families with a dozen or more children because we didn't have to change diapers or help with homework or pay for designer jeans.

The blooming flowers were in the back and the wash of color, even in the dim light, was breathtaking. Yellow daffodils and lilies, white babies breath and statice, tulips, daisies, and roses, of course, because of the Finnish preference for yellow and white blossoms at our funerals.

Another table held pink, red and orange carnations and more roses. Just beyond that, up against a wall, was a workstation composed of a wooden bench topped with open shelves that contained plastic bottles and containers. I read a few labels: Thrive Alive, Seaweed, Nitrogen, Phosphorous, Potassium, Sulfur. Vitamins and supplements, I assumed, to contribute to healthy plants. There was even a bottle of Ibuprofen and a container of Vicks Vaporub. I picked up the later but a disembodied, none-too-happy-sounding voice behind me almost made me drop it as I (figuratively) jumped out of my skin.

"Hatti?" There was a slight edge in Pauline's pleasant voice and the heat of embarrassment rushed through me. I had shamelessly invaded her privacy and in a time when she was grieving for the loss of her surrogate daughter.

She turned on an overhead light and thus could see me holding the jar of Vicks. As if just being in her space wasn't enough of a violation. She was as pale as a pearl but her makeup was perfect, as always, and she wore a beige wool pantsuit with a Christmas green turtleneck and a silver modern art Christmas tree pin.

"What are you doing?"

Her tone was not accusing but it lacked the usual ring of friendliness. It seemed as if she was too tired or sad to make the effort and I realized that it was an effort. Pauline Maki, lover of plants, was undoubtedly an introvert who had made herself into a public figure to please her husband. I wondered if Arvo knew how lucky he was. I finally realized she was waiting for an explanation.

"Geez Louise," I muttered when I could catch my breath. "Pauline, I apologize. I was walking home and, oh, it just seemed like a good time to take another look at the crime scene."

Her faintly accusing expression didn't change.

"You are, of course, aware that the death occurred in the sauna."

"I know. I got sidetracked. The greenhouse just looked so magical and restful and I couldn't resist poking my nose in. I've never been here before."

The older woman drew in a deep breath as if to calm herself with the familiar scents around her.

"Would you like a tour?"

It was an olive branch and I decided to take it. Besides, I wanted to learn more about this oasis.

"Yes, please."

"Well, you've seen my work station." She waved toward a pegboard filled with tools, including different-sized trowels and little rakes, pruning shears, weeders, scoops, and dibbers for planting seeds. "And my medicine chest." She eyed the jar in my hand.

"Speaking of that, I said, trying to sound nonchalant, as if she hadn't just scared the breath out of me, "do plants get sore throats?"

"Not specifically. The Vicks and the Ibuprofen are for me. But they definitely feel sick and melancholy. The supplements are intended to keep them in the pink."

"And the Mozart?"

"To lift up their moods."

"Plants have moods?"

"Like children. Like pets. I imagine everything with a brain and a heart is subject to mood, don't you?"

"I hadn't thought about it."

She was kind enough not to comment on that.

"The seedlings over on this side of the nursery are my hybrids. I'm of two minds about the experiments. There's nothing quite like coming up with something unique but the downside is that they can go fatally wrong."

I realized then, if I hadn't before, that Pauline viewed the plants as almost human; as, in fact, her offspring.

"Was Liisa interested in the greenhouse?"

The color that had returned to the woman's face faded a little.

"Yes. She found it interesting. At least she did when she first moved in. After school started and voice lessons and choir practice, she got busy."

"That must have been disappointing."

"Oh, no. To each his own, you know."

We'd wandered over to the blooming flowers where I noticed a majestic purple-blue flower with individual blossoms that reminded me of the business end of a saxophone.

"That looks like some kind of delphinium," I said.

"It's called monkshood," she said. "Because of the scoop on the end."

A bell rang in my head.

"Is that the same as wolfsbane?" She nodded. "I think that was what was in the witch's potion in the Harry Potter series."

"Quite possibly," Pauline said. "Monkshood or Wolfsbane contains the poison, aconite, which is powerful enough to stop the heart. I wouldn't have it in the house if we had young children around but, as it is..." Her voice trailed off and, for a moment, there was a gleam of moisture in her eyes.

"What about that iris," I asked, hastily, moving over to another flower. "It's almost a cerulean blue. I can't remember ever seeing that color before. Is it a hybrid?"

"Actually, that one is not. But I have done some experimenting with some of these others," she said, leading the way to a table laden with mature blooms in colors ranging from sapphire to midnight to cobalt, cornflower and royal blue. They were exquisite.

"Arvo is partial to blue," she said, by way of explanation. "Because of Finland."

Of course.

I gazed with admiration at a single blossom the color of lapis lazuli.

"That's a hybrid called Blue Mystique. Arvo calls it my robot orchid." She swallowed, painfully.

"Pauline?"

"Forgive me," she said, not denying the emotional reaction. "Arvo used to come up here to sit and watch me work with the plants but he has been so busy with the festival and everything else, he hasn't been here in a while."

"The festival's almost over," I said, encouragingly, "and it's been successful. I spoke with him this morning and he said he's certain the committee will grant us a stop on the Snow Train. What's this violet-blue flower?"

"An iris hybrid. I did that one the old-fashioned way—with grafting. You can't graft just anything. There are compatibility markers."

"Next thing we know there will be plant marriage counselors."

"That's not as far out as it seems." I was pleased to hear the enthusiasm return to her voice. "There are botanists who believe plants have memories. Take nightshade," she said, pointing to a row of velvety midnight blossoms with tiny berries. "A hundred years ago, a scholar hypothesized that the reason nightshade is so deadly is because it harbors a lot of anger. Nightshade's other name is *Atropa bella donna,* because centuries ago Italian women squeezed the juice out of the roots and used it to dilate their eyes which was considered a mark of beauty."

"Beauty and anger and danger," I said. "Are they connected?"

"Everything in life is connected," she said.

"Pauline," I said, impulsively, "do you think Liisa was killed because she was so beautiful?"

"We don't know that she was killed at all, but, no, not just because of that. Beauty in and of itself is not lethal. If she was killed it was probably because of disappointed hopes."

"You mean like a boyfriend."

"I'm afraid so."

I suddenly thought of my own marital mess.

"What's the secret to a long, successful marriage?"

Her smile was small and tight but it seemed sincere.

"This," she said, waving her arm to include the entire greenhouse. "This sanctuary. It's my crack in the teapot."

I stared at her as I recognized the reference to a W. H. Auden poem I'd studied in English Lit.

"The glacier knocks in the cupboard,
The desert sighs in the bed,
And the crack in the teacup opens,
A lane to the land of the dead."

A poem about death, the great, frightful ending, the abyss that awaits us all. We know it is coming and we construct our own defenses to fight the knowledge. In Pauline's case, it was the peace and inspiration of the greenhouse. I felt a spurt of admiration for this woman I'd known all my life. I hated to jerk her back to the misery of the present but knew I needed to do it.

"Could you run through the events of yesterday?"

All emotion and peacefulness seemed to vanish from her eyes and she was, as always, courteous and businesslike.

"Of course. We rose at six."

"Six a.m.?" I wouldn't have been surprised to hear Pauline Maki say she started the day that early but Liisa had been a teenager.

"Oh, yes. Always. Liisa was not a slug-a-bed."

"All right. Then what?"

"I made her breakfast: scrambled eggs, fresh orange juice, and bacon. Oh, and *korvapuustit*," she added, referring to the cinnamon rusks that taste best dunked in coffee.

"Do you cook like that in the morning?" She shook her head.

"Sometimes we just have homemade granola. Yesterday was special because of the parade. And because it was her birthday."

I winced, inwardly, at the emotion in her voice.

"After we ate," Pauline continued, without prompting, "Liisa and Arvo left to string more lights downtown. She was supposed to go from there to pageant rehearsal at one."

"What happened?" I asked, even though I'd already heard versions of this story.

"She didn't get there. Not until just before the parade. She told me she'd gone to the Frostbite Mall in Houghton," Pauline said, slowly, so slowly that I knew she hadn't believed the story. "She wanted to buy a new dress for the Snowball Dance last night."

"She'd intended to go to the dance?"

"I don't know. So she said."

I looked at Pauline for a long moment.

"Did she keep many secrets from you?"

Pauline drew herself up as if offended but before she could issue a strong denial, she seemed to change her mind.

"Liisa was an angel," she said, "a daughter. But she was also a teenager. I'll admit I sometimes thought she had secrets. I tried to remind myself that everyone—even a child—is allowed some privacy within her own mind."

I thought that over.

"It must be hard for parents, trying to figure out when to interfere and when not," I said, examining that idea for the first time.

"You want to keep them from getting hurt, from being frightened," Pauline said, gazing into the distance. "You want to protect them. But you can't protect them from life."

Or death. I kept that corollary to myself.

"Do you know whether Liisa was with someone during the time she said she went to the mall?"

"I don't know. I've thought and thought about that. I conclude she must have been but, for the life of me, I can't tell you who it was. Liisa," she added, her voice sharpening, "as you know, was very attractive."

"Matti Murso?"

She waved a hand. "That was just a date. One date."

"Was she involved with any other boys?"

Her pale eyes focused on me and in them, I read a mixture of pain and what I thought was protectiveness.

"I don't think so. She was a good girl, you know."

"Of course, of course. Did she buy a dress?"

"What?"

"For the dance. Did she buy anything at the mall?"

"I don't know that, either. All I could think about was how she'd missed the rehearsal and that it was too late for her to put on the longjohns. I was afraid she'd get sick."

"Couldn't she have worn a parka?" The question had been asked and answered the previous night but I thought there was no harm in bringing it up again.

"That was my fault." Pauline's voice trembled. "I didn't want the line of the costume to be ruined. I knew it was important to Arvo." She dipped her head for a moment and then continued. "After the children placed their candles at the cemetery, I whisked her home and into the shower, gave her some tea with honey and spread Vicks on her chest. I hoped a good night's sleep would take care of her scratchy throat and slight fever."

"Did you consider staying home with her?"

A flash of pure anguish crossed Pauline Maki's face.

"Not really. She was eighteen. And she would have been asleep."

Except she wasn't asleep. She'd gotten up and gotten dressed and gone down to the sauna to meet her death.

"Can you think of anyone who might have wished to harm her?"

"No. She was such a lovely girl. Did you know she never even knew her own mother?"

I smiled at her. "Isn't it wonderful that she got to have a surrogate mother at least for a few months of her life?"

This time the tears welled up in Pauline's eyes and one slid down her cheek.

# NINE

The sauna was as clean as a whistle and there was nothing at all to see there. I was about to leave when I thought of Jane Marple and all the other detectives who would scorn to leave a stone unturned.

"Pauline," I said, "I'd like to take a look at Liisa's bedroom."

She hesitated for an instant and I thought I could read her mind. She didn't want some morbid curiosity seeker poking around in the personal belongings of her beloved, dead, surrogate daughter. But Pauline Maki knew it wasn't an idle request and her sense of duty took over. With her head high and her spine straight, she led me to the downstairs kitchen and up the backstairs.

I don't know what I expected but I was both shocked and impressed by the second floor of the funeral home. Unobtrusive skylights had been installed in the main rooms and recessed lighting in the others provided a pleasant, warm glow. The kitchen was a symphony of pale gray with gleaming stainless steel appliances and thick white marble countertops. The white walls in the living room provided a pleasing contrast to the grass-green, cross-hatched fabric on the rattan furniture, the thick green carpet and the stands of living ornaments including seagrass, hanging baskets of ferns and pots of succulents.

I kept opening my mouth to compliment Pauline on the décor but the grim line of her mouth and her firm, relentless stride seemed to discourage any conversation. We arrived in front of a door in the center of the white-carpeted hallway and she paused, sucked in a breath, and said, "This is it." She emphasized the last word in the subject as though announcing the Second Coming. "Liisa's room."

She turned the knob, opened the door and stood aside to let me enter.

The instant I stepped into the pink paradise I understood one more thing about the woman I had come to know and admire in the past hour. She had wanted the displaced girl to whom she and her husband had offered a room to be happy here. As much as Arvo, Pauline had wanted this girl to become part of their family.

I stood still for a moment drinking in the extraordinary vision. Everything was pink and ruffled from the curtains at the windows to the canopy over the four-poster bed. A frilly pink shade sat on a bedside lamp and even the pink carpet on the floor was overlaid with a furry area rug of a lighter shade of pink. The mirror on the pink dressing table was embellished with round, pink lightbulbs and one of the pale pink walls was covered with a large, framed quilt that depicted a family of pink elephants on green grass but each was wearing a pink crown.

A pink jewelry box sat on top of a dark pink dresser scarf on a fuschia-toned dresser. An iridescent pink backpack hung on a pink hook and there was a rose-gold laptop sitting on a powder pink desktop.

The room would have delighted a six-year-old, I thought. It reminded me of nothing so much as Pepto Bismol.

Pauline was still standing in the door. I turned to her and smiled.

"You went to a lot of trouble for Liisa," I said, hoping to dismiss her. She nodded, but didn't leave.

Not everything in the closet was pink. There were a few sweaters in other pastel shades and the designer jeans were denim. But there were also pink corduroy slacks, pink-and-white sweaters, a blouse with rose-buds embroidered on the collar and a warm, flannel nightgown trimmed in lace and small, pink unicorns. I checked when I spotted the garment. Was that what Liisa had worn to bed last night? Had she gotten out of her sickbed to change into jeans and a sweatshirt then made her way through the empty house to the sauna? The answer had to be yes but the question remained; why?

I forced myself to focus on the room itself and the inevitable question of how a woman with the common sense and good taste displayed by Pauline Maki could have thought a seventeen-year-old girl would appreciate this bubble gum nightmare. Or had Liisa liked it? I thought not. There was no sign of anything personal here. No posters on the wall or selfies of herself and friends. There was no teenage novel by the bedside, no cosmetics on the dressing table. Nothing to indicate that a real person lived here.

"She didn't like it."

I'd forgotten about the older woman's presence and the sound made me jump. Pauline didn't seem to notice.

"I tried to anticipate what she would like. I invited her to tweak it in any way she wished." She sounded tired. "I guess I am too much out of touch with today's young people. Perhaps Mrs. Laplander is right that I couldn't understand about St. Lucy because I don't have a daughter of my own."

It was such a delicate moment. Pauline Maki revealing vulnerability and at a loss. I wanted to throw my arms around the taller woman and reassure her. I wanted to say I was sure Liisa had loved the room. But I knew, with every fiber of my being, that Pauline had missed the mark and that Liisa Pelonen had never felt this room was home.

"It doesn't mean she didn't care for you," I finally said, softly.

The fine eyes focused on me and I thought I detected new lines of strain in the pale skin around them.

"Thank you, Hatti."

I finished looking through the drawers and found, as expected, piles of neatly folded pink underthings, camisoles, bras, panties. The jewelry box contained only a set of beautifully matched pink pearls.

"We gave those to her for the homecoming dance," Pauline said. "I wanted to make her a dress and I let her choose the fabric. When she chose white, I knew the pearls would be the perfect complement."

A clock chimed from somewhere in the house and both of us realized it was getting late. It was time to head over to the church. Pauline offered me a ride and I accepted. In the silence of the luxury car, I thought about what I had just seen.

On the one hand, it was disappointing. Liisa Pelonen had had secrets and the room she'd occupied for six months hadn't revealed them.

On the other hand, the room told me a lot about Liisa's hostess. Pauline had seen motherhood through rose-colored glasses. The room had fulfilled a fantasy about welcoming a child into the house. Had Liisa been able to live up to the expectations for that dream? Could anyone have measured up to it? Had disappointment colored Pauline's attitude toward the girl? Had it diminished her interest in the surrogate daughter? And, most important of all, had it prompted Pauline Maki to get rid of the girl who hadn't really wanted to be her daughter?

I glanced at the grim but calm face of the woman beside me and thought not. Pauline had decades of learning to cope with disappointment. She'd found her talisman, her defense against the chaos. There was no reason for her to kill Liisa Pelonen.

I found myself praying that Sonya would give us a verdict of accidental death.

# TEN

Visitors to Red Jacket were always dumbstruck by the soaring spire and flying buttresses of St. Heikki's Finnish Lutheran Church, to say nothing of the gargoyles.

Today, despite the cold temperatures and the relentlessly falling snow, the arched doors stood open. The Reverend Sorensen and Mrs. Moilanen stood inside to offer a welcome, shake hands and direct pageant-goers to the front pews of the sanctuary. The chancel was swathed in white sheets studded with foil-studded stars that matched those on the cone-shaped hats of the starboys and girls and on the tips of their wands. A large, evergreen advent wreath sat on the baptismal font and ropes of holly hung from the choir stall.

Arvo and I stood together in the narthex while Pauline and the other mothers fussed with the costumes of the participants. Astrid Laplander, short and squat, her dark unibrow particularly prominent against her white costume, tried to stand still while her mom teetered on a step stool trying to attach the heavy evergreen crown of electrified candles on the girl's head.

"Why is that wreath slipping down over her eyes," Arvo asked, in a whisper.

"It's too big," I said, and added without thinking, "it wasn't made for her."

"*Ei.*" No. The single syllable made my heart ache.

"I'm so sorry," I said, grabbing his arm. "Liisa would have been perfect. Astrid is just a girl."

He made an effort to smile.

"The first St. Lucy was just a girl, too, Henrikki. Maybe we—I—have made it too much about beauty. Do you think it was her beauty that got her killed?"

The comment shook me. Luckily, there was no time to answer, as Miss Ianthe struck the opening chords of the traditional song and the children set off in pairs toward the altar as they sang the familiar words.

> The evening is beautiful,
> little breeze blows fresh and light.
> Or to be late? The evening is beautiful.
> Come quickly my boat,
> Saint Lucy! Saint Lucy!

The tight expression on Arvo's face eased and I thought about how much he loved our Finnish-American customs. Was this, like Pauline's greenhouse, his answer to the terror? Did everybody have a passion that filled in the crack in the teacup? If so, what was mine?

Pauline joined us and Arvo put his arm around her spare shoulders. The gesture looked awkward rather than natural, no doubt because they were nearly the same height. She swayed toward him but did not attempt to lay her head on his shoulder and I got the sense that there was no real comfort. Each of them felt the grief alone.

After the pageant, the Makis and I made our way down the stone steps to the basement kitchen, where Pauline joined the women of the Martha Circle, who were setting up punch, coffee and plates of pastries including *Joulutorttu*. Normally even the whiff of the seasonal prune tarts sets my stomach on edge because it reminds me of the day, a year ago, when Jace told me it was over. Today, though, there was too much to think about to dwell on the past. Arvo and I stepped into the parlor that was currently functioning as a green room. Coats, jackets, boots and mittens, empty juice cartons and food wrappers littered the shabby furniture and every surface.

The performers and their parents poured into the room to change out of their costumes, exchange greetings and compliments and gather up their belongings and Arvo took my arm and drew me back into the now-empty hall.

"So, Hatti-girl. Any progress?"

I wanted to remind him that I'd only been working on the investigation for a few hours, that we didn't even know yet whether Liisa's death was accidental or otherwise. I swallowed the urge to make excuses.

"I haven't been able to find out too much about her. It seems nobody knew her well and there was nothing personal in her bedroom."

"Ah," he said, separating his fingers and running them through his rug of hair. "Her room. It is something special, yes?"

I thought I detected a hint of disapproval but his eyes twinkled and I realized it was more complicated. He was acknowledging that the decorating was over-the- top, but that he understood Pauline's need to make what she felt was a perfect environment for their surrogate daughter.

"Liisa did not spend too much time in that room," he said, with just a touch of dryness. "She was at school or choir practice or out. In the evening, she liked to visit me downstairs."

I was startled.

"Downstairs in the embalming room?"

"Yes and the office. Wherever I was working. She liked to talk about her dream of becoming a famous singer."

"I'd have thought the greenhouse would be more pleasant to visit."

"Yes, yes. She did so at first. But her skin began to itch and it turned out she was allergic to the fertilizer."

"That must have been hard on Pauline."

"*Joo,*" he said. Yes. "I asked her once and she said it was all right, that she spent time alone with Liisa after school."

An idea suddenly occurred to me.

"Did Liisa like to use the sauna?" Naturally, I pronounced it sow-na, in the approved Yooper dialect.

Arvo chuckled. "She did, then, but not for bathing. She likes to do her homework in there."

She studies in the sauna with the wooden benches and the lack of heat? Apparently, the pink really had been too much for the girl.

"What about friends?"

"We told her she could have people over but she never did. She must have been friendly with Barb Hakala and Astrid. They were in her class, but they never visited her here at the mortuary."

"What about boyfriends?"

"Just Matti. And just that once. For the Harvest Dance. Liisa," he said, his eyes moist, "was a homebody."

"Arvo," I spoke as gently as I could, "Liisa was dressed when you found her. Do you think she could have been going out somewhere?"

"No." The word was definite but I noticed he didn't meet my eyes.

"Is it possible she was running back to her father's house?"

"No." This time he looked directly at me. "She would have said." He squinted at me. "You look stressed, Hatti-girl. The festival is nearly over. Why don't I call the sheriff."

He was trying to let me off the hook, I thought, and possibly he just wanted the whole business over and done with.

"Let me stay on it a little longer," I heard myself say. "At least until we know why she died."

My cell phone rang and I excused myself to answer it.

"You'd better come over to the funeral home." Sonya's voice was grim. "I've found something."

I'm ashamed to say that the lurch in my stomach was excitement. It was the first concrete step. I was going to find out how Liisa Pelonen turned up dead on the floor of the Makis sauna.

Arvo had answered his phone at nearly the same time and he said, "Pauline wants to leave. She's calling to ask if you want a ride back to Calumet Street." I nodded and he disappeared down the corridor toward the kitchen. An instant later I felt big hands cupping my shoulders from the back and a word was whispered into my ear.

"Umlaut."

My stomach flipped again and my heart galloped but even before he turned me to face him, I knew it was Max. I found a smile for him despite the shock of hearing the nickname my husband had used for me.

Max's weathered face with its craggy features and the deep crinkles around his smiling brown eyes, was always a welcome sight, I reminded myself. He smelled of snow and pine and some sort of sexy soap. It was probably Lava, but it smelled sexy to me.

Max Guthrie has way more than his share of testosterone.

"Helluva show," he said. "So, just for the record, what was this St. Lucy supposed to have done to rate a yearly festival?"

"She turned down an offer to marry an Italian nobleman because she wanted to keep herself pure for God. His friends stabbed her in the eye and she bled to death which is why the costume includes a red sash."

"Ye gods. What about the candle thing on her head?"

"St. Lucy Day is also about bringing light to the cold, darkness of winter."

"Are the stories related?"

"Nah."

"Huh. I've told you this before, Umlaut, but you've got one weird little community up here."

There was affection in his voice and a twinkle in his eyes. Max was not only attractive, he was likable. I know some people (Sofi, Elli, sometimes me) thought he might be perfect for me since we were both in the fish business and for-all-intents-and-purposes, single. All I knew was that I got a tingle in my spine when he showed up even when he used the unfortunate nickname. I suddenly remembered what Sonya had suggested in our telephone call that morning.

"Max, do you have a law enforcement background?"

"Who says so?"

For whatever reason, I was reluctant to bring Sonya's name into the conversation. I waited and he finally answered.

"U.S. Marshal Service, among other things."

Pauline Maki appeared in the hall behind us and I knew I didn't have much time.

"I need to talk to you about something sensitive."

He glanced at the approaching woman, nodded, slightly and said, "tonight?"

"At my house. After the smorgasbord."

"I'll bring the wine and doughnuts."

"Doughnuts?"

"For breakfast." He winked, then turned in one easy, coordinated move and nodded to Pauline before excusing himself.

*Breakfast?*

# ELEVEN

Sonya greeted Pauline and me at the funeral home's front door. I was struck, as always, by the midwife's serene beauty. Her eyes appeared as dark as her hair except when the light caught them at a certain angle and it was obvious they were dark blue. Her complexion was soft and creamy as if she'd cruised through the thirty-five years of her life.

I sensed it wasn't true although Sonya never complained nor had she ever talked about what had brought her to the Keweenaw.

"Let's sit down somewhere," Sonya said. Pauline, hauling on her hostess hat, invited us up to her remodeled kitchen. "I'll make tea."

It was a gracious gesture but underscored, at least for me, how Pauline had never completely blended into our community. No one else in Red Jacket would have offered anything but coffee.

A few minutes later, the three of us, seated at a charming, enamel-topped table, were sipping tea from fragile bone-china cups. I couldn't help wishing it was coffee.

"I don't believe Liisa's death was an accident," Sonya said, getting right to the point. "I'm sorry. I know that makes this more difficult for you."

Pauline's hand, the one that held her teacup, trembled. My reaction was different. I felt an odd sense of excitement.

*Not an accident.*

"What makes you think that?" Pauline asked.

Sonya nodded. "The cut on her head isn't deep enough to have killed her. I'd be inclined to say she fell on something sharp."

"There was nothing in the sauna where she was found," I said, thinking aloud.

"Is it possible she had an accident somewhere else and that she staggered to the sauna and bled out?" Pauline asked.

The midwife shook her head. "There isn't enough blood for that scenario." She sighed. "In fact, there is so little blood I'm inclined to think she was hit after she died."

"But, why?" Pauline sounded as if she were about to cry.

"As a distraction? To cover up a murder?"

"But what makes you think there was foul play?" Pauline's voice shook. All the color drained out of her face and I thought I knew why. She was worried about how Arvo would react to a theory like this.

"I don't know for certain," Sonya said, gently. "Death may have been due to natural causes. Do you know whether Liisa had any medical condition that would have put her at risk?"

"No, no." She hesitated. "Well, nothing serious. I remember she told us she'd had a little flurry with Afib a year ago but that it was all cleared up."

"Afib?" Sonya peered at the older woman. "You mean an irregular heartbeat?"

Pauline returned the midwife's gaze.

"I don't know precisely what it is."

"I don't know precisely what it is. I just remember she told us she'd had a bout with it in the past but she wasn't on medication." She hesitated, then pinched her nose with her forefinger and thumb. "I would have known. If it had been a life-threatening condition, I would have known."

I exchanged a look with Sonya.

"Is it possible the trauma of the blow to the head affected her heartbeat?"

Sonya shook her head. "I'm afraid I don't know enough about the condition. I think the danger is that the heart rate can slow to a point where the oxygen simply isn't getting to the brain which causes a faint. She may have fainted but that wouldn't have killed her."

I said nothing. Pauline had hunched over. Her right hand shaded her eyes as if she couldn't bear to look at the present. Or the future. I suddenly wished I'd thought of holding this conference in the greenhouse; Pauline's sanctuary.

"I found something else," Sonya said, in a low voice. Her gaze, fixed on Pauline Maki, was compassionate and I tried to brace myself for bad news. "I found a possible motive for murder."

I let out an involuntary yelp and Pauline's eyes filled with despair.

"I performed an internal exam on her," Sonya said, speaking slowly and carefully as if aware she was navigating a minefield. "It's something I'm qualified to do and with a young girl, well, it seemed appropriate. In any case, I discovered her uterus was enlarged."

I stared at Sonya and was aware of Pauline doing the same thing.

"What does that mean," I finally asked. "Cancer?"

Sonya tried to hide an involuntary smile.

"Far from it. There's no easy way to say this. Liisa was pregnant, Hatti."

We heard Pauline's cup clatter against the saucer and neither of us looked at the woman's face. The news was a shock on so many levels. I wanted to give her time to absorb it and so, I suspected, did Sonya.

"That's just not possible," the older woman said, in a faint gasp. "She didn't have a boyfriend. She wasn't seeing anyone. We knew where she was at all times. It couldn't have happened." Her eyes met Sonya's. "You must be wrong."

Sonya's midnight eyes glowed with compassion.

"I'm sorry, Pauline."

"How pregnant?" I asked, in a low voice. "I mean, um, when did it happen?"

"About six weeks."

"Six weeks?" Pauline repeated the phrase as if it presented another shock. And then, all at once, her face turned the color of clown paint and she collapsed against the back of her chair. Sonya reached her before she could slide onto the floor.

"Get her a glass of water, Hatti," she said. She held the woman with one arm and slapped her face gently.

When she'd revived, a moment later, she accepted a few sips of water and allowed us to lead her into the green-and-white living room and prop her on the sofa. She sucked in a breath and apologized.

"I'm so sorry to be so much trouble," she murmured. "it's all been such a shock."

I patted her hand and Sonya told her it would be best if she'd lie down in her room but Pauline shook her head.

"Oh, no. I have to get over to the smorgasbord." When we started to protest, Pauline held up a hand. "I appreciate everything you've done for me but I want to go. I can't bear to think of Arvo worried about me." She looked at me. "Hatti, please. If you want to help don't tell him about this. Not yet. He adored that girl, you know, and this will simply break his heart."

As soon as we stepped into the hall, I saw the question in Sonya's eyes. And then she was asking it.

"Do you think Arvo will be surprised at this news?"

I knew what she meant. Statistics tell us that when a young woman is raped and/or murdered, the perp is most likely a family member.

"Arvo didn't rape her," I said, one hundred percent certain. "And I don't believe he killed her, either." Then I pictured Liisa, standing on the back of Ollie's sleigh, her face pinched and white with cold. Or, was it worry? And then there was the fact that she'd been dressed to go out last night. Had she been running away? If so, from what? Arvo?

"What about the timing? Does six weeks mean anything to you?"

I counted backward to the middle of October.

"Geez Louise! The Harvest Dance."

One of Sonya's smooth, dark eyebrows lifted.

"She attended it with a date. Matti Murso."

"I think," Sonya said, "he should be your first official interview."

The inn was very festive for the Saturday night dinner, the last smorgasbord of the St. Lucy Festival. Elli had substituted real candles for the electric ones on her Christmas tree and on the Scandinavian candle stand in the window and she'd decorated the antler chandelier in the parlor with the red-and-white Nordic Christmas balls the circle had knitted in November. Aunt Ianthe was plunking out Jingle Bells on the upright piano and several guests, including those from Lansing, were standing nearby with cups of spiked eggnog, singing along. Miss Irene, waiting to play the more musically complex carols, was ensconced in one of Elli's plump armchairs, working on a dainty project in pink—no doubt for Mrs. Kaukola's baby girl.

In the dining room, Elli had pushed her small, square pine tables to make two long, parallel tables—she liked to call them crocodiles. Both were covered with bright red linen runners and strategically placed evergreen wreaths as well as formal place settings. The food would go on the wide coffee stand at one end of the room.

The dining room itself was deserted but we could hear talking and laughing in the kitchen, including one male voice, and just as we reached the swinging door, it opened to reveal a man carrying a giant tray over his shoulder with such ease that he must have been a professional waiter in a previous lifetime.

Max Guthrie.

Pleasure surged through me and I greeted him only to find myself totally ignored. He set the tray down on the serving table and unloaded it. By the time he turned to speak to us, Sonya had slipped out a side door into the corridor.

"For goodness sake," I said to him, "what's the matter?" He found a smile for me and produced a little laugh.

"There was a lot riding on my shoulder," he quipped. "I just didn't want to drop it. So I'll see you tonight." He moved fast, brushed a quick kiss on my cheek and disappeared. When I stepped into the kitchen a few seconds later, he'd left the inn.

"What happened to Max?" I asked Elli.

"He had to get back to Namagok. He's got some guests checking in tonight."

"For fishing?"

"It must be ice fishing," she said. "Listen, I need you to make the coffee and set out the cups. Lickety-split, okay?"

Sofi arrived a few minutes later and she, Elli, Sonya and I set up all the food including, among other things, Mrs. Sorensen's ham and prunes, Aunt Ianthe's *kulta salantti*, or golden salad composed of carrots, mandarin oranges, orange juice and honey, Diane Hakala's corn pudding, Ronja Laplander's calico beans and the tender whitefish filets called *mojakka* that were Elli's specialty.

The dozen or so guests had lined up at the serving table and the Reverend Sorensen was about to offer a prayer of thanks, when we heard the front door open. A moment later, Pauline and Arvo Maki appeared in the dining room. There was a forced smile on Arvo's handsome face and Pauline looked like the proverbial image of death warmed over. They should both, I thought, be at home under warm blankets, but I wasn't surprised that they had made the effort to be here. It was typical of both of them to do their duty.

The Makis tried to smile at the greetings; *Hyvaa Joulu!* and Merry Christmas! They'd obviously been devastated by the death of their visitor. How would the others react when they knew? Ronja, for example, who was basking in the compliments about Astrid's performance as St. Lucy. Would she take some satisfaction in the girl's demise? And what about the Hakalas? They would express horror, of course, because they are civilized human beings but would some part of Diane feel that, with Liisa's death, justice had been done?

It was human nature to have mixed feelings but that was a far cry from committing a murder. And yet someone in our tight-knit community had crossed the line that separates the folks who occasionally say, "I'd like to kill her" from the ones who are willing to do the deed. Was it Matti Murso? Or was there someone else, someone cleverer than Toivo Murso's son? Someone I hadn't yet identified?

It was very weird eating traditional Finnish foods on this holiday, with neighbors I'd known all my life and wondering which, if any of them, had spent last night murdering the girl who'd been chosen to play St. Lucy. I picked up my too-hot coffee, burned my tongue and let out a gasp and that caused Aunt Ianthe's head to snap around like the rubber band on a slingshot.

"*Voi!* Henrikki! Don't tell me you ate a bite of Edna's cabbage! You know it does not agree with you." Miss Irene had clapped her hands together and brought them to her mouth in an expression of horror. "You know, Irene! You know! Remember that time Hatti ate the cabbage and her whole face swelled up and we had to rush her to Doc Laitimaki over in Frog Creek?"

The scene had been re-enacted many times over the years. Many, many times. Miss Irene, the loyal sidekick, as always played her part.

"Oh, mercy me," she exclaimed, her hands at her breast her eyes on me. "Oh, Hatti, you were so sick that time, then."

I had been sick. It was nearly twenty-five years ago, now, at a church potluck. My folks were on a trip and the aunts were in charge of Sofi and me. I was caught (according to Aunt Ianthe, I confess I do not remember) with my fingers in or near Mrs. Moilanen's vinegar cabbage and within a few minutes, someone noticed my face had swollen to beach-ball size. Doc Laitimaki said it was the mumps and the proximity to vinegar cabbage was a mere coincidence but Aunt Ianthe had never believed that and I had long ago stopped trying to convince her that I never had and never would eat vinegar cabbage.

"I didn't eat it," I said when my aunt had quieted down. "I choked on the coffee. It was too hot."

There was a brief, universal silence as we waited for the familiar benediction. In just a few seconds, Miss Irene's fluting voice filled the room.

"Heal the sick, raise the dead, cleanse those who have leprosy, drive out demons. Freely you have received, freely give. Matthew."

The visitors appeared mildly puzzled but mostly resigned. Apparently, they'd become accustomed to our odd quirks.

Edna Moilanen, while very fond of both Miss Irene and Aunt Ianthe, was understandably weary of the periodic attacks on her most famous dish and she was the one who changed the subject.

"Pauline, are you certain we can obtain the proper wool to make authentic Shetland wedding ring shawls? Perhaps we should settle for something less rare and costly. Some of us are, you know, fledgling knitters."

All the locals knew Mrs. M. was not referring to herself. She had learned to knit, she was fond of saying, at her grandmother's knee and had, over her lifetime, made dozens of scarves and hundreds of mittens. She had a tendency to point out projects that might be too difficult for new knitters. She may have been thinking about the beginners but I suspected that, mostly, she wanted to preserve the distinction (and superiority) between them and the masters.

There was also the strong possibility that her nose was slightly out of joint as I had agreed to Pauline's project idea without consulting her. In fact, I'd barely thought about the suggestion. I'd been distracted with the festival preparations and the police job and, perhaps, most of all, with the approach of the anniversary of my marital implosion. I hadn't cared what project the knitting circle chose.

Now, though, I was willing to go to the mat for the grieving surrogate mother.

If Pauline wanted to make lace shawls, then, by Jiminy, as Pops would say, we'd make them.

"The yarn arrived yesterday," I fibbed. "And Pauline has made photocopies of the directions. I have a dozen size 00 circular needles and we can start the lace knitting as soon as this week." Thursday night had been designated for circle meetings to avoid conflicts with the town council meetings on Mondays, the school board meetings on Tuesdays, potluck and choir practice on Wednesdays, family night on Fridays and, of course, the Saturday night sauna.

"Hatti, dear," Mrs. Sorensen said, "I understand it is easy to lose your place while working on heirloom lace."

"Goodness me," Aunt Ianthe interjected, at the spectre of not being able to knit and chat at the same time.

"Pish-posh," Mrs. Moilanen put in. "Lace is lace. It is just a bunch of yarn-overs and knit two together."

I held up a hand to forestall other comments.

"Luckily," I said, "Pauline has offered to walk us through the pattern, stitch by stitch, until we have memorized it."

"Like bingo," Mrs. Moilanen said, dryly.

"I'm afraid I don't have much of a memory," Miss Irene said, which, of course, was absurd since she'd memorized the entirety of the King James Version.

"I'll help you, dear," Aunt Ianthe said, patting her hand. "We'll get through it together. And, don't worry, Henrikki, dear. Irene and I will bring a fresh batch of *Joulutorttu.*"

# TWELVE

Sofi left early to meet Charlie who had been with her father, while Elli settled her guests then set the tables for the morning smorgasbord. Sonya and I washed by hand Elli's lovely Danish Christmas plates and then it was time to leave. The midwife and I put on our parkas and boots and stepped out onto the back porch. There was no wind and the snow seemed to float on the air. I yawned.

"Sorry," I said, belatedly covering my mouth. "I'm just so danged tired." Sonya had stopped and was fumbling with something in her pocket. "What's up?"

"I found something during the pseudo autopsy."

"You mean besides the pregnancy?" It was a weak attempt at a joke and she didn't laugh.

"Jewelry. Liisa was wearing it around her neck. I didn't want to mention it in front of Pauline in case she had given it to her, but the more I thought about it, the less likely that seemed."

"Very mysterious," I said, holding out my hand, palm up, as she drizzled a chain into it. The pendant on the end was the last thing to drop.

"The spider web in the middle of the circle is intended to catch and hold bad dreams and the feathers are supposed to transport the good dreams back to the sleeping child. The bad dreams disappear with the rising sun. It's an Indian dreamcatcher."

I stared at the object in my hand as if it were a moon rock or the Hope Diamond. Unfortunately, it was something much more familiar.

"Do you recognize it?" Sonya asked, softly.

"It belonged to Miriam Night Wind, a fifteen-year-old from the Copper Eagle Reservation. She got pregnant and fled to Canada. Her son, Jace, gave it to me on our wedding day."

Sonya made a startled sound. "Oh, Hatti. I'm sorry." I nodded.

"The real question is how did it wind up, eighteen months later, around the neck of a dead girl?"

Neither of us had any answer to that.

"Let me walk you home," Sonya said. I declined. I felt buffeted by memories and I wanted to be alone with them. There were plenty of good times. In the beginning, it had seemed like a fairytale. I hadn't been looking for Prince Charming but he'd showed up anyway. He'd been tall, dark and enigmatic, a man of few words and so smitten that he claimed he could not let me go. Until he could, and did.

I was still waiting for answers.

I'd met Jace Night Wind during my first year at the University of Michigan law school in Ann Arbor. The mid-sized college town with its thousands of students jaywalking across the streets and tens of thousands of fans streaming toward the stadium on football Saturdays, the pizzas and beer that replaced pasties and *pannukakku* and the general clamor had been something of a culture shock to a girl brought up on the remote Keweenaw Peninsula but I'd loved it. Finally, I was getting to see the world.

Toward the end of my first year, I went to see a guest lecturer speak on Indian rights. He wore his hair in a straight black ponytail but his eyes were gray. Silver-gray. With long, dark lashes. The talk was fascinating, or so I was told. I spent the entire event reminding myself there was no such thing as love at first sight. It turned out I was wrong.

I'd never felt like that before and I hated the heaviness in my heart that I felt for the rest of the day. I was glad, in fact, to get a call from a rescue group I belonged to and happily trotted to a home on the edge of town to accept a cardboard carton of homeless puppies even though by the time I made it back to campus, it was sprinkling.

A few blocks from my graduate dorm, the deluge increased and the puppies began to squeak with alarm as the soggy box began to collapse on them. Just as I was wondering what to do, an ancient Jeep Wrangler pulled up next to me and a tall, lean man unfolded himself from the seat, grabbed the limp box and bundled it and me into the vehicle. It should have been frightening or at least intimidating but the thing was, even with rain pelting down on him, Jace Night Wind looked appealing. I think it was those eyelashes.

"Where to," he shouted, against the noise of the pelting downpour.

I told him the name of my dorm and he shook his head.

"They don't allow dogs."

"Oh, I know. I'll hide them for a few days until I can find homes for them."

By now the puppies were squalling with fear and Jace put the standard shift vehicle into gear and headed off in the wrong direction.

"Hey," I protested. "Where are you taking us?"

"Home," he'd said. "To my home. And don't give me any lip about being abducted by a stranger. I saw you in the lecture this morning."

He had? He'd noticed me? I felt as dizzy as Cinderella and I did not protest again as he parked behind a student apartment building and put his finger to his lips as we hustled the puppies up the backstairs.

Several hours later, when everyone was dry and fed, and the six puppies were asleep, I asked the question that had been on my mind.

"The dogs aren't allowed here, either. How is this better than taking them to my room?"

The gray eyes kindled and I felt engulfed in warmth.

"If you don't know yet, you will, Henrikki Lehtinen."

He turned out to be right. Apparently, Cupid had struck twice that day and from then on, for the next eighteen months, I'd experienced the incandescent joy of loving and being loved.

A week later, after we'd found homes for the puppies and I'd dropped out of law school, we got married at the Washtenaw County

Courthouse then we drove the Olive-green Wrangler to Washington D.C. where Jace started a Native American Law Center and I worked as his unpaid office manager. We lived in a tiny apartment on Capitol Hill and, at first, spent weekends exploring the city and the nearby Virginia countryside. And then the nonprofit began to grow and Jace began to travel.

His trip to the Pine Ridge Reservation in South Dakota happened during the first week of December and he told me he intended to make a stop on the Keweenaw to visit his grandfather, Chief Joseph Night Wind on the Copper Eagle Reservation just fifteen miles away from Red Jacket. He invited me to come with but, by then, we had a couple of other lawyers working with us and my presence was essential to the running of the office. I thanked him, spent more time on the phone with my sister and Elli and my mom and dad, and began to decorate for Christmas. I thought it was important to represent both our cultures so I lugged home a much-too-large pine tree and covered it with straw ornaments and baskets and colored lights. I bought the ingredients for the fry bread Jace loved and for *Joulutorttu* the Christmas prune tarts.

I was, in fact, in the middle of blending the stiff dough on the Friday afternoon Jace was due home. I was beyond excited and kept turning off the mixer to listen for his key in the front door.

Finally, irritated with myself, I turned on the radio and in the middle of "Grandma Got Run Over By A Reindeer" I heard the key in the lock. I flew to the foyer, launched myself into his arms and hugged as hard as I could. It wasn't the first time I'd greeted him that way and before he'd hugged me back so hard I could hear his heart beating fast and he'd buried his face in my waist-length hair.

This time was different.

I didn't want to believe it but I knew it was true. He relaxed his hold on me and I stepped back and looked up into the gray eyes. There was no welcome there. No blazing heat. Just an expression of soul-deep empathy and I knew it was for me.

"I'm sorry, Umlaut."

I swallowed around a sudden lump in my throat.

"Sorry for what?"

"It's over." He paused. "We're over."

At first, I was a fish caught under the ice. I couldn't speak. And then the ice melted and I couldn't stop speaking. I couldn't stop asking. Why? Why, why, why?

He never lost his temper, never yelled at me. He repeated the apology and, eventually, told me to take the Jeep.

"Take the Jeep where?"

"Home," he'd said, in a parody of the first time he'd referred to the place as ours. "Back to the Keweenaw. It's over."

I don't know how I got back. I don't remember much about the eighteen-hour drive except for the stop in Toledo for gas when it occurred to me that I'd left the *Joulutorttu* dough on the counter in the mixer, like the Hebrews fleeing Egypt with only unleavened bread.

The reactions to my precipitous return were varied. My mom harped on about the folly of ever leaving Red Jacket. My sister wanted to know what the scoundrel had done to me. Elli didn't talk about my troubles. Neither did Pops, at least for the first few months. About February he suggested that I might like to run Carl's Bait Shop and I agreed. He approved the addition of yarn and knitting supplies and spoke of selling me the business if that's what I wanted.

I don't know. And when I say that, I mean I don't know whether I want to stay in Red Jacket and run Bait and Stitch. I don't know what happened to destroy my marriage. And I don't even know whether I am still married, although I imagine I am since I haven't signed a divorce paper.

My sister wants me to be more proactive about dissolving the union and maybe I will.

But first, I have to find out why Liisa Pelonen was wearing my dream catcher pendant around her neck.

I could barely lift my feet as I slogged up the front porch steps. I hadn't locked the door but I hadn't left on the porch light, either, so I was pretty much operating on instinct. I'm not sure when I realized I wasn't alone on the front porch. No one had spoken or made a move. I just sensed it. Or maybe I smelled it. There was a definite tang of something woody, fresh and masculine. And then I remembered.

Max.

The prospect did nothing to lift the heaviness I felt and, just for an instant, I regretted asking him to come over tonight. And then the masculine scent turned into a touch on the shoulder. It was a gentle touch. I felt it against my skin even through my quilted parka and sweatshirt and I knew it wasn't Max.

"Jace."

# THIRTEEN

"In the flesh."

His tone didn't match the cockiness of his response and I knew he wasn't sure of his reception. With good reason, I thought.

"What are you doing here?"

"I need to talk to you." He produced a bottle. "And I've got wine."

I hadn't expected to see him again until after I'd made my mark in the world, you know, married Brad Pitt or won a Pulitzer Prize...something along that line. I didn't know what to do and I couldn't seem to think. He reached past me, opened the front door and flicked on the light in the foyer.

"Before you offer me coffee, I should probably confess to something."

I looked at him. We were both soaked from the snow but while I knew I looked like a drowned rat, he looked beautiful, with his high, sharp cheekbones and the long, feathery dark lashes framing those silver eyes. There was something different, I thought, but I wasn't sure what.

"Confess?"

"Yeah. I didn't bring the wine with me. I got it from some guy who was loitering on your doorstep. He gave it to me when I informed him that you and I were married. Apparently, it was news."

*Max.* I made a mental note to apologize to him in the morning.

"What is it you want to talk about," I asked, "that couldn't have been handled in a phone call?"

He glanced at my stringy hair and my soaked jacket.

"It can wait." He turned me toward the stairs inside the door. "Your room up there? Go on. Dry your hair and change clothes before you catch cold. Hell, you might as well put on your p.j.s."

The whole thing seemed like a dream. I had the feeling that if I did go upstairs and change into my pajamas, I'd fall asleep and when I awoke none of this would have happened. How dare he come back and act as if everything was fine between us? As if we were still married?

I returned a short time later, wearing jeans and a sweatshirt emblazoned with an outline of the Upper Peninsula and the words: Michigan's Better Half. He'd made his way to the kitchen and had put on a pot of coffee. Two wine glasses, filled with a Chablis, were set out on my mom's oilcloth-covered table.

"Got anything to eat?" he asked, turning to look at me.

"I know what it is," I said. "You've cut your hair."

He set two mugs on the table then looked at me.

"It's more professional. You've cut yours, too."

"Easier to take care of."

My chest hurt as we lied to one another. At least I lied. I'd hacked off my hair out of rage and frustration and grief. Short hair is a mourning tradition in some Native American cultures and the idea had appealed to me.

I had no idea about Jace and he clearly did not intend to explain.

"What's the story with the wine guy?"

I blinked at him. "Max? I invited him. He was here to do me a favor."

"What kind of favor? Change the bulb on the front porch?"

"No. I wanted to pick his brain about something."

Jace scowled and I noticed that, in addition to the short hair, his face was thinner and more heavily lined. He'd probably been working too hard. My heart twisted inside my chest and when Jace said something, I didn't hear it. "What?"

"Food."

"Oh." I moved toward the shiny, new jade-colored breadbox that was supposed to look like an antique, removed a plate covered with plastic wrap and set it on the table. Jace stared at it.

"*Joulutorttu?*"

I was surprised he remembered.

"Yeah. Sorry. I wasn't expecting company tonight."

"What about mysterious Max?"

"Do you want them or not?

"I absolutely do," he said, pouring the fresh coffee into the mugs, pulling out a chair for me then seating himself. I'd always wondered how he had learned such good manners during his dysfunctional childhood. "I love prune tarts. I baked the ones you left behind, you know. And then I ate every one of them."

I stared at him. "I'm glad to hear they didn't go to waste."

He ate three tarts in quick succession and, for once, I didn't interrupt the quiet. This was his idea, his party. I'd asked all my questions a year earlier and the only response had been a year of silence. I realized I had lost that frantic need-to-know somewhere along the line. My heart still sped up in his presence but somehow it was different. I had finally fallen out of love.

I wondered why I didn't feel happier about that.

A contented sounding snuffle reached my ears and I realized Jace was rubbing the skin behind Larry's ear. I wanted to shout at him not to be nice to my dog. I wanted to order him to leave my home—well, my parents' home—and never come back.

"All right," I said, not bothering to hide my irritation, "what is so important that you had to shlep to the UP?"

He held my gaze and said, "it's about the girl who died."

Something lurched in my chest and I could feel warmth in my cheeks. He was here about Liisa Pelonen. At almost the same moment, I remembered the dreamcatcher. Coincidence? I didn't think so.

"Liisa Pelonen," I said, trying not to reveal how much it hurt that this trip wasn't about me.

"Yes. The St. Lucy girl. My grandfather called me last night and I got here as soon as I could."

"Your grandfather? I don't understand. What did Chief Joseph have to do with Liisa?"

But I knew. That is, I didn't know what it was exactly but I knew there was a connection because of the dreamcatcher. Suddenly I realized what he had said about the timing.

"Your grandfather called you last night? She only died last night, sometime between seven and nine. How could he have known?"

"Reid told him."

"Reid?"

His sensuous lips twisted into a half-smile. "Out of sight out of mind. Reid Night Wind. My half brother."

Of course. I had forgotten. Or, maybe I'd just pushed everything to do with Jace to the far recesses of my mind.

"How did your brother know about the death?"

He hesitated. "This conversation is strictly off the record, okay, Umlaut?"

"I'm not a journalist."

"No, but you're the acting top cop and you're heading up this investigation, aren't you?"

A part of me wondered how he knew that. It was supposed to be a secret between Arvo and Pauline and me. Another, bigger part, was busy being hurt. Jace really had come to the Keweenaw to protect his family—his real family, not his temporary wife.

I took refuge in toughness.

"Are you gonna tell me or not?"

He nodded. "I trust you not to hurt Reid. The trouble is, he was there."

I nearly jumped out of my seat.

"When she died? He was there when she died?"

"Just afterwards. They had planned to meet in the sauna at the funeral home but when he got there, she was already dead. He didn't kill her, Hatti."

"How can you know that?"

"Because he told grandfather he didn't and no one, in their right mind, would lie to grandfather."

Fear for Jace slammed into my gut. Chief Joseph, who had to be a hundred and ten, and Reid Night Wind, were his only family. If Reid were to be convicted of murder, Jace would spent most of the rest of his life alone. I fought, for a minute, to remind myself that it was not my problem.

"What was the relationship between your brother and Liisa?"

"They were friendly. He was like a big brother. Something was bothering her and she confided in him. The plan, last night, was for them to run away together."

"You mean elope?"

He looked uncomfortable.

"Not literally. She wanted to leave Red Jacket and he was going to help her get away. They'd met a few times in the sauna because nobody used it except Arvo Maki on Saturday nights. She'd told him everyone would be at the smorgasbord at the inn and the coast would be clear."

I thought about that.

"If she was running away, wouldn't she have had a suitcase?"

He nodded.

"There wasn't one. Not in the sauna. Not in her room. No sign of a suitcase. No sign of clothes missing, either. It must have been stolen, by the person who killed her."

"Not Reid. Grandfather said the girl was afraid of something or someone. That's why Reid wanted to help her."

"You said she was bothered."

"Well, afraid sounds kinda melodramatic. Like something a teenage girl would say. But that was the term. Afraid. Frightened. Scared."

"I don't buy it. Arvo loved her like a daughter. She'd have told him."

"Unless he was the threat."

"She couldn't have been afraid of Arvo."

"Why not?"

"He would never hurt anyone and, like I said, he loved her like a father."

He sneered at that. "Nine times out of ten violence against young women comes from the men in their lives and that includes fathers."

We'd reached an impasse.

"All right, tell me this. If your brother is innocent, why didn't he contact the police when he found Liisa's body?"

"Are you nuts? He's an Ojibwe kid who's already got a rap sheet. The cops would have slapped him in jail and thrown away the key before I could catch a flight out of Reagan."

"Not," I said, with some pride, "if he had contacted me."

"Come off it, Hatti. I know you're standing in for your stepfather but you don't have any real authority over this kind of crime. My guess is you're investigating it undercover, the way you did the lighthouse business last summer."

"How do you even know about the lighthouse murders? You haven't been in my life for a year."

"Never mind. The point here is that Reid couldn't take a chance."

I wondered what he meant. Had he kept tabs on me? But why, when he wanted nothing more than to send me packing with a flea in my ear.

"What are his priors?"

"He got busted five years ago for running a cat lab up in the Porkies."

Methcathinone, or "cat," was the poor man's methamphetamine, and cat labs had proliferated in the UP during the past twenty years, partly because of the remote location and partly because the substance could be made using household items including lithium batteries, aquarium tubing, starter fluid, acetone and Gatorade bottles.

"He was cleared of that charge. He was also cleared in the other complaint," he added, with a slight grimace.

"The other charge?"

He didn't want to tell me. I could tell because he paused as if waiting for me to jump in to ease the awkwardness. He knew me so well. For once, though, I waited. I really needed to know. Finally, he spoke.

"It was a paternity suit."

*Hell's bells!* Reid Night Wind was the father of Liisa's baby. I felt a wave of pure terror for Jace. There was going to be no way out of this. And he didn't know. I'd have bet my Jeep Explorer on it. I wished, suddenly, fervently, that I could talk to Pops. He would know how to handle this. I didn't realize I'd said it out loud until Jace's dark brows met between his eyes.

"Pops? Are you referring to your paragon of a stepfather?"

"I don't know that he's a paragon but he's a great father." I was only half listening. "He's wise and fair and he's kind, Jace. He's the kind of person you want with you in times of trouble."

The sneer twisted his mouth again.

"I can see you really believe that."

It was not the first time we'd argued about fathers. Jace had a life-long, totally justified grudge against the man who had abandoned his mother and him. Miriam, never very stable, had drifted into prostitution and alcoholism and Jace had been responsible for himself, his mother and, eventually, his half brother.

"I need to talk to Reid."

"Yeah. I know. That's why I came to see you. I'll take you to him."

I swallowed this last cruel reminder that Jace had not come to discuss our marriage.

"No, thanks. Just give me the address. I've got Google maps."

"I hate to be the one to tell you this," he drawled, "but your cell-phone's not gonna work up in the Porkies."

The Porcupine Mountains or Porkies is the name of a small mountain range located just south of us in Gogebic and Ontonagon Counties.

"Reid and I built a cabin up there when we first came to the Copper Eagle when I was eighteen and Reid was eight. It's where he had his meth lab."

*Geez Louise.*

I've always been a little ashamed of the fact that I grew up in a rural wilderness and yet I'm happier with a pond than a lake, a rosebush than a white pine and, quite frankly, a sidewalk instead of a dirt path. The lack of outdoorsman skills (and interest) is just one of the reasons I value Einar's sure hand at the bait shop.

I tried to visualize myself hiking up a steep mountain path, knee-deep in snow. No picture materialized.

"He'll have to come here."

Jace's spontaneous laugh was more of a bark than an expression of pleasure but I was still glad to hear it.

"That's not going to happen, Hatti. Either you go with me or you don't get to interview him."

"I could just turn this information over to the sheriff," I pointed out. He regarded me with a grave expression.

"You could but you won't. I know you pretty well and I know that despite your justifiable anger at me, you would never revenge yourself on someone I loved." I said nothing. I was remembering what it had been like to be loved by Jace Night Wind. "So. I'll pick you up in the morning?"

"Fine," I said, getting out of my chair. "Goodnight."

"Hold on there, Umlaut. If I'm not mistaken, we've just forged a partnership." He waited to hear an objection but I just looked at him. "Right," he said. "Well, I'd be pleased if you would tell me what you know about this case so far. We're on the same side, you know."

"Even if Reid is guilty?"

"I'm a sworn officer of the court. I want to find the truth."

I took a minute to consider. I'd believed that Jace was like Pops, as ethical as they come and focused on helping others. He was devoting his career to finding justice for Indian tribes and individuals all over the country. On the other hand, he had not honored his commitment to me. But, perhaps, that was different. I'd long ago concluded that our flash-fire romance had been a flash-in-pan for Jace. He was young. Only thirty-one. Why should he tie himself to a woman he no longer wanted?

I understood. Kind of.

I just wish he'd told me how he felt; that he'd spelled it out.

I have to admit I'm not all that good at reading between the lines, especially if I'm not fond of the narrative.

"Okay," I said and detailed Liisa's schedule for Friday, December 12, everything from breakfast to the (alleged) impromptu trip to the Frostbite Mall in Houghton, to being late for the parade which prevented her from wearing long underwear.

"She got a chill and a sore throat and the Makis decided she should stay home in bed while they went to the smorgasbord. Pauline left the house around six fifteen but returned twenty minutes or so later to pick up some thimbleberry jam. She didn't peek in on Liisa because the girl is a light sleeper and she didn't want to wake her. When Pauline and Arvo got home a little before nine they looked in on her and found her bed empty. It took fifteen or twenty minutes to find her because the sauna was the last place they looked."

His brows knit. It was an expression of deep concentration and brought back a flood of memories.

"She never called for help?"

"No." And then I frowned, as I realized I didn't know. If Liisa had called Arvo or Pauline, the likelihood was that the ring wouldn't have been heard in the din of the smorgasbord. "They would have told me if she'd called."

"Hatti." He looked at me sternly. "The first rule of investigating is never trust a suspect."

I wanted to protest that the Makis had been heartbroken about Liisa's death, that they weren't suspects or even witnesses and then I thought of something else.

"I hope you will remember that when we talk to your brother."

His face cleared in surprise and he nodded.

"How did the Makis explain that Liisa was fully dressed and, apparently, on her way out?"

"They didn't. They didn't know. Until a few minutes ago nobody knew she was planning to leave town with Reid Night Wind."

Jace shook his head. "Somebody knew. Somebody wanted her dead and decided to set him up as the killer."

"That's a pretty big leap."

"Is it? There's too much inside knowledge, Hatti. How many people knew she had a sore throat and wouldn't attend the smorgasbord? Add to that, who knew the Makis would leave her home alone? Who knew that she was scared of something and intending to run away as soon as Arvo Makis back was turned? Where's the suitcase? Where's her purse?"

I gazed at him steadily as the answer presented itself. Only one person knew all of that. Only Reid Night Wind. He looked away but said, "he had no reason to kill her."

"Jace," I said, gently, trying to protect him as much as I could. "Reid did have a motive. Sonya Stillwater, the local midwife, examined her body this afternoon." There was no easy way to say it so I just blurted it out.

"Liisa was pregnant."

The muttered oath contained so much anguish that Larry got up from his kitchen bed, padded across the floor and put his chin on Jace's knee.

Just for an instant, I wished I could do the same.

# FOURTEEN

A n hour later I stretched out on my childhood bed and stared up at my glow-in-the-dark stars and wondered what I'd gotten myself into.

It wasn't so much the investigation of Liisa Pelonen's suspicious death, although that's where it had started. It was this new complication that had my stomach twisting in knots.

"Dress in layers tomorrow," Jace had said, on his way out the door. "And bring whatever food you've got. And a bottle of water. I'll take care of the sleeping bags."

"The what??"

He'd turned to smile at me, the grim expression erased if only for a moment.

"It's a six-hour hike up and back and impossible to do in the dark. We'll come back in the morning."

"What?"

"You know, Umlaut," he said, his finger lightly brushing my cheek, "Either your vocabulary has regressed or you're afraid of spending the night with me. I'm not going to ravish you, you know."

I knew that. He'd made it clear, a year ago, he no longer wanted me.

"It isn't that. I don't like camping, especially in the winter."

"We're not going to be outside. The cabin has a fireplace and besides, we'll have a chaperone, remember?"

I clamped down on the urge to argue. There really was no choice if I wanted to interview Reid Night Wind before this whole thing got handed over to Sheriff Clump and I did want to. Jace was right in believing the lawman would make short work of Reid. It seemed to me the kid was guilty, dead to rights, but I wanted him to have a chance to prove his innocence. I had to go.

"One other thing," he'd said, as he opened the back door and started to head toward his grandfather's truck. "That guy that was here tonight."

"Max?"

He nodded. "What's the deal with him?"

I'd been tempted to say that Max and I were embroiled in a hot and heavy affair. There would have been some satisfaction in showing Jace that I'd moved on, and, in fact, there was a chance that Max was my future. But he wasn't my present. Not in that way and I found I couldn't lie.

"He's got a law enforcement background and I wanted to talk to him about the case so I invited him over."

"What about the wine?"

I shrugged and answered as honestly as I could.

"We're friends. Maybe a bit more. I don't see that it's any of your business."

"It is if you intend to talk to him about my brother."

I cocked my head to one side.

"What happened to I'm-a-sworn-officer-of-the-court and I-want-to-find-the-truth?"

He scowled. "Still stands. I'll find it. And without help from your boyfriend."

His voice had gotten louder and I replied in kind.

"Max isn't my boyfriend."

And Jace, as he often did, got in the last shouted word.

"Good!"

I smiled into the darkness as I remembered but the amusement didn't last long.

"What was I thinking," I asked Larry, who was curled around my feet. "I must be out of my mind."

With the prospect of spending a day and a night with my ex to say nothing of the responsibility for finding out what had happened to Liisa Pelonen, I didn't think I'd be able to relax enough to sleep but before I knew it Betty Ann's chirp sounded in my ear:

"Good morning, Keweenaians! Rise and Shine! Today is the perfect time to trek out to the woods to search for your tree!"

Just for a moment, before I fully regained my senses, I pretended it was an ordinary December Sunday and that my husband and I were headed out to the wilderness, not to interview a suspect in a murder investigation but to cut down our own Christmas tree.

Reality hit with Betty Ann's next words.

"Take a bottle of water and a compass. You don't want to spend a night on Bald Mountain."

I threw my legs over the side of the bed, got to my feet and tried to summon some *Sisu*, which is a highly prized Finnish concept of inner strength. Nowhere in Luther's Small Catechism, as my mom would say, did it promise that life would be easy, only that it was important to address it with dignity and a moral code. I had a job to do and I intended to stiffen my spine and get on with it.

As soon as I had some coffee.

I dressed in layers of long underwear, flannel-lined jeans, heavy socks, a gray turtleneck and an ancient forest-green sweatshirt that had once belonged to my ex-brother-in-law, Lars. It read, Eh, B, C, a play on the Yooper tendency to end a sentence with the meaningless syllable, eh. I'd chosen it because I wanted to make clear to Jace that I was not getting dolled up for him. Also, because I hadn't done laundry in a while.

Using the same logic, I bypassed mascara and eyeliner, applied just enough strawberry lipgloss to keep my lips from chapping and ran a brush through my spiky hair. I coaxed Larry to accompany me through the snow to the Leaping Deer with the promise of syrup-drenched *pannukakku.*

The crowd had thinned out. Neither Sofi nor Sonya were there. Mrs. Moilanen and Diane Hakala helped Elli and me serve the smorgasbord and it wasn't until I spotted Arvo dining with the guests from Lansing, that I realized Pauline wasn't there, either.

"Is Pauline all right?" I asked Arvo, when I got a chance to talk to him alone.

He shook his head. "She's taking it very hard, Hatti-girl. She says it's her fault. I encouraged her to stay in the greenhouse this morning. It is her happy place." I nodded. "Listen, Pauly and I are going to take the guests up to Copper Harbor this morning then, this afternoon, they will catch flights back down south. (South is shorthand for the mitten part of the state.) After that, you and I will talk, eh?"

By mid-afternoon, I expected to be half way up a mountain.

"Arvo, you said I could have until the end of the weekend to investigate. I want to hold you to that."

He shook his head, as though thinking.

"We will be in enough trouble, Henrikki, for holding out so long."

I hesitated. I didn't want to tell him about Reid. Heck, I didn't want it to be Reid. But there were so many signs that pointed to him and I wanted some answers before Sheriff Clump got involved.

"I have a lead," I said. "I'll tell you all about it tomorrow. Just keep it under wraps until then, okay?"

I could tell he didn't want to. The horror had subsided a little and now he was just a sad, surrogate dad with an unresolved situation and a body in his mortuary.

"All right, then," he said. "Tomorrow. Bright and early. First thing."

I wouldn't be back until afternoon but there was no way I was going to get into that.

"Thank you," I said, and kissed him on the cheek.

It didn't occur to me until he had walked off that I'd just blown my opportunity to avoid an overnight trek with Jace and, because I am fundamentally honest with myself, I acknowledged that a part of me—the impulsive, risk-taking part of me that had married a man I'd known less than a week—wanted to go.

I shoved my arms into my parka and found Elli in the dining room brushing crumbs off the tablecloth.

"Listen, can you keep Larry overnight for me?"

"Sure," she said, then she stopped what she was doing and looked up. "Overnight? Is this part of the investigation?"

I was glad I'd found a moment the previous night to tell her about Liisa.

"Yep."

My cousin studied my face with her guileless blue eyes and I found myself telling her the surprising story of Jace's return and his brother's involvement.

"Holy moly, Hatti," she said. "Do you think it's a good idea to go into the mountains with him?"

I shrugged. "I don't have a choice."

Her delicate features were twisted in concern for me.

"I could go in your place."

It was an idea and not a bad one. Elli would not come back home in an emotional body bag after spending time with Jace. And she'd know what questions to ask Reid, as well as I.

"Thanks, anyway," I said. "I want to go."

She gave me a worried half smile.

"I know. That's what worries me."

---

Jace was lounging against the railing on my parents' front porch. He reminded me of a lean, hungry jungle cat who'd strayed into the snow belt and I felt my heart slam against my ribs. *Dang.* Maybe Ellie was right. Maybe this was a mistake.

He never took his eyes off me as I waded through the foot of snow and my heart pumped harder. Was he thinking about how much he'd missed me? Had he changed his mind about us? What would I do if he asked me to get back together with him? What would I do if he didn't?

I decided to call him out.

"What are you looking at?"

"Your walk," he replied. "It's a kind of glide, isn't it? That the best way to get through knee-deep snow?"

He was interested in the mechanics of navigating the snow? Well, I'd asked.

"Yep," I said. He nodded.

"We'll take the pickup."

"Fine." I said, suddenly exhausted. "Just let me get my backpack."

I hadn't heard him follow me inside, but when I hoisted the pack up off the kitchen table it flew out of my arms and found its way onto Jace's back.

"I can carry it," I protested. He just grinned at me.

"Save your strength. Where's the dog?"

Not only did he think I couldn't carry my own things, he thought I'd neglected to make arrangements for Larry.

"At a spa. He signed up for a massage and a colon cleanse. The works."

"No need to be sarcastic, Umlaut. I didn't mean to second guess you. Seems I've developed some dictatorial habits since I've been responsible for everything at work and at home."

And whose choice was that I wanted to ask, but there was no need. He seemed to read my mind and the half-smile dropped off his face.

The pick up was composed of two colors, white and rust, but the engine started at once and the heat worked. We belted up and I scanned the horizon as he turned it around in the alley and headed out to Tamarack Street toward M-41 going west.

"Coast clear?"

"What?"

"You seem jumpy, like you don't want any of your friends to see you with me."

"I think we should get one thing straight right from the get-go. This is a fact-finding mission, nothing more, nothing less. It isn't personal."

He turned left and then right.

"You should know by now, Umlaut, that everything between you and me is personal. Even a murder investigation."

I ignored the first part of the comment and focused on the second part.

"You think it was murder, too, then?"

"Hell, yeah. A carefully planned, well-thought-out execution, complete with a prime suspect."

"But why? Why would anyone target a teenaged girl?"

97

"Money."

"But Liisa didn't have any money. Neither does her natural father who lives in a remote cabin out near Ahmeek. I suppose it's possible that Arvo could have written her into his will but he's still a relatively young man. And he's healthy. That just doesn't make sense."

"Greed is the most common motivation for murder," Jace insisted.

"What about jealousy and revenge?"

He shrugged. "She was a teenager."

I thought about Ronja Laplander and her soul-deep disappointment in the St. Lucy pick. And I thought about Diane Hakala who had expected her daughter to get married after graduation.

"Teens have feelings as strong as ours," I pointed out. "Sometimes stronger. And they haven't yet learned that time eases disappointments."

He shot me a quick glance.

"Did that work for you?"

"We're not talking about me."

He must have heard something in my voice because his tone softened.

"I'm sorry, Hatti. Have I failed to tell you that? I'm sorry about everything that happened between us."

The apology was small comfort against the grief of loss I'd grappled with for the past year and I couldn't bring myself to be gracious.

"Whatever," I muttered.

Jace drove in silence for a moment. I hoped he was re-living (and regretting) his actions of that grim December day in D.C. It turned out, he was not.

"So who was jealous of the girl?"

I wanted to scream but, for once, I controlled my impulse and focused on the topic at hand. I told him about the Laplanders and Arvo's highhanded decision and I told him about Barb Hakala and her break up from Matti Murso.

"Mind you," I finished, "I do not think any of them were responsible for Liisa's death. Aside from the fact that Diane, Barb, and Astrid were at the dance, they are all upstanding members of St. Heikki's. None of them would kill except in self-defense."

"What about Astrid's mother?"

"Ronja? She helped out at the smorgasbord then, I assume, she went home."

"To brood about the unfairness of the St. Lucy pick? Or to do something about it?"

"I'm sure Armas Laplander can provide an alibi for his wife," I said, stiffly.

"Right. Anybody ever tell you an alibi is suspect when it comes from a spouse?"

"Well, maybe you'd believe Ronja's four daughters."

"That isn't the point, Umlaut." He didn't sound angry. "You have to look at everybody who had any sort of a motive."

"You're just trying to save your brother's skin."

"That, too."

I was silent for a minute.

"Jace, I should tell you that Arvo is ready to turn this whole thing over to Sheriff Clump. He's normally a very law-abiding person and I think his conscience is bothering him."

His lips tightened, so I sought something comforting to say.

"The sheriff won't know about Liisa's connection to Reid, you know."

"Don't kid yourself. Nothing is more efficient in a small town than the grapevine. You were probably the last to know about my brother's connection to the deceased."

The bitterness in his voice caught at my heart.

"Was that how it was on the rez?"

He nodded. "No secrets."

How painful that must have been for a boy with a mother like Miriam.

"The good news was that I never got caught for shoplifting. Now I believe that people would step up to pay for milk or bread or cereal."

"That was kind."

He said nothing and I thought about how frightened and guilt-stricken he must have been every time he stole something, even though he got away with it.

"You're wrong, you know," he said, after a minute. "I never felt guilty." He glanced over at me. "Just like I don't feel guilty about whisking you into the mountains to spend the night with me."

It wasn't so much the words as the amusement in his voice. Rage boiled inside me and exploded.

"Turn around."

"What?"

"I want to go back. I was doing this as a favor for you, Jace. You can spend a night on the mountain with Sheriff Clump instead."

"What did I say?"

I could feel the heat in my cheeks and I knew they were bright red.

"Are you kidding? You were flirting with me. *Flirting!* That's so inappropriate."

"You're right," he said, finally. "I wasn't thinking about the separation. It just seemed like old times, you know? I've missed you, Hatti."

"Huh."

He drove in silence for another mile.

"If you want me to turn around, I will."

"No. This was bound to be awkward."

"I'd have said so, too. The thing is, it feels natural being together again." He caught my eye again and there was no humor in the gaze. Instead, it was bleak.

"Somehow," he added, "that's worse."

I knew what he meant.

The drifting flakes began to gather strength as we headed down the interstate. The grassy fields and stands of pine trees were covered from a previous snowfall but the newly plowed pavement started to disappear under the white stuff.

"What about the girl's father? Where does he fit in the picture?"

I settled into telling Jace about Jalmer Pelonen, his cabin and his annual fishing trip.

"He's lived around here a long time, but no one seems to know him except Einar, my shop assistant. Liisa lived with him until last summer and only moved to Red Jacket because her high school was down to like five or ten kids per class and the district couldn't afford to keep it open. The other kids are at the high school in Lake Linden but Liisa wanted to attend Copper County High School because of the music program. She was a singer."

"Another Britney Spears?"

"More classical, I think. My great Aunt Ianthe said she sang like an angel."

"The fishing trip seems like kind of a fishy alibi."

"I know. But Jalmer was her father. He'd never have killed her."

"Hatti," he said, in a world-weary tone, "grow up."

"But why would he kill her? He'd lived with her for years. Why now?"

"Maybe she defied him. Maybe he didn't want her to leave. Maybe he was afraid people would criticize him for letting his daughter move out when she was only seventeen."

I shrugged. "It's not like Jalmer Pelonen cares what people think about him." I shook my head. "He just doesn't have a motive."

"Who does, then? Reid?"

"They could have had a lover's quarrel."

"He told grandfather the relationship wasn't like that." But there was a lack of conviction in his voice and I heard it.

I gave him a moment to collect himself and then I gave him my gut-level opinion.

"I just don't think any normal father would kill his daughter. Not for any reason."

"Define normal. If I remember correctly, your father took off when you were just a baby."

"That's true. But he didn't kill me. And, anyway, I was lucky. I got Pops."

Jace's expressive lower lip curled.

"The perfect stepfather. You've made that point many times."

"Then I communicated badly. He has been the perfect father to Sofi and me. I just wish someone like Pops had come along for you and Reid."

He dismissed my sentimental comment with a shake of his head.

"You have to consider Maki. He lived in the same house with Liisa. He may have been the baby's father."

"No. There's no way. He and Pauline loved her. She was the

daughter they'd been waiting for. Arvo would never have abused that trust."

"If you're gonna go on your gut you might as well give up now. You want me to keep my mind open about Reid. Shouldn't you do the same?"

He had a point and, after a moment, I agreed.

The pickup ate up the miles despite the worsening conditions of the roads. Soon I saw the Quincy Mine's shaft rise up out of the ground, and I knew we were just north of Hancock. The city is built on a rise, and we zigged and zagged as M-26 led us past weatherworn houses built into the hills, then onto Quincy Street past Finlandia University, Humalalampi's Flowers, Rissanen's Jewelers, and Ryti's Market. The ethnic influence is so pervasive in Hancock that each street sign carries both an English and a Finnish name, and every winter the city hosts *Heikinpaiva*, a festival to celebrate the feast day of Finland's patron saint, St. Heinrik, for whom I am named.

"You know," I said, "I really feel that someone should find Jalmer Pelonen. Imagine how horrible it will be to come home and find out your daughter has been dead for days?"

Just then we passed a billboard advertising an investigating agency and I had a stroke of genius. I fumbled in my pack for my cellphone and punched in a number.

Lars Teljo, my ex-brother-in-law, answered on the second ring.

"Oh, great, you're there!"

"Hello to you, too, Squirt. What can I do you for?"

"I need a favor."

"You got it."

That easy acquiescence was one of the many qualities I'd always loved about him. There was no muss, no fuss, no equivocating. Just straight answers, support, and good judgment. Except for that one time, three years earlier when he'd spent the night with a barmaid at the Black Fly. I told him about Liisa Pelonen and about her father purportedly ice fishing on Lake Gogebic.

"I think someone should try to find him. Can you do it?"

"No problem. You want me to tell him about the girl?"

"Yes. No. I don't know."

"I'll use my judgment."

"And let me know when you find him, okay, Lars?"

"You got it," he repeated.

I hung up and Jace glanced at me.

"Squirt?"

"Lars is my sister's ex," I said, marveling at how little we knew about each other's families. "They married in high school and lived with us for years. He was Clump's deputy sheriff for a while but they didn't get along. Now he's a private investigator."

"Why the divorce?"

I hesitated. "It sounds worse than it really was."

"He cheated on her."

I made a face. "How'd you know?"

"There are only so many reasons."

I studied his profile and wondered, for the millionth time, which reason had driven Jace to leave me. I tried to explain about Lars and Sofi.

"Things were hard. They'd been married a long time and parents nearly as long. Neither had a chance to go to college. It was all right for Sofi. She stayed home with the baby. But Lars wanted something better for him and the family. He wanted to go the police academy downstate but Sofi wouldn't let him go. He was working for Clump, and, pretty much at a low ebb and drinking too much when he got involved with the insect."

"The insect?"

"Cricket. The barmaid at the Black Fly. He said it was just a one-night stand and he promised it would never happen again. She divorced him, anyway."

"Do you blame her?"

"I do and I don't. He's a good guy and a great dad. His kid, Charlie, misses him a heckuva lot. And he loves Sofi. He always has. I think she should give him another chance. The whole family wants to see a reconciliation."

"Ah," he said, "but he didn't cheat on the whole family."

We stayed on M-26 as we crossed the Portage Lake Bridge that spans the Keweenaw Waterway and connects Copper County with the more prosperous lower half of the peninsula. Houghton, Hancock's sister city, is the home of Michigan Technological University, and usually there are students thronging the streets. Not today, though. It was Christmas break.

The pickup's windshield wipers fought to clear the snow that fell more and more heavily as we headed south through the countryside. Our world felt insular and, thanks to the pickup's heater, toasty warm. I must have started to doze, because his next words seemed like something out of a dream.

"Did you know that the Ojibwe have a creation legend like your Kalevala?"

# FIFTEEN

I stared at him, shocked that he'd mentioned the Kalevala. I didn't know he'd ever heard of it.

"It's the story of Waynaboozhoo, the original man, who was both a human and a spirit."

"Kind of like Jesus."

"Hmmm." Jace kept his eyes on the slippery pavement. Visibility was decreasing fast, but he drove with confidence, the same way he did everything else.

"The Creator, Gitchee Manitou, told Waynaboozoo to go all over the earth and name everything he saw, plants and animals and bodies of water, the seasons, the sun, moon, and stars."

"Big job."

He glanced at me but continued the story. "In his travels, Waynaboozoo met his mother, the earth, his grandmother, the moon, his father, the sun and his uncle, the wind."

I didn't interrupt him again. I was busy trying to figure out why he was telling me this.

"One day Waynaboozoo learned that he had a twin brother. He set out to find him, but didn't know where to look. A spirit guide, Bugwayjinini, appeared to help him out."

Jace's voice shifted from a narrative singsong to a slow, rhythmic monologue. I could imagine him sitting cross-legged in front of a campfire, holding the other members of the tribe spellbound with his story.

"Your shadow brother is your other side, Bugwayjinini told Waynaboozhoo. There are differences between you. You will walk the path of peace, while he would not. You are kind, while he is not. You are humble and generous. He is not. You seek the good in others, but he does not. You are the light, Waynaboozhoo. He is the darkness. Know that your brother is with you. Understand him but do not seek him."

I felt tears prick the backs of my eyes as Jace told the story and, in doing so, became once again the man I'd fallen in love with. I thought I understood the message. He wanted me to know that he, like Waynaboozhoo and every other person who has walked the earth, had a dark side. Was this his way of accepting the responsibility for what had happened between us? Would he finally explain? I wouldn't ask again but I couldn't help hoping that he would tell me why he ended our marriage. Perhaps it would bring me closure.

We continued the trip in silence, eventually turning onto an unmarked road that, almost immediately, slanted upward at a nearly forty-five-degree angle. I recognized the area, as the route to Silver City and Lake of the Clouds, a pristine body of water located between two ridges of the Porcupine Mountain Range. The lake's name comes from the placid surface that mirrors the sky.

Another hour brought us to the end of an old logging road, where we found an ancient, rusty pickup truck covered in several inches of snow.

"Reid's?"

Jace nodded. We parked and slung our arms into our backpacks. Jace carried the larger one, and loaded on top were not one, but two, sleeping bags. I frowned.

"I can carry my own."

His smile was slow and teasing, and it did unfortunate things to my insides.

"I'd rather carry two sleeping bags now than have to carry you, too, when you finally collapse."

"I'm not going to collapse," I snapped.

"Don't be so prickly. You're not exactly a Campfire Girl. Remember how I had to bribe you with the promise of a hand-churned ice cream cone before you'd take a walk on the Potomac River's C and O canal path."

I remembered that day. It was fall and the trees along the canal were changing colors. I'd pretended to resist the proposed walk but the truth was, I'd have gone anywhere with him.

"Hey," he said, ripping through my reverie. "What the hell have you got on your feet?"

I glanced down.

"They're Zamberlan Three-tens, the Jimmy Choo's of hiking boots," I said. "I got them from Max at a great discount."

"Max? That presumptuous cowboy?"

"He stocks outdoor gear for his clients. When he found out Zamberlan was planning a big promotion with cut-rate prices, he got boots for Sofi and me and Elli. Good thing, too, eh? I mean, who knew I'd have to climb a mountain?"

He scowled but said nothing more about the footwear.

"Let's go. Stay behind me on the narrow parts. There are holes and rocks under the snow and I know where they are."

"You must have spent a lot of time up here."

He didn't answer. He just strode off and left me to trot along in his wake.

It was a long, hard slog. Not only did we have bits of hail the size of baby peas pinging against our faces, but the path was narrow and mostly uphill. Some of the trail was bare, but more often we ran into drifts, and negotiating them was like trying to wade through oatmeal. Fallen branches hidden under the snow presented additional hazards, as did patches of camouflaged ice.

After two hours we reached a treeless plateau where we paused out of deference to my heavy breathing and beet-red face. Jace, of course, looked as fresh as a mountain goat. He extracted two bottles of water from his pack, and, even though I had my own, it was easier to just accept the one he handed me. I chugged, my hand shaking with fatigue.

"Not so fast," he murmured. "You'll get cramps."

I slowed down. After all, he was the one with woods experience. I, however, was the one who called the Keweenaw home so, as I looked around the clearing, I began to talk about the history of the land.

"This is a tailing field." It was a guess but an educated one. I'd spent some time last winter in Pops' study reading books about the local terrain.

"What's that?"

"It refers to a field that was used for dumping poor rock which is the bits of rock left over after the copper was extracted. The rocks on this plateau have been in place for seventy plus years which is why you know where they are."

"Speaking of that," he said, finishing his water and grabbing both our bottles to return them to the pack, "if you don't want to break an ankle, you'd better take my hand."

I didn't want to break an ankle nor did I want to hold his hand. Well, maybe I did want to hold his hand but I knew it was dangerous. I could feel his heat through his glove and my mitten. He guided me through the clearing and back onto the path and when he dropped my hand to step in front of me, I felt a deep sense of loss.

By the next break, two hours later, I was no longer thinking about my companion at all. I just wanted to lie down in the snow and drown in my bottle of water. I leaned against a tree and closed my eyes.

"No sleeping, now, Umlaut. Tell me how you got saddled with the job of top cop."

"What? Oh, you know how it is up here. Everybody has to wear more than one hat. " I kept my eyes closed. "Pops got injured in a snow-mobile hit-and-run accident in November and Arvo asked me to take the job. I figured it was a favor for Arvo but mostly for Pops and there's hardly ever any crime up here."

"Famous last words."

"Yeah."

"Take heart," he said, again taking my empty water bottle off my hands. "We're almost there. The cabin's just up around that rise. No more than two hundred yards. I have to warn you, though. It's pretty primitive."

I gasped. "Is there indoor plumbing?"

He grinned and nodded.

"Then it's Xanadu."

A few minutes later I spotted the small, square structure built against a hillside and buffered with pines. It looked as solid and dependable as a good marriage. Then the peace was shattered when a harsh expletive split the air.

"What's wrong," I asked.

He cursed again.

"No smoke from the chimney. Reid's not here." His eyes were grim as they met mine.

"We'll be spending the night here alone."

"But we came all this way just to see your brother."

Humor flashed, briefly, in those silver eyes.

"You know that and I know that. He didn't get the memo."

"Maybe he's just out for a little fresh air," I said, trying to look on the bright side.

Jace did not bother to point out that the short day was racing toward nightfall, that the temperatures had already dropped well below freezing and that the snowfall was thickening as if someone had mixed it with starch.

He just smiled.

"Thanks, Umlaut."

"For what?"

"For not accusing me of planning this. Some people would think I lured you up here to keep you from investigating the murder or my own nefarious reasons."

The fact was that neither of those possibilities had occurred to me. I had thought that I understood Jace Night Wind's character almost from the moment I met him and, despite the fact that he'd left me without a word of explanation, I still believed he was as honorable as Pops.

"Maybe he's left us a note," he added.

"Or, even better, a written confession."

Jace grinned at that but shook his head, opened the unlocked door and preceded me into the single, small, dark room. I must have made a sound of distress because he handed me a flashlight, took my arm and led me across the room to another door.

"Xanadu," he said, with a gesture. "After you."

# SIXTEEN

J ace set about building a fire and, within a few minutes, the small room was warm and there was enough light to see the rolled-up sleeping bag in one corner, which I assumed was Reid's, and the kitchenette in the other.

A shallow shelf held cans of fruit and soup, a plastic container of granola and a package of beef jerky. A battery-operated hotplate sat next to a sink and there was a college dorm-sized refrigerator on the floor. I opened the door of the latter and found it loaded with Escanaba Black Beer. I hadn't heard Jace cross the room but the door squeaked when it opened. I wondered suddenly, wildly, if he intended to abandon me in the cabin.

"Where are you going?"

He held up a bucket. "Getting snow to make coffee."

"But there's a sink."

"A sink, yes. But no running water."

Twenty minutes later, when we'd spread out the food on a blanket and held mugs of instant coffee made with the snow Jace had boiled on a hob in the fireplace, he asked me why I'd been suspicious.

I shrugged. "Paranoia, I guess. I mean, you could save money on our inevitable divorce."

He didn't laugh.

"Do you want to talk about that now?"

Suddenly, I didn't. It felt good to be warm, inside and out, and to be comfortable. The makeshift picnic of ham-and-cheese pasties and clementines hit the spot and, to be honest, it felt good to be with Jace.

"No. Let's have a truce, the way the soldiers on the Western Front did on Christmas Day during World War I. No personal talk tonight."

His dark brows knit over the silver eyes but he didn't answer. He just handed me a piece of chocolate walnut.

"That's my favorite," I said, "how did you know?"

"It's everybody's favorite. It wasn't easy to find in the midst of all that eggnog and peppermint stuff your sister sells at this time of year."

"You met my sister?" He nodded.

"Did you tell her who you were?"

He lifted an eyebrow, a talent that never failed to distract me. I have never understood how a person can move their eyebrows or their toes one at a time. Or how they can roll their tongue.

"Have another piece," he said, instead of answering. "Mountain climbing builds one hell of an appetite." He chuckled. "By the way, you surpassed expectations."

"You mean in my goat-like ability to hike uphill?"

"Well, if you recall the time we decided to hike the Appalachian Trail, we only made it about two hundred yards."

I'd wimped out. I started to get cramps and, because I thought-slash-hoped I was pregnant, I didn't want to take a chance on a miscarriage. It turned out to be a false alarm and, because we had not discussed children yet, I had never told Jace.

"I'm tougher now," I said, by way of explanation.

"Speaking of tough, I seem to remember you were averse to anything that crawled. How'd you wind up with a bait shop?"

"Pops. He asked me to run it just to give me something to do, I suspect, but it has worked out because he's busy being the police chief and he let me add yarn supplies so it's a little more up my alley. Anyway, I have Einar."

"Einar?"

"Pops' assistant. He handles everything in the refrigerator and all

ANN YOST

the other fishing gear, too. He knows everything there is to know about fishing." I paused. "And the weather. And sauna."

"Why do you call it sow-na?"

"Finns pronounce every letter and always put the emphasis on the first syllable. It's just how we say it."

He nodded. "So you get along with this Einar?"

"Well, he's not much of a conversationalist. You can't get more than a few words out of him on any given day unless its commentary on my lack of a husband."

"You don't lack a husband."

The words were spoken in a neutral tone but there was a remote expression in his eyes.

It came to me in a flash that a relationship like ours, between two people who had once been wildly in love, was the most difficult to navigate. If we had just met, we'd be chatting easily, sharing anecdotes or an easy silence. As it was, nearly every topic was loaded and the gun always pointed back to our failed marriage.

"Détente," I said, lightly. "Remember?"

He looked into the fire and spoke.

"So. How does Einar feel about Max?"

I didn't get the connection at once.

"Max admires Einar's flies and respects his fishing knowledge. They don't go fishing together or have slumber parties."

"How about you?"

I knew what he was asking and I felt a rush of sadness. Nothing could bring us back together but, clearly, a friendship between us wasn't possible.

"No slumber parties. Let's talk about something else."

"How do you like living in Red Jacket?"

This had to, I thought, be the strangest conversation. I was living in my hometown because, twelve months ago, and for no stated reason, he had kicked me out of the marriage.

"I like it fine."

"You liked living in D.C., as I recall."

I thought back to the culture shock I'd experienced in the fast-paced lifestyle of the nation's capital. I'd gotten adjusted to it because I'd loved being with Jace.

"I'm really more of a small-town girl."

He didn't answer. He got to his feet with his usual masculine grace and punched up the fire. His hands were quick and efficient and something flashed in the jumping flames.

"You're still wearing your ring."

He frowned, then sat back down just a little closer than he'd been before.

"We're still married," he said. In the following pause, I imagined the unspoken words, *I've missed you.*

My heart jumped a little but I couldn't decide whether that was a good or bad thing. I'd worked hard to come to terms with what had happened and I didn't want to fall back into the what-might-have-been-slash-if-only frame of mind.

"I'm sorry," he said, suddenly. "It was so unfair to you. I'm sorry I never explained."

I froze. Did that mean he was going to explain now? Could I stand to listen to it? Could I stand not to? I was conscious of a strong inclination toward peace. Like I said, a Christmas-time cease-fire. No more pain. He seemed to read my mind because he dropped the subject. We cleaned up, spread our sleeping bags in front of the fire and crawled into them.

"Tell me about St. Lucy," he said, as we watched the flames. It was a good topic and I was happy to comply.

"Celebrating St. Lucy day is a Swedish tradition and practiced in areas of Finland where there are Swedish-speaking Finns. Since most of us are Lutherans, we don't have much to do with saints in general but somehow St. Lucy really caught on in Sweden and has been continued in this country.

"Anyway, St. Lucy or Santa Lucia, was supposedly a young girl who wanted to keep herself pure for God and rejected an offer of marriage from an Italian nobleman. The suitor's cronies killed her by thrusting a sword into one of her eyes and making her bleed to death. That's the dark side of the story. The other side is that St. Lucy represents light— which is illustrated by the crown of candles on her head. The lightness is very welcome during the long, dark nights and short, gray days of December."

"The whole thing's apocryphal, right? Like the stories in the Bible."

"You could make a case for both of those," I said, "but I wouldn't do it around here. We're very attached to our traditions."

"So how is the St. Lucy girl chosen?"

I nodded. I thought it was like him, thorough and thoughtful, to have hit on an aspect of this case that might not be evident to someone else.

"Normally the high school seniors choose St. Lucy and there's a very short list. This year, Astrid Laplander was the frontrunner but then Liisa Pelonen arrived in town and she looked exactly like every poster you've ever seen of St. Lucy. Arvo Maki unilaterally decided to name Liisa to the position and the rest is history."

"Do you think that had anything to do with her death?"

"Not if your brother killed her."

"Let's—for the sake of argument—say he didn't. Could this Astrid person have been angry enough to have committed murder?"

"She was angry," I admitted. "And her mother, even more so. It's a big deal in Red Jacket. St. Lucy is a status position among the girls and the mothers, like Ronja Laplander, really believe good things will come to a girl who plays the martyr."

"It didn't work in the case of Liisa Pelonen."

"No."

"Did you ever take the part?"

"Yes. You have to remember that while it's a coveted part we have a very small community."

"What about your sister and your cousin?"

I was frankly surprised that he remembered Elli.

"Sofi was picked all right, but not Elli who was a senior the same year as me. Only one of us could be St. Lucy. She didn't mind."

"Are you sure?"

I thought back to high school and the St. Lucy festival.

"I'm sure. One of the superstitions is that St. Lucy will get a good husband. Elli was practically engaged to someone at that point and she figured I needed the karma more than she did."

"Ah. I didn't know your cousin was married."

"She's not. It didn't work out. In the end."

It hadn't worked out for me, either, but neither of us pointed that out.

"So how much anger was there this year?"

"Quite a lot," I admitted. "Ronja, the mother, was furious with Arvo for taking the decision into his own hands. Physically, Liisa was the perfect St. Lucy, but it wasn't fair for Arvo to completely ignore the Laplanders' hopes."

We sat in silence for a few minutes watching the fire. Suddenly Jace ran his fingers through his short hair and spoke.

"Let's pool our resources, Umlaut. Maybe if we go over every detail of what each of us knows, some direction will occur to us."

I thought it was a good idea. It seems to me that trying to solve a crime is like trying to put together a puzzle, only first you have to find all the pieces. We were still in gathering mode.

I told him about Liisa's day starting with breakfast.

"She'd gone downtown with Arvo to help put up more twinkle lights and then, a couple of hours before she was supposed to be at the church to line up for the parade, she told him she needed to go shopping for a dress for the high school dance scheduled for that night. According to Pauline, she went down to the Frostbite Mall in Houghton with an unknown friend and got back just in the nick of time for the start of the parade at 3 o'clock. The parade is scheduled so when it ends down at the Old Finnish Cemetery, dusk is settling in and the lighted candles the children prop up next to the headstones are visible.

"The fact that Liisa was late meant that there was no time for her to put on longjohns under her costume and she caught a chill."

"Why didn't she just wear a jacket?"

I made a face. "She should have. Apparently, Pauline was afraid it would detract from the impression of the delicate saint. Anyway, as a result, she had a scratchy throat and a bit of a fever when she got home. Pauline gave her tea and Vicks and tucked her in bed."

"Vicks?"

"Vaporub. Guaranteed to cure anything that ails you."

"Then what? The Makis left the house?"

"That's right. They were expected at the smorgasbord at Elli's bed and breakfast. Pauline went home once, about six forty-five, to pick up some jam but she didn't hear anything and she didn't peek in on Liisa because she didn't want to wake her. They returned at nine and it took them fifteen or twenty minutes to search the house when they found her not in her bed."

"How'd they know to look in the sauna?"

"I imagine it was the last place they did look."

"And, at that point, she was back in her clothes."

I nodded. "She had to be planning to leave."

"With Reid, you mean."

I nodded, again.

"So where's her suitcase?"

"I wondered the same thing."

"So the last time anyone saw her alive it was Pauline Maki and that was, what time?"

"About six-fifteen."

There was a short silence.

"Hatti, does it occur to you we have only Pauline Maki's word that Liisa was alive and in bed at six-fifteen?"

I stared at him. "You think Pauline Maki killed her? But why? There's no motive. Pauline and Arvo loved Liisa."

"Maybe Arvo loved her too much."

I shook my head. "You didn't see them after they found the body. He was weeping and she was pale and hollow-eyed and shaking. Pauline told me that Liisa's coming to live with them made up for all the years of childlessness. They honestly considered her a surrogate daughter. And you should see what she, Pauline, that is, did to the bedroom. She must have spent a fortune on pink furniture, clothes and accessories."

"All right, all right. It was just a thought."

"And, anyway," I rushed ahead, impulsively, following my own train of thought. "Pauline didn't even know about the baby."

"She couldn't have had anything to do with the pregnancy," I added.

"No," he said, finally, "but it's possible her husband did."

"Arvo? No way. He would never have abused the trust of a young girl living in his house. Why he's as honorable as Pops."

The look my husband turned on me was positively reptilian.

"I'm sure you believe that," he finally said. He looked so miserable that I reached out a hand and laid it on his arm.

"I realize the baby makes the case worse for Reid."

"Not necessarily. He told Grandfather that his relationship with Liisa was purely platonic. He was helping her get out of Dodge because she was afraid of something or somebody."

"He might have lied," I said, thinking of the dreamcatcher in my pocket.

"Why should he lie? There was nothing stopping them from being in a relationship if that's what they wanted."

I shrugged. "That baby came from somewhere."

"My money's on Arvo Maki."

I struggled to control my temper. Nothing could be gained by getting into a knock-down, drag-out with Jace.

"Sonya believes Liisa was hit with a rock but that it didn't kill her. We don't know the cause of death but there is no rock on the floor of the sauna so the blow must have been deliberate."

"So we know there was an attack but not how she came to die."

"There's just not that much blood at the scene."

"Maybe she was killed somewhere else."

"It's possible." I sighed and decided to share my theory. "Sonya suspected that Liisa had a heart condition and Pauline corroborated that. Unfortunately, that doesn't explain the blow on the head. You know what I think?" He raised one eyebrow. "I think she was poisoned."

"Poisoned with what?" But he knew. "You think my brother has a stash left over from the old days. You think he killed her with an overdose of methamphetamines."

I could hear the disgust and the concern in his voice and I didn't know how to answer either.

"I need to talk to your brother," I said. "In the meantime, I'm going to sleep."

# SEVENTEEN

I gnatius Holomo, Red Jacket's oldest living inhabitant since my *mummi* died, had surrendered his title and was, as Pops put it, "at long last heading to the marble orchard."

I walked over to the funeral home with my parents and Sofi to pay my respects. Everyone in town was there, queued up to file past the coffin while Miss Irene played Sibelius on the old, upright piano, the way she does for all our funerals whether they are held in the chapel at the Maki Funeral Home or at St. Heikki's. The scent of roses was strong and it triggered a familiar feeling of anxiety.

I am not a fan of funerals in general, and my least favorite part is the mandatory "viewing of the body." As a child, I'd developed the trick of focusing on a corner of the raised coffin lid, thereby avoiding a face-to-face with the dearly departed. Sometimes though, like today, my conscience intervened and I forced my gaze to Ignatius's grizzled mug, intending to suck it up and offer him a silent "R.I.P."

I never got the chance. A series of short, sharp, shrieks halted Miss Irene's playing and shocked me awake. I shot bolt upright, hyperventilating, sweating, gripped by panic. After a moment, I calmed down enough to become aware of strong arms holding me and a husky voice in my ear.

"You're all right, babe. It was just a bad dream. I'm here."

I laid my head against a muscular shoulder as conflicting emotions assailed me. Gratitude and relief on the one hand and resentment on the other. I'd hoped to awake to those words every morning for the past three hundred and sixty-five days.

"What was it, Umlaut?"

I breathed deeply a few times before answering.

"I was at a funeral service. When I looked into the coffin, it was you."

"Ah. I imagine you've had that dream more than once during the past year."

I shook my head but kept silent. I did not tell him that my standby dream was of him holding me and repeating the same words he'd just said. *You're all right, babe. It was just a bad dream. I'm here.*

His fingers drew a line down my cheek, and then I felt his lips against mine. It was a chaste kiss, sweet and comforting and so non-sexual that I wanted to cry. That impulse, thank goodness, was checked when the cabin door burst open letting in a blast of snow and cold and a bright, harsh light. Jace cursed and rolled away from me.

It was a scenario that was all too familiar, and in that moment, I felt lonelier than at any time in my life.

"Well, damn, big brother," said the newcomer. "And here I thought you were coming up here to rescue me."

Luckily, the brash words banished my self-pity. *Geez Louise.* If there was a less dignified, more embarrassing way to get introduced to a murder suspect (or anyone else) I couldn't imagine what it was. I struggled to sit up.

"Don't get up on my account."

He propped his flashlight on its end so that it illuminated the room without blinding us and I was able to get my first glimpse of Reid Night Wind, my soon-to-be-ex-brother-in-law. I was not surprised to see that he was as devastatingly handsome as Jace. About six feet tall, rangy shoulders, lean and tanned with a shock of thick, raven hair and matching eyelashes. His nose, like Jace's, was straight and narrow, his chin square, his cheekbones as sharp as flint.

Straight, white teeth flashed in the shadows and I found myself wishing I could have combed my hair.

"I'm Hatti Lehtinen," I said, trying to take some kind of command of the situation.

"I'm relieved to hear it," Reid said, bending over to take my hand then raising it to his perfectly sculpted lips. "I'd hate to find my brother on top of someone else's wife."

Smooth, I thought. Too smooth for someone who was not yet twenty-two. He might very well be capable of planning and executing a crime. The thought saddened me.

"I'm glad you dropped by. I've got some questions."

Reid nodded. "Grandfather said you were Red Jacket's top cop."

"Temporary top cop."

"Temporary, acting," Jace put in. "Temporary job, temporary husband. Temporary is Hatti's middle name these days."

The edge in his voice surprised me and I shot him a look intended to remind him that the separation had been his idea. Naturally, he wasn't looking at me.

"Where've you been, Reid?"

"Visiting a friend."

"Is your friend a timber wolf?"

He chuckled as he took off his boots and grabbed a sleeping bag to sit on.

"I spend a lot of time up here. There's a whole community if you know where to look." He settled into a cross-legged position and grinned at me and I was willing to bet my last pasty that his friend was female. "Go ahead," he said. "Ask your questions. I'll tell you what I know."

"Did you know Liisa Pelonen was pregnant? Did you kill her?"

I hadn't planned to start with that. It just came out. And I thought it surprised him. I studied his face as he composed his answer. His eyes were dark, almost black, compared with the light gray of his half-brother. Like Jace, he'd already learned how to mask his response.

"Yes, I knew about the baby. No, I didn't kill her."

"Do you know who did?"

"No."

Well, what had I expected? That he'd confess?

"Were you the father?"

"Also, no. We were friends."

I thought about the breathtaking beauty of Liisa Pelonen at eighteen. Was it possible that any young man could have withstood her magic?

"Very good friends," he amended as if he'd read my mind. "I wanted to protect her."

*Protect.* The word triggered another thought and I dug my fingers into the pocket of the jeans I was still wearing. I held up the pendant and it gleamed in the ray of the powerful flashlight.

"This was found around her neck," I said, with only a slight waver in my voice.

I was looking at Reid, knowing the muttered curse hadn't come from him.

"What the hell," Jace added, an instant later. I ignored him.

"You gave her a family heirloom," I pointed out. Something in my voice must have alerted him because he slapped his forehead.

"Oh, lord, was it yours, Hatti? I didn't know. I just found it in a box of stuff at Grandfather's trailer."

"It's not mine anymore," I told him. "You were right to give it to Liisa."

I glanced at Jace just as the flickering fire revealed an expression of anguish on his harsh features but I knew this wasn't the time to talk about our old business.

Reid shrugged. "I figured she could use some good luck. I told you. I was trying to take care of her."

That talisman hadn't brought Liisa any better luck than it had me. I was starting to feel distinctly undignified sprawled out at the feet of my suspect so I suggested making coffee which, I figured, would provide an opportunity for a little musical chairs. It worked.

Ten minutes later we were sitting cross-legged in a semi-circle around the fire in a parody of a pow-wow.

I sipped at the hot brew then focused on Reid.

"Tell me about Friday night."

He nodded. "We had made plans to meet in the sauna." He pronounced it in the correct Finnish tradition. I waited for an explanation. "Liisa had told Pauline Maki that her throat hurt in the hope that she'd be told to stay home from the dinner at the inn and that's exactly what happened. I was to come by at seven-fifteen to pick her up."

"Why?"

He shrugged again and looked mildly embarrassed.

"It sounds kind of melodramatic but she wanted to run away."

I nodded. We had pretty much figured that she was planning to leave.

"Away from the Makis?"

"Just away from Red Jacket. Something had spooked her. I should probably give you some background on my relationship with her."

"Please. How did the two of you meet?"

"Believe it or not, I met her at your house." He grinned at me. "Your dad introduced us."

"My dad?"

"Her stepdad," Jace snapped. I glanced at him and wondered why he always insisted on that distinction. I made a mental note to ask him about it, later.

"Hatti's stepdad, Carl Lehtinen, stopped me for speeding one night in October. Instead of writing me a ticket, he invited me over to play pool."

That sounded like Pops. He wasn't a pushover but he firmly believed that old adage that the devil finds work for idle hands and he was well aware there was very little for teenagers to do on the Keweenaw. And, anyway, he liked young people.

"It was fun and it developed into a weekly thing."

I cocked my head at him. "I never saw you there."

"We got together on Thursdays."

"Ah." I turned to Jace. "Thursday, the knitting circle meets at the shop and Mom plays bingo at St. Heikki's. Pops gets the house to himself."

Jace's only response was a grunt.

"A few weeks into it, the funeral director, Maki, came over. Liisa was with him and while the old guys played pool, she and I talked."

"Well, sure. She was a gorgeous girl and you're a handsome guy."

Reid waved the comment away.

"I never thought of her as anything but a kid. An unhappy kid."

I nodded and thought about that. "Do you remember the date you met her?"

"No, but it was early November. She had something on her mind right from the get-go and whatever it was, seemed to escalate. By the next time I talked to her, she knew about the baby and she was in a panic. She told me she'd pay me a hundred grand to get her out of town."

"A hundred grand?" Jace and I spoke in unison, my high voice and his low one creating a sort of harmony.

"She has, I mean, she had a trust fund." Reid peered into his coffee mug as he spoke as if he didn't want to meet my eyes. Or, more probably, his brother's.

"It's a weird deal. The money comes from her late mother's family and it was put in a trust that was not to be touched until she reached twenty-one." He paused and looked up at me. "Or, until she married."

"Geez Louise," I breathed. "Did you marry her then?" He nodded.

"Friday morning. That's why she was late for the parade. She skipped choir practice one day last week and we got a license. Friday we drove over to Eagle Harbor and got married by the justice of the peace."

There was a short silence.

"I did it partly for selfish reasons," Reid said. "Jace will tell you I'm no Sir Galahad. But she was pregnant and I convinced myself that this was the right thing to do."

"But you're not the baby's father," I pointed out.

"No." He made an aimless gesture. "Liisa wasn't interested in marriage. Not really. She was only eighteen and she'd hoped to have a professional singing career. And, once she was married, she'd get her trust fund so she wouldn't have any money problems. We never thought it would be a till-death-do-us-part marriage. I got a sublet in Marquette and I told her I'd stick around for as long as she needed me. We planned to go our separate ways at some point.

"And what about the baby?" Jace asked.

Reid hung his head. "She'd spoken about abortion at first but then she changed her mind. The head was willing, the heart wasn't, I guess."

I could certainly understand that.

I stared at Reid.

"You said she was afraid. Of what?"

"I just don't know. I keep trying to figure it out. She was freaked about something. I thought maybe she'd worked herself into a delusion because I couldn't imagine anything threatening in Red Jacket."

"Do you think she was afraid of Arvo?" I made myself ask the obvious question. Reid shook his head.

"No. She thought a lot of him and Mrs. Maki. She always said they'd done so much for her and I think she was fond of them. The truth is, Liisa was beautiful and she had a sweet way about her but she was a bit, I don't know, aloof. That's one reason I never got interested in her, you know? She didn't give off that kind of vibe." He glanced at the sleeping bag where he'd seen Jace and me when he'd come through the door. I thought I understood.

"Why didn't she leave Red Jacket and go back to her father?" I asked.

"She should have," Reid said, regretfully. "At the time she just didn't want to reopen that can of worms. Her father, Jalmer, loves her but he didn't want her to go to Hollywood or New York and she was afraid that if she went back to the cabin, especially with a baby, she'd never get her chance at a career. She needed the trust fund money."

"So you married her to help out."

Reid turned to his brother. "Yeah. I married her because I wanted the money. I wanted to help her out, too. You and I both know how hard it is for a very young mother alone in the world."

I thought of Miriam Night Wind and Jace's disastrous childhood. Reid most likely had fared better because he'd had Jace to lean on.

"Was that when you gave her the dreamcatcher?"

The brother's eyes riveted on me and Reid cursed.

"I'd forgotten all about that. Yeah. I'd gotten her a cheap ring but I wanted her to have something significant to welcome her into the family —such as it is."

"Whatever the threat to Liisa was," I said, slowly, "she must have thought she could escape it by moving to Marquette. That seems to imply that it was a situational threat, you know, someone local." I looked at Reid as a cold finger worked its way down my spine. "Do you think she was raped?"

"I don't know. She never said anything like that but it could have accounted for the fear."

I could only imagine that agony Arvo would suffer if we discovered it was true. He'd never forgive himself.

Again, Reid seemed to read my mind.

"That would also account for why she wouldn't go to Maki. She knew it would hurt him."

Jace got up to punch up the fire.

"Tell me about that night," I said to Reid.

"Okay. I had a key to the sauna. We'd met there a few times because it was never used except by Maki on Saturday nights. Like I said, I was supposed to be there at seven-fifteen but I got there late and she was already dead."

"Did you touch anything?"

"Yeah. I knelt down to feel her pulse and then I grabbed a rag out of my backpack and cleaned up the wound."

"You did what?"

Reid turned an apologetic glance toward his brother.

"All I could think of was how much she would have hated that blood running down her face."

"You destroyed evidence," Jace said. "We believed the cause of death was something other than the blow to the head but this changes everything."

"I know. I almost took her with me but common sense prevailed. Belatedly."

"And you didn't think to call the police?"

He looked at me. "I've found the police to be distinctly unhelpful," he said. "Except for your dad."

We both waited for Jace to mutter, "stepdad" but he remained silent.

"What about a suitcase?" I asked. Reid looked puzzled. "Did you see one there in the sauna?"

"As a matter of fact, I didn't. She should have had one with her."

"A suitcase would help your story," Jace said. "Without it, who will believe she was running away? And speaking of that, running away isn't going to look great for you, either."

Reid shook his head. "Not many people knew we were even acquainted."

"They will when your DNA and fingerprints show up in the autopsy," Jace pointed out.

"I know. I'm hoping we'll have come up with another suspect by then. I mean, the fact is, I didn't do it. Which means someone else did."

"Reid," I said, trying to find some sliver of hope that would exonerate him, "don't you have any idea about the baby's father?"

"No. None. Like I said, she gave off a don't-touch-me vibe. I can't see her succumbing to a moment of passion."

None of us replied to that but I was sure we were all thinking the same thing: this was looking more and more like rape.

"How big was the trust fund?" Jace finally asked.

"A couple of million."

"And you were going to accept a hundred grand in exchange for marrying her?"

"It was a loan. I want to get off the Keweenaw, too. I figured I'd go to school. Become a lawyer." His beautiful lips twisted. "Like my big brother."

"Oh my gosh!" I slapped my cheeks like Kevin in Home Alone. "You were married to Liisa when she died. That probably means you inherit the entire trust fund."

Reid nodded and Jace closed his eyes for an instant, immediately aware of the implications.

"I'd say, little brother, that you are in a world of hurt."

"I know," Reid answered. "That's why grandfather called you."

We all moved at the same time, preparing our sleeping bags for slumber. It was as if we all knew that things were so bad there was no further point in talking about them. The fire was low and the room quiet when a thought occurred to me.

"If Liisa was so frightened, why didn't you just go from Eagle Harbor up to Marquette? Why come back for the parade?"

"I asked her that," Reid said, with a sigh. "She said she felt badly enough about skipping the pageant, that she couldn't miss the parade, too. She couldn't disappoint the Makis."

Well, that answered one question. Liisa's nemesis had not come from inside the funeral home.

# EIGHTEEN

I awoke to the soft light of morning, the smell of coffee under my nose and Jace's striking features in my direct line of vision. I wanted to freeze the moment in time.

"I've been thinking about the suitcase," Jace said. "The likelihood is that the murderer took it intending to dump it into Lake Superior but what if he didn't have time?

We know Liisa was still alive at six forty-five when Mrs. Maki came back for the jam and that she was dead at seven-thirty, when Reid got there. The murderer may have heard Reid and had to get out fast."

I looked at the younger brother.

"Did you hear or see a car leaving?" Reid shook his head.

"So the perp was on foot, most likely," Jace said. "He may not have been able to run with the suitcase in which case he'd have stashed it somewhere."

"In the yard," Reid suggested.

"Or in the house," I said. "If he heard Reid coming up to the door or inserting the key, he'd have had to backtrack through the house. And that brings up another question. How did he get in?"

"Key in the milk chute," Jace said. "Isn't that the Red Jacket tradition?"

I nodded. "Of course. So it's possible the suitcase is still in the house."

"How can we search for it?" Jace asked. "You can't tell Arvo Maki."

I knew that. Even though Reid had indicated that Liisa was fond of the mortician, he couldn't be eliminated as a suspect. Not yet.

"I'll find a way to do it." I made a mental list that included search for a suitcase and have a little chat with Matti Murso down at the Gas 'n Go.

Jace and I packed up but Reid decided to stay up in the mountains for a while.

"Whoever did this is smart," Jace said to his brother. "I don't think it's a coincidence that it happened when Liisa had plans to meet you. I think the perp knew or suspected the marriage and knew or suspected that Liisa had promised you money from her trust fund. I think you've been set up like a duck at a shooting range. You're the perfect prime suspect. You'll have to come back to face the music at some point but let us see if we can at least get another name on the list."

"No one knew about the marriage," Reid said, "And no one knew about the trust fund, either."

Jace and I looked at each other.

"Some banker must have known," I said.

"And her father," Jace added. "Jalmer Pelonen. I think we'll drop in on the man on our way back to Frozen Paradise."

---

Jace and I shouldered our packs and headed back down the path. After the early morning meeting of the minds, I expected there to be less tension between us on the return trip. I should have known better.

We had learned some important things about the case but none of the information had helped Reid, and we had not touched on the bruised skin around the wound of our marriage. It was obvious that Jace didn't want to talk about it because even though there was room for two on most of the paths, he went ahead of me and I got to spend the hours looking at the same scenery: A set of wide shoulders, a long, rigid back that somehow managed to look uncommunicative. I relived the day he broke up with me and asked myself, for the eleventy-millionth time, why.

I was stiff and sore and heartsick by the time we climbed into the truck.

"Where's Pelonen's cabin?" he asked, the first words either of us had spoken in six hours.

"Ahmeek. He is due home from a fishing trip today."

Jace shrugged and I thought he looked pale and cold. "Either way we'll check out the place."

He turned the key and gunned the motor and I prepared for another hour of silence when my cell phone jangled. I answered quickly, hoping it was Lars and that he'd have a chance to tell me what he'd discovered before the power ran out.

"*Hyva*, Henrikki," said a voice I hadn't expected to hear. Arvo sounded ten years older than he had the day before, partly because he'd lapsed into Finnish and largely because the customary lilt had gone out of his voice. "I wanted to let you know the jig is up, eh? Somehow Clump found out, and he's taking charge. The meat wagon's on its way."

I could hear the pain in his voice.

"I'm sorry, Arvo. So sorry."

"Have you learned anything?"

He was fishing for a scrap of encouragement that might make it easier, emotionally, for him to release the body.

"I'm working on some leads," I said. "What about the sheriff? Do you know if he has anybody in his sights?"

"The Murso boy," Arvo said. "He was in love with my Liisa and everybody knew it. But I can't believe that young man would hurt our girl."

"So, just Matti?"

He answered, absently, as if his mind was on other things.

"What? Yes. I have to go now, Hatti-girl. Time to get Liisa ready for her trip to the sheriff's office." He meant the morgue which was located behind the tiny office on Main Street in Frog Creek but he didn't have the heart to use the word.

"How's Pauline?"

"Sad, Henrikki. We are both so sad. And we still have not talked to Jalmer Pelonen."

"Tell you what," I said, inspired, "why don't I take care of that? I'm heading in his direction now."

Arvo agreed to it and we hung up.

"I've got our entrée," I said. "We are going to tell Jalmer Pelonen about his daughter."

He nodded and then sucked in a long breath.

"Listen, Umlaut. I'm so sorry about the dreamcatcher. You'd left it on top of the dresser and I just sent it back to the rez along with some other things. I'd meant for you to have it."

"Doesn't matter," I said. "It's lovely but it belongs in your family."

He said nothing after that and we drove in silence through a light snowfall north on M-26, bypassing the exits to Houghton, Hancock, Lake Linden, Red Jacket, and Frog Creek until we came to a hand-lettered sign for Rimrocks, one of the many ghost towns in Copper County. What had been a thriving mining community was now a collection of empty, rotting structures that were, season after season, disappearing back into the earth.

I shivered.

"Turn up the heat if you're cold."

"I'm not cold. I'm sad. I hate the way towns and people just kind of disappear from the Keweenaw."

"You mean the miners? Cheer up. They'd all be dead by now, anyway."

"That makes me feel much better."

He shrugged. "Life is economics. In the case of the Keweenaw, the economy was based on natural resources, which meant at some point they were bound to run out. There was never any hope for permanent wealth and prosperity up here."

"So what are people supposed to do?"

"Move. They're supposed to follow the jobs."

I thought about the community of my youth and now, of my future. I knew Jace was right. Schools were closing, businesses folding, young people moving, old people dying. At some point, in the not-too-distant future, nature would reclaim the Keweenaw. At some point. Not yet.

We finally reached Ahmeek, which consisted of a handful of dilapidated homes with the ubiquitous steeply pitched roof-lines and the saunas that looked like tumors attached to the sides. The old logging road that led to Jalmer's cabin was undedicated and unplowed, and the pickup struggled in the eighteen inches of virgin snow. Finally, Jace turned into the driveway that led from the spur to an open carport. The bay where Jalmer's truck should have been looked like a first grader's missing front tooth. Next to the inside wall was a pile of neatly stacked firewood and, hanging from a hook, was a large, rounded piece of equipment. A snow scoop.

"He's not home," I said.

"Great detective work."

I hopped out of the cab and collapsed into a foot and a half of snow. Instead of rescuing me, Jace just laughed.

"I thought you said you were a native. How come you can't handle snow?"

I sputtered, wiped my face and struggled to my feet. A couple of minutes later I found the square metal door inside the carport. To the uninitiated, it probably looked like a fairy door or something out of Alice in Wonderland. I opened it and grabbed the key.

"Does every house on the Keweenaw have a milk chute? Even the new ones?"

"There are no new ones. That's the point. We're a throwback to the sixties and earlier when there was home milk delivery."

He held out his hand for the key and then he opened the door to the kitchen.

"Hey," I protested. "This is my investigation."

"Yeah, well, just in case there is someone here, and that someone is a murderer, I thought it would be best if I went first."

"Oh. Well, thanks."

I followed him into a tiny, compact kitchen and down the world's shortest hall where he stopped short and I crashed into his body. It was like smashing into the Pictured Rocks on the southern shore of Lake Superior.

"Good Lord," he whispered. The hair on the back of my neck stood up and I knew why. He'd found a body. Jalmer Pelonen was my first guess. I put my hands on his upper arms, trying to get him to duck so that I could see the crime scene. When I finally got him to move, I discovered the shades were all pulled and the room was pitch black. If there was a body, he couldn't have seen it. But his focus—and mine—was on a battery of blinking lights on the banks of computers that circled the room.

"Holy guacamole," I breathed. "It's the bridge of the Starship Enterprise."

# NINETEEN

I managed to find a floor lamp and turned it on as Jace examined the computers.

"I figured Pelonen would be one of those beaver pelt-slash-eight-point-buck-head-on-the-wall guys. This is sophisticated. So sophisticated that I suspect he's either trading stocks or leading an underground militia. It also means he's got access to money. So why couldn't he have bought Liisa a car or sent her to boarding school? Why agree to have her live with strangers in Red Jacket?"

"He couldn't have known what would happen," I said. "Jalmer's lived around here a long time. We hardly have any crime and we never have murders." Even as I spoke I realized that spiel was no longer accurate.

Jace is not officially a tech expert but he's one of those lucky people who finds computers interesting rather than intimidating and I left him with the machines while I explored the rest of the house. It didn't take long.

In addition to the small kitchen, there were two small bedrooms, a postage-stamp-sized bathroom, and what had to be the world's smallest wood-burning sauna. If it hadn't been for the computers, I'd have suspected Jalmer Pelonen of being a latter-day Henry David Thoreau.

I picked through the drawers and closets, finding only a few pieces of men's clothing, all of them clean and folded or hung neatly on hangers. Next to one of the twin-sized beds was a snapshot mounted in a wooden frame. It was of an angelic, blond child, obviously Liisa. She was sitting on the lap of a young woman, also blond and pretty but whose face was scored by faint lines of tension. Or, maybe it was unhappiness. I felt a wave of sadness so sharp that tears started in my eyes. Liisa's mother? She had died young. I couldn't help wondering if she'd taken her own life.

I carried the photo back to the living room and showed it to Jace.

"What do you make of this?"

He studied it. "Like mother, like daughter."

"Meaning what?"

"Reid said Liisa wasn't happy. Possibly they both suffered from depression. The mother obviously took off."

"What makes you think that?"

He looked up at me.

"She isn't here."

"She died."

"Did she? It's one way out of an impossible situation."

I felt tears pricking the backs of my eyes and I snatched the photo and stalked out of the room. His voice followed me.

"Are you crying, Umlaut?"

"Not really," I said, returning to the room. "I just think it a shame that this woman had such a short time with her beautiful daughter. Sometimes I wonder if beauty is a curse."

He shook his head. "You know what they say, beauty is in the eye of the beholder. That suggests that all perceived beauty is personal and based on more than just physical appearance."

"That's what they say," I agreed, "but I've been thinking about this a lot with this case. There are universally recognized elements of feminine beauty and both Liisa and her mother embodied most of them. I think those extraordinary good looks set them up for disappointment whether because others expected too much from them or because they came to expect too much themselves."

"You mean a sense of entitlement?"

"Well, yes, but I also wonder if people held their beauty against them. My niece told me that when Liisa Pelonen walked down the corridor, the boys and even grown men would sort of freeze and just stare at her. It was as if she'd cast a spell on them."

He nodded, thoughtfully, and I remembered one of the reasons I'd fallen in love with him. He listened.

"Maybe you're right. Beauty is a factor in the doom of mythological figures and the fairytales based on them. Still, beauty didn't kill Liisa Pelonen. It was a rock. And, in any case, the decision to take someone's life is life-altering for the murderer, too. It seems to me there would have to be a strong motive."

"You mean like life or death?"

His lips thinned. "Or two million dollars. Find anything else?"

"Frozen rabbit stew and some beer in the refrigerator. Nothing fresh, which makes sense since he was planning to be gone for two weeks." I looked around, guiltily. "He could come back at any time."

"We've got a legitimate reason to be here, remember?" Jace's gray eyes were ice cold. "Someone killed his daughter. Meanwhile, we should try to get into his computer." He pointed to a desktop model with a large keyboard and an oversized monitor.

"What are you hoping to find?"

"Ideally? Some sort of evidence that he's been siphoning money from Liisa's trust fund."

"Come on, Jace. You can't really think Liisa's father would have killed her."

"Happens all the time," he said. "In some circles." He worked the keys and pulled up a screen that was password protected. There were dozens of bright little icons present, though, and it seemed to me they revealed something about the man.

"Let's take a crack at the password," Jace said, cutting off my train of thought. "It's usually something common, like a birthdate or a pet's name."

"Sauna," I said, "Suomi. Keweenaw. Fishing. Snow. Beer."

"No," he said, as he tried them one by one. "No, no, no, no and hell, no."

"Lake, trout, woods."

More clicking. "Negative."

"Cabin, snow scoop, Stormy Kromer."

He paused, his fingers curved above the keyboard.

"What the heck is a Stormy Kromer?"

Inspiration struck belatedly.

"Never mind that. Try Liisa."

"Bingo," he said, but he sounded less than enthusiastic and I thought I knew why. A father who would memorialize his daughter's name in a password would be unlikely to kill that same daughter. If Jalmer was innocent, the light shone that much brighter on Reid Night Wind.

Jace squinted at the screen.

"I've got a menu but need another password to get to the files."

I stepped close enough to inhale the scent of him (pine, appealing sweat, industrial-strength testosterone) and feel his warmth and I had to make an extra effort to focus so I started to talk about the icons.

"Lots of information here," I said. "Look at this. Disaster Preparedness. Doomsday Skills. Sharpshooters, Inc. Michigan Militia." I met Jace's eyes. "Liisa's father seems more like the Unibomber than Henry David Thoreau."

"He may be a vigilante," Jace said, "but I think he's just a survivalist who knows how to kill."

"Or, at least, how to open a can of hash with his teeth. Do you really think it is Jalmer Pelonen?"

Jace shook his head. "But I'll tell you this, Umlaut, the killer is someone who knew she was home alone that night which means he or she is one of your nearest and dearest."

"Or yours," I replied. I cursed my own thoughtlessness when I saw Jace's long lashes drop over his eyes.

"Look," I said, trying to distract him, "there's a separate icon for Jussi & Jussi, a Hancock law firm. They do everything from divorces to wills to settling neighbor disputes. I'll check with them tomorrow to see what I can find out about the trust fund."

Jace turned the computer off.

"If there was a trust fund. The girl may have lied to Reid to get him to marry her." I said nothing and he seemed to think better of what he'd said. "Probably not. But I've learned that you can't go wrong expecting the worst from people."

I blinked at him.

"Is that what happened with us, Jace? You expected the worst from me and you got it?"

"No," he said, after a minute. Then he swung me up in his arms and carried me through the snow bank I'd tripped in earlier and deposited me in the passenger seat of the pickup. "I don't know what I expected from you, Hatti, but I got the best."

There was silence during the thirty-minute ride back to Red Jacket. Well, outward silence. Inside I was screaming. Why? Why? WHY? Neither of us spoke until he pulled up in front of Bait and Stitch. I was still waiting to hear his voice when I opened the car door. And then I did.

"Hatti," he said, "I need Sonya Stillwater's address."

It felt like a slap in the face, not the least because Sonya is totally lovely and one of the best people I know and I was sure that Jace would instantly fall in love with her.

"Third Street," I snapped. "Above her medical clinic. There's a sign."

# TWENTY

E inar was, as always, perched on his high stool behind the cash register and Arvo, leaning on the counter, was conducting a one-way conversation.

Both men looked at me as I came in the door and I realized the night on Kilimanjaro hadn't done me any favors. My eyes felt puffy and my hair sprouted like a dandelion gone to seed.

"What's wrong Hatti-girl?"

"Conniption fit," Einar diagnosed out of his vast knowledge of female behavior. "Needs husband."

Four words. I was impressed. It was a masterly output from my monosyllabic assistant. My cheeks flamed. It was bad enough being in a jealous temper. It was hateful to get caught. I shook my head.

"I'm fine. Just tired." And heartbroken. And ashamed that I was thinking about my wretched love life and not about the lovely girl who had just died.

Arvo looked at me sideways. "You look like you slept in the woods."

My involuntary laugh disrupted my internal pity party and I almost told him about the sleepover.

"Were you looking for me?"

"Hmm? Oh, yes, yes." Arvo frowned as he felt the pockets of his overcoat until he came up with a folded piece of paper. It was such a familiar gesture that I had to smile. Pauline was always making lists for him then tucking them into his pockets. He was the big concept guy, and she was the detail person. Yin and Yang. One of the reasons they had a successful marriage.

"Doc Laitimaki is doing the autopsy," he said, consulting the list. "I thought you'd like to know." Viktor Laitimaki, a septuagenarian general practitioner, is one of five physicians who share autopsy responsibilities for the three counties on the Keweenaw. He's been our family doctor since before I was born. I was glad to hear the news. Doc L., as we called him, would come up with answers.

"In time for my angel's services," Arvo said. His blue eyes shone with unshed tears. Pauline and I will give her the Sweetheart. That's our best model, white with carved rosebuds on the lid and inside, pink satin."

I suppressed a shudder. The description of the coffin sounded eerily like that of a jewelry box or a dollhouse. Or Liisa's room at the funeral home.

Arvo looked back at the note.

"I am supposed to ask you about a necklace, whether you know where it is. A dreamcatcher on a chain."

I sucked in a breath and my chest hurt as if I'd cracked a rib. This time it wasn't because the pendant had once belonged to me. This time I was terrified that it would connect Reid Night Wind to the case.

"Does this mean anything to you, Hatti-girl?"

"A dreamcatcher on a chain?"

"Maybe a gift from the Night Wind boy. Nothing romantic, you know. He was just a friend."

Of course Arvo knew about Reid. He'd been at our house with Pops, playing pool, the night Liisa and Reid had met. I was mildly relieved that Arvo still considered the two young people mere friends but knew that would change when it came out that they had married. And that Reid Night Wind, a reckless young man from the rez, was now a millionaire. I realized, belatedly, that Arvo was crying and I hurried to put my arm around him.

"There is something you don't know, Henrikki," he said, wiping his eyes. "Liisa, she was *raskaana*. Pregnant. We, Pauline and I, were going to be grandparents."

Arvo's nose dripped and Einar handed me a tissue for him.

"You knew about the baby?"

"Of course, of course." He wiped his eyes and blew his nose. "Liisa told me it had been an accident but I was so happy. It meant we would have our Liisa and another child."

My mind started to click over like a very old, very slow engine.

"Pauline didn't know."

"Eh? No. That's right. We were saving the news for a very special Christmas present. When Pauly got the idea to make a lace shawl it seemed like a sign from God."

"It's a wedding ring shawl," I said.

"But it can be used for a christening, too, eh?"

Almost immediately his face fell.

"How can I tell her, Hatti-girl? How can I tell her we were so close to having our own family?"

At least I could lighten one burden for him.

"Pauline already knows. Sonya discovered it during the examination."

He nodded. "Poor Pauline. She has to bear the sorrow and pick up the pieces."

"Arvo, how was it that Liisa told you about the baby?"

"One night. After supper. We got in the habit of going to the office to do paperwork and to clean up there and in the embalming room. She told me lots of things, Hatti."

"About her father and mother?"

"She didn't remember her mother much but she said Jalmer was good to her except he didn't want her to leave the UP. She wanted to go down to Interlochen to study after the Ahmeek school closed. Coming to Copper County High School was a compromise between them."

"Did she tell you her father is a computer geek?" He nodded.

"Sure. He trades stocks and bonds. That's how he makes his living."

I wanted to ask about the trust fund but I was afraid to find out. Meanwhile, Arvo sniffed one last time, nodded to Einar and said goodbye to me.

There was something I needed to ask him, but whatever it was floated in the back of my brain and wouldn't come to the surface so I let him go out the door. An instant later he was back, his list once against in his fingers.

"Pauline needs three dozen yellow roses for the grave blanket. Can you ask Sofi?"

I nodded. "I'll bring them up to the house myself."

After Arvo left I took a quick look at the mail before going over to the Floral and Fudge. At the last minute, I remembered to ask Einar whether there had been any messages for me.

"*Joo,*" he said. "Miss Irene wants yarn."

"Did she say which yarn?"

He nodded. "*Joo.*"

"Did you write it down?"

He shook his head.

"Okay. Good job. Did she say anything else?"

He closed his eyes then recited. "God hath clothed me with the garments of salvation; he hath covered me with the robe of right-eousness, Isaiah."

I doubled-over with laughter. Apparently Biblical verses did not count as words spoken toward his daily self-imposed limit.

"Any other messages?"

"Sofi husband."

Lars! He must have gotten in touch with Jalmer Pelonen. I wondered why he hadn't called on my cell, but it didn't really matter. I figured I'd call him after checking in with my sister.

Sofi's shop smelled of freshly cut flowers and an odd combination of peppermint, eggnog and chocolate. I wrinkled my nose. Holiday foods are all well and good, I thought, but not when they interfere with coffee or fudge.

Charlie was at the cash register and I greeted her and waved to the shoppers then slipped behind the counter to snatch the last square of chocolate walnut, which is nearly always good for a mood boost.

Sofi's shop is a narrow rectangle, an exact replica of mine, but where most of mine is showroom, most of hers is backroom. Her three spacious coolers are nearly always filled with buckets of freshly cut flowers. The shelves are neatly stacked with containers and pots, spools of wire and ribbon, Styrofoam inserts, and all the rest of the paraphernalia needed for flower arranging. The view and the scent reminded me of Pauline's greenhouse.

Sofi, one strand of hair loosened from her braid and hanging in her moist, rosy face, was laboring over an arrangement in a ceramic bowl. It contained snapdragons, carnations, tiny yellow rosebuds, and baby's breath and it was exquisite. Unfortunately, as it was yellow and white I knew it was an order for a funeral. Probably Liisa's.

"Everybody and their Aunt Sadie has been in here today either ordering centerpieces for Christmas or flowers for the Pelonen funeral."

"So I guess the word is out."

"You can say that again." She blew the wheat-colored strand up in the air. "Everyone knows she's dead but so far they think it was an accident. Listen, if you're going to stand there, could you strip the leaves off those asters? And maybe the daisies, too?"

It was the usual request. As I have no eye for floral arranging my only value is in such things as stripping leaves or driving the delivery truck. I got to work.

"So," she said, "how was your sleepover?"

I lifted my eyebrows. "It wasn't a party, Sofi. It was a fact-finding mission. I went up there to talk to a witness."

"If you're talking about Reid Night Wind, don't you mean a suspect?"

"It's too soon to tell."

"Well, did you learn anything?"

I told her about the marriage between Reid and Liisa and about the trust fund. "The thing is that he looks as guilty as sin."

She shrugged. "If it looks like a duck and quacks like a duck…"

"I know, I know, but I just don't think he killed her. I mean, why should he? She'd promised him a hundred thousand dollars. Why risk life in prison just for a little more?"

"Two million is not just a little more. But, as it happens, I think I agree with you. It seems like someone really wanted to shut Liisa up or send her away. The killing had to be very precisely timed and planned and there would have been a great risk. I can't believe it would have been worth it to Reid."

"Jace thinks Reid's been set up."

Sofi's big blue eyes held mine. "Well, that seems to me to be another problem. How many people knew about his relationship with Liisa?"

"Edna Moilanen, apparently, which means all the rest of the Ladies Aid."

"Yes, but who knew she would be alone at the funeral home and that she expected to meet Reid Night Wind there at seven o'clock?"

"I don't know."

"Well, somebody knew, Hatti. And if you don't want your brother-in-law to spend the rest of his life in jail, you'd better get busy finding out who."

"Maybe Mrs. Moilanen knows," I said, with a touch of bitterness.

"Well, if she does, you're in luck. Pauline Maki has called a special meeting of the knitting circle tonight."

"Why?"

"For some reason, she thinks that working on delicate, cobwebby lace is going to cheer us all up."

"Oh."

"Did Reid Night Wind admit to being the baby's father?"

"No. The reverse."

"Looks like Edna M. is right about that, too. She's put her money on Matti Murso. Hatti?"

"Yes?"

"You're still in love with Jace, aren't you?"

I wrinkled my nose. "That's like asking if you're still in love with Lars."

"I know."

That reminded me that I still needed to speak with Lars. I started to excuse myself when Sofi stopped me.

"Oh, and on the subject of Matti Murso, Diane Hakala stopped in this morning to let me know she's going to need, and I quote, a whole boatload of flowers for a wedding in March."

"Whose wedding?"

"Barb's. Turns out Matti has rebounded back into her hands.

They're tying the knot early so they can honeymoon at the Ellsworth Cheese Curd Festival over spring break." I looked at her.

"Not a shotgun wedding then?"

Sofi laughed. "That would really be the final straw, wouldn't it? I mean Matti Murso's a good hockey goalie, sure, but when all's said and done he's just a gangly kid with pimples. Hard to imagine him as the father of two simultaneously conceived babies and a murderer."

But I wondered.

"I need to go," I said, "but I was supposed to remind you that Pauline needs three dozen roses for the grave blanket. I said I'd deliver them tonight."

"You can't," she said. "Knitting circle, remember? Tell her we'll get them over in the morning. They can't have the funeral for a few days at least. The body's still at the morgue."

Sometimes my sister's plain-spoken practicality knocks me off my feet.

"Get another piece of chocolate walnut on the way out," Sofi called, "you look like you could use it."

# TWENTY-ONE

The Gas 'n Go, a convenience store-slash-service station owned and operated by Tauno Murso, sells motor oil, coffee that tastes like motor oil, red vines, gum, canned soup, boxed cereal and milk that is always perilously close to its expiration date.

I found Tauno where he seemed to spend most of his time, under the chassis of a pickup.

"Mr. Murso?"

"*Mita?*"

He responded with the Finnish word for "what", which was encouraging, but he did not come out from under the vehicle, and I found it a little awkward to introduce myself to his left boot. I did it anyway.

"I'm Hatti Lehtinen, and I'd like to speak with Matti."

There was a long pause while he digested my words. Did he know why I was there? Was he afraid his son was in trouble with the law? Was he working on a mechanical problem that took up all the space in his cerebrum? The response came, at long last.

"Ei tanne." Not here.

I tried again. "Where can I find him?"

"*Mita?*"

I sighed. This was going nowhere fast. I doubted whether Tauno

146

would be this uncooperative with Pops. But, of course, I was not a card-carrying member of the Finnish-American good 'ol boys club.

"Don't bother Tauno, Umlaut. Can't you see he's busy?"

I jumped, not so much because I hadn't heard him come into the garage behind me, but because he'd used the nickname. Jace's nickname. Again. I forced a laugh to camouflage my accelerated pulse rate. Max couldn't have known. And there was no patent on the word.

"What're you doing here?"

"I saw you come in, figured you wanted to talk to Matti and deduced that you'd need a little help with translation."

I knew he wasn't talking about Finnish to English but about the great communication gap that exists between taciturn men of a certain age and younger women.

"As it happens," he continued, "I'm in a unique position to help you, madame. Let me help you into my carriage, er, truck." After a small hesitation I placed my fingers in his outstretched hand. The contact felt secure and warm. I hadn't even realized I was cold. He whispered in my ear. "I know where to find Matti."

Max's pickup was a late model and much more luxurious than the one Jace had borrowed from Chief Joseph. It was spacious, warm and comfortable just like his touch. I felt myself melt into the seat, mildly surprised that you could even get heated cushions in a truck.

"Whither bound?" I asked, then disgraced myself with a huge yawn.

He laughed and put the truck in gear. "Hockey practice."

Of course. Matti Murso was a hockey star. The reference reminded me that we were talking about a teenager—a kid—in connection with a murder. It also reminded me of that kid's status. Hockey is the most popular team sport in the UP and folks followed the Copper County High Muskrats with the same enthusiasm the Brits follow Manchester United.

"What's your connection to the team?"

"I keep score at the games."

"You play hockey? I thought you were from Texas?"

"The southwest," he replied, vaguely. "In any case, we've all got ice. Mainly in refrigerators and indoors. I played some as a kid and I know the rules so I help out with the Muskrats in my leisure time."

"You're a man of many dimensions." He laughed.

"You know the old saying about the UP. Everybody's got to wear multiple hats."

Another massive yawn interrupted my laugh and I apologized.

"No need," he said. "Just sit back and relax."

I allowed my eyes to close and my bones to sink into the warm seat cushions and I realized that, for the first time since Jace Night Wind turned up on my parents' front porch, I felt no tension at all. In fact, I felt safe. A feather-light touch on my cheek opened my eyes and my ears and I heard Max's voice.

"Hey, sleepyhead."

I sat up. "Oh geez. I'm so sorry, Max."

"Rough night?"

"It's complicated."

"Something to do with the ruffian who claims to be married to you?"

There was something besides a touch of humor in his voice and I remembered our interrupted date.

"Oh my gosh," I said. "I haven't even apologized for Saturday night."

"Forget it."

"No, no. I want to explain if you'll let me." It occurred to me I hadn't yet picked Max's brain and this might be a good time.

"Is it true? Is he your husband?"

I searched his face for signs of regret but I could only see his profile. I realized we'd reached the frozen lake and he was watching the practice.

"Officially. For the moment, anyway. Like I said, it's complicated."

"Okay."

He didn't seem all that put out and I wondered if I'd overestimated the bonds between us.

"You wanted to talk to me about something," he said, helping me out. "Was it Liisa Pelonen's death?"

"Yep. Sounds like you know something about it."

"Pretty much only what Betty Ann had to say on her program this morning. Arvo and his wife found Liisa in the sauna with a wound on her head. Investigation is ongoing and Sheriff Clump would appreciate any and all relevant information." I groaned, even though I already knew Clump had been brought in.

"That tears it. Arvo and Pauline wanted me to look into the situation quietly before anyone contacted the police. But there are no secrets in Red Jacket and the sheriff won't want me anywhere near his case. I wanted to ask you some questions. The case is a bit of a puzzle.

"Sonya Stillwater did a sort of unofficial autopsy on Saturday afternoon..." I paused when he growled.

"She what?"

"Just a preliminary look-see, you know? Just to try to figure out whether it had been an accident, natural causes or murder."

"Damned interfering woman."

That reaction seemed a bit extreme to me but I was anxious to make the most of my time with Max.

"Anyway, Sonya didn't think the blow had killed her. Apparently the girl had a bit of a heart condition."

"Stillwater told you that?"

"No, no, there's no way she could have known. I think it was Arvo who told me. Anyway, Doc will find out what killed her."

"You're thinking that someone bashed her on the head and counted on the shock to trigger her heart condition, right?"

"Seems like it could have happened like that."

"If so, it doesn't rule out your brother-in-law."

I stared at him, my jaw dropping.

"How, in the name of the Father, Son and Holy Ghost do you know about Reid?"

Max's grin contained no humor.

"I was a professional investigator. After my little set-to with your midnight visitor, I made some inquiries. His kid brother's got himself in some deep doo-doo."

I nodded. "Jace and I talked with him last night."

After a silence stretched to more than a minute, Max said, "You gonna tell me about it or don't you trust me?"

Everything I knew, I reflected, would soon become common knowledge and, anyway, I did trust Max. I told him about the quickie wedding, the plan to meet at the Makis' sauna at seven fifteen and the plan to live in a sublet in Marquette.

Max appeared to listen carefully.

"That surprises me a little," he admitted. "Those brothers don't seem like the marrying kind."

I actually twisted to the side to try to avoid the knife prick into my heart but I knew he was right.

"She was pregnant," I said. "She wanted to get married because of that and because she'd be eligible to inherit a two-million-dollar trust fund. She promised Reid a hundred thousand of that."

"Geez Louise," he said. "Sounds like a slam dunk for Clump."

"I know. But Reid says he didn't do it."

"That's what criminals all say, Umlaut. None of them ever did it. Not in a million years."

A sense of hopelessness descended on me.

"But why should he kill her?"

Max shrugged. "Who gets the trust fund now that she's dead? Her husband, right? More than that, what other suspects do you have?"

I thought about Ronja, so thrilled with Astrid's star turn as St. Lucy and about Diane Hakala joyfully planning Barb's wedding to Matti now that Liisa was out of the way. And I thought about Matti himself, desperately in love but rejected after one date.

"Look at him," Max murmured, as the tall, lanky teenager loped over to the truck. "He's just a baby with a good left hook. I don't think Matti killed anyone."

I wanted to point out that the murder had most likely been accidental, the unexpected result of the blow on the head, but it didn't matter what I said. Besides, I wasn't an apologist for Reid Night Wind.

"See what you think," Max said, getting out of the car and hailing the kid carrying a helmet in one hand and a hockey stick in the other. "Hey, Matti!"

"Hey, Max," Matti said. He grinned then trotted over to the truck. "What's up?"

Except for his wiry build he couldn't have looked less like his father who was short and dark. Matti's hair was angelically blond and he had a pair of dreamy blue eyes whose effect was only slightly dimmed by the outbreak of acne on his cheeks. I was sure that Barb Hakala regarded him as a Nordic god.

"You getting ready for Menominee this week?"

"You know it. Shoot-a-mile, we're gonna clobber them good."

"Matti, do you know Hatti Lehtinen?" The boy's smile disappeared. "Ah. I can see that you know she's serving as temporary police chief. She wants to ask you a few questions about Liisa. Is that all right?"

"I don't know nothing about it."

"Well, then that's what you tell Hatti. Here, I'll take your gear and you slide into the driver's seat for a few minutes."

He didn't want to talk to me. That much was obvious. Was it because he was afraid he'd give himself away? I looked into the hunted eyes and felt desperately sorry for him. He'd fallen in love, been rejected and she'd died. Any one of those things would have sent most teenage boys on a long walk off a short dock, as Pops would say.

"I just have a few questions," I said, gently. "I know you cared about Liisa and I'm sorry about what happened to her."

"I'm sorry, too," he mumbled.

"Do you know what happened?"

"Barb's mom told me she slipped in the sauna and hit her head on a rock."

"That's partly true," I said, deciding to level with him. "She had a blow to the head but we don't think it was bad enough to have killed her. What I want to know from you, Matti, is what was she like?"

There was a faraway look in his eyes and I got the feeling he wasn't seeing me at all.

"She was perfect," he said, simply. "Just like an angel."

"Because of her looks?"

"Yes. And her voice. She sang like an angel."

"So I understand."

"But it was more than that." He leaned toward me, suddenly eager to make himself understood. "She was good, you know? Nice to everybody."

I nodded. "I understand you took her to the Harvest Dance."

"I did. It was the most wonderful night of my life. I thought she was my girl and everything, but," his voice trailed off, "it didn't work out that way."

"Why not?"

He shrugged his wide shoulders then let them droop.

"She just wanted to be friends."

"Because there was someone else?"

"No. There was no one else. She just, well, she just wanted to focus on her singing."

"I see. Did that make you angry?"

"Some. Mostly it made me sad." He looked up at me. "It still makes me sad."

"What about Barb?"

I shouldn't have asked. It wasn't relevant to what had happened to Liisa.

"We're gettin' married in March. I'm looking forward to the cheese curd festival."

I felt a pit in my stomach for Diane Hakala's daughter. She wouldn't even be first on Matti's mind during her own honeymoon.

"Do you know whether Liisa had girlfriends?"

"I guess. I mean, I saw her talking to girls, but they were mostly jealous of her. People think it's lucky to be that beautiful, you know? But there's a lot of it that's just a burden."

I could hear Miss Irene's voice in my head. "Cast your burden upon the Lord and He will sustain you. Psalms."

"Matti, what were you doing Friday night?"

He didn't make the connection at first. I could tell the minute he did.

"I didn't kill her," he said. "I didn't even see her. I was at the parade and I knew she was sick and I knew, if she was sick, Mrs. Maki wouldn't let her go to the dance. So I didn't go, either."

"What did you do instead?"

"Played video games. In the basement. Alone."

"Was your dad in the house?"

"Yah, sure. He's always there if he's not at the gas station. I didn't see him."

I thought he was telling the truth. He certainly could have said he'd spent the evening with his dad which would have given him an alibi.

"It was her birthday, you know," he said, in a broken voice. "I bought her a bracelet." He pulled a box out of his pocket and opened it to show me a silver chain with an angel charm hanging from it.

"It's lovely," I said.

"She wouldn't have wanted it."

"I think you're wrong. Any girl would love it. Will you give it to Barb?"

Again, I wasn't sure why I'd asked the question. He shook his head.

"Would you like me to see that Liisa gets it?"

"Yes, ma'am," he said. Suddenly, I felt a hundred years old.

"One last question. Can you think of anyone who would have wanted to hurt Liisa?"

"Not really. But she did seem scared of something. I thought it was her father."

"Why?"

"I'm not sure. Something about the way she seemed stuck. Like, whatever it was that was scaring her was something she couldn't get away from."

It seemed to me to be a good description of someone resigned to her fate and, again, I was impressed with Matti Murso's insight. Maybe it was Jalmer Pelonen, after all.

"Can I go now?"

"Sure. And thanks. Oh," I slapped my forehead, "one more thing. Did you know about the baby?"

Color jumped into Matti's face and his eyes were like china blue saucers.

"Baby?"

"Liisa was pregnant," wishing I hadn't had to tell him, but knowing it was inevitable. "About six weeks. Is there any chance you could have been the father?"

"No."

The word came quickly but it was quiet and unemphatic. I couldn't tell whether it was the truth but, for some reason, I didn't think he'd lie about something like that.

"Matti," I said, impulsively, "do you think it's wise to marry Barb so soon?"

"It'll happen sometime," he said, wearily, "and she wants it to be now. And I kind of owe her."

His answer reminded me of *The Moomins,* a series of adventures about a tiny troll family that Elli and I had read and re-read as children. In one story the main character, Moomintroll summed up his life's goal saying, "I only want to live in peace and plant potatoes and dream."

As Matti Murso climbed out of the truck and spoke with Max, I offered a silent prayer for him: *Goodbye, Moomintroll. And godspeed.*

Dusk had darkened the sky when Max pulled up in front of my parents' home. I could see the lights inside, and I knew Sofi and Elli and Charlie would be there waiting for me. Even though I was beyond tired and grimy and more than a little discouraged, I felt a comforting sense of belonging. My friends and family had helped me through the worst time in my life, and now they were helping me again—just by being here. I decided that I'd lay the case out for them to get their thoughts, maybe after the older ladies left. I turned to Max, felt a surge of warmth and realized I wanted him to be part of the tribe, too.

"Have you got dinner plans?"

He looked surprised. "What do you have in mind?"

I nodded at the house. "Elli and Sofi are setting up a little smorgasbord of leftovers from the festival, and we'd love to have you join us. I should warn you that my aunts and Mrs. Moilanen and the Reverend Sorensen and his wife will probably be there, along with Diane Hakala and Ronja Laplander. We've got a knitting circle meeting scheduled for right after supper."

"It sounds nice," he said.

I thought I understood his hesitation.

"Jace won't be there. Here, I mean. He's gone off with Sonya Stillwater."

"Fine," he said, but he didn't smile and I found his face unreadable. "I'd like to contribute something."

"They'll have enough food for both armies of the Winter War," I said. "What we really need is a Christmas tree."

"Christmas trees I've got. Give me an hour."

# TWENTY-TWO

**M**ax returned an hour later with a freshly cut Frasier pine tree of
the perfect shape and size (I was beginning to think that
anything Max put his hand to would be the perfect shape and size).
Without any direction from me at all, he and Charlie set the tree in the
stand and began to decorate while the rest of us ferried food from the
kitchen to the dining room table for a family-style smorgasbord.

"You have to string the lights so that no two lights of the same color
are too close to each other," I heard Charlie explain. Sofi and I
exchanged an amused glance. "And that angel, the knitted one, goes on
the top. Most important, when we get to the tinsel, no clumping!"

"Yes, ma'am," Max said, in a meek voice.

"They sound like an old married couple," Elli said, in an undertone,
with a little smile. "Or else he's just really good with teenaged girls."

"I get the feeling he's really good with everybody," Sofi said,
shooting me a pointed look. "He's a keeper."

I felt a little rush of pleasure and wondered about it. Was I really
interested in Max Guthrie? Was he really interested in me? Was it time
to cut my losses and move on? I had no answers.

"You have to put the homemade ones up high on the tree," Charlie
said. "I don't know why."

"It's because when he was a puppy, Larry liked to lick the pieces of macaroni," Sofi said, as she stepped into the parlor. "Listen, Charlie, Max is doing us a big favor with this tree and you sound just the tiniest bit dictatorial."

"Nonsense," Max replied, in a mild tone. "I like a woman who knows her mind."

I smiled to myself. Max would make a great dad. I stepped into the parlor to admire the tree.

"The last thing we need is the snow," Charlie said.

"Snow?" Max blinked at her. "You're going to put snow on our beautiful tree?"

"Fake snow," Charlie said. "Flocking." She looked at me. "Down in the cellar?" I nodded.

"There are some people," Max said, with a slow grin, "who might think it odd that you bother to spray the tree with foam when there is an abundance of the real stuff outside the windows." I laughed.

"Tradition is very big in Red Jacket."

"Yeah," he said. "I'm starting to get that."

The others had been arriving, bringing with them cold air, frozen crystals in their hair, covered dishes, pies and bar cookies for dessert. The Reverend and Mrs. Sorensen, Mrs. Moilanen, Aunt Ianthe and Miss Irene, Diane and Arnold Hakala, Ronja Laplander and the Makis admired the tree, en route to the dining room. After the pastor's blessing, we tucked into Elli's special omelets made of eggs, butter, onions, potatoes, Gruyere cheese and *Joululimppu*, which is a treacly Finnish Christmas bread. There was an awesome assortment of casseroles, molded salads, vegetables and special dishes, including Mrs. Moilanen's vinegar cabbage. And there was coffee. There was always coffee.

I had set out my mom's hand-painted wooden candle stand and the warmth of the flames made every face at the table bright and hopeful. Even Pauline and Arvo appeared cheerful and the latter encouraged a series of toasts to family and friends, near and far, hoisting his short glass of egg nog.

The sense of peace might have been due to the magic of the season but it seemed to me it was more about the magic of community and I felt lucky to be a part of it.

After supper, the non-knitters (Arvo, Max, the reverend, Arnold Hakala and Larry) tidied up the kitchen and the rest took seats in my mother's parlor. Pauline Maki distributed cloth knitting bags that she had made and filled with the essentials for attacking heirloom lace. She sat in a ladderback chair at the head of what was essentially a horseshoe arrangement and began to talk about the contents of the bags which included a copy of the pattern, size-two needles and single skein of the softer-than-a-baby's-butt wool that she, Pauline, had already wound into a yarn cake.

"This is the finest, softest yarn I have ever felt," Aunt Ianthe said, feeling a strand with two fingers.

"It is very special yarn," Pauline explained. "It comes from the hair under the chin of the musk-ox on the Shetland Island of Unst. There is only so much available every year as the herd is small."

"It has an aura," Diane Hakala said, holding hers up to the light. "It seems to glow."

Pauline nodded.

"True lace weight yarn often carries a halo," Pauline said. "That adds to the beauty of the finished project."

"All around him was a glowing rainbow, like a halo shining in the clouds on a rainy day." Miss Irene quoted. "Ezekiel."

"On the other hand, it is the so-called glow that presents the difficulty of knitting with the yarn," Mrs. Moilanen pointed out. The widow habitually indulged her oppositional streak with the justification that she was just "telling it like it is."

"The halo makes the stitches on the needle appear to run together and it is easy to shred the ply," Pauline said, nodding. "But we welcome the challenge."

"Why do we get only one skein," Ronja Laplander asked. "We can hardly knit an entire shawl with one skein."

"This is just to start," Pauline explained. "I have more at home and will hand out fresh yarn cakes at every circle meeting."

I interpreted that to mean we were to have finished our allotment in the days between meetings. Pauline did not intend to let any grass grow under her feet-or to let any project languish.

"This wool must be expensive," Mrs. Sorensen said. "You must let each of us pay our share, Pauline."

"Certainly not." Pauline smiled at her. "It is our gift—Arvo's and mine—to the knitting circle and the community as each of you, no doubt, will make a breathtaking cobweb shawl for someone local. Perhaps a young bride."

"For I am jealous over you with godly jealousy: for I have espoused you to one husband that I may present you as a chaste virgin to Christ. Second Corinthians." Miss Irene beamed.

I decided we'd had enough comments from the peanut gallery. I clapped my hands.

"All right. Would anyone like more coffee before we start the class? No? Then I think we should let Pauline begin."

Pauline sat up straight in her chair and favored the assembled women with a smile.

"One of the interesting aspects of the Shetland shawl is its background," she said. "Centuries ago people had very little money to provide the things they could not grow and some enterprising women found a way to earn money by producing very fine lace to sell. The finer the lace, the more they could charge for it. Color projects fetched even more money.

"The ladies on Unst, a Shetland Island that is inaccessible to the Scottish mainland, created the most delicate of the delicate lace, sometimes called cobweb. The six-foot shawls were so fine they could be drawn through a wedding ring, hence the name. The yarn was two-ply and easily split and difficult to work with and the spinners and knitters tended to be older women whose job it was to knit and spin and to mind the children. They worked during the day when the others were out in the fields, as they needed quiet to follow the intricate patterns."

"Oh, dear," Aunt Ianthe said, distressed. "Does this mean we will have to adopt *omerta* for all our meetings?"

This reference to the mafia's code of silence drew a muffled giggle from Sofi but the unflappable Pauline took the comment at face value.

"Perhaps at first. These patterns are complicated. This is not your average yarn-over lace."

Aunt Ianthe, Miss Irene, and Mrs. Sorensen looked properly

impressed but Ronja, no doubt, still hugging her grievance about the St. Lucy pick, was quick to strike at Pauline's all-knowing air.

"This is stupid," she thundered. "I thought we'd agreed to work on something simple this winter, like socks."

Pauline gazed at her, a pained look on her face.

"Then I have more bad news for you," Pauline said, with a barely perceptible tinge of irony, "with a lace project, it is vital to swatch."

Swatch, for the uninitiated, means the knitter must work a square of material in with the yarn to test for gauge based on needle size and tension. For all that most of us love the process of knitting, it seems that no one likes the process of knitting something just for practice and I have heard all kinds of excuses from knitters anxious to avoid making the practice squares.

I could tell by the belligerent look on Ronja's face she was about to condemn swatches as a waste of time but Pauline wasn't fazed. She threw me a quick, amused look, then plunged ahead.

"First we will do a loose cast-on," Pauline said. "Let's say forty eight stitches." She produced a bowl of stitch markers, small metal circles with colorful charms hanging from them. "Then we'll knit eight stitches, place a marker, knit another eight inches, do the same and so on to the end of the row. Purl back. When everyone has gotten that far, I will read the specific directions to you, as in knit two, yarn over, knit two together, slip one, knit one, pass slip stitch over. I will read the same for each section of six stitches."

"The markers are simply adorable," Aunt Ianthe caroled.

"So cunning," Miss Irene agreed.

"This is more like Morse code than knitting," Ronja complained.

"No, I'd say it's more like bingo with Pauline as the caller," Mrs. Moilanen said.

"No talking," Pauline said, with a smile. "As soon as you're finished, purl another row. We are making a cockleshell pattern and it will be extremely difficult to unravel any mistakes, so I would caution you not to talk."

As no one wanted to be the first to get into the deep water of trying to unravel a mistake, the room was silent except for the clicking of the metal needles.

"I want to introduce you to the concept of lifelines," Pauline said.

"I thought you said no talking," Ronja interjected.

The mortician's wife smiled at her.

"This is a technique you will be glad to know."

"Are you saying I will screw up?" Ronja's spine had stiffened lifting her substantial bosom a couple of inches.

"Oh yes," Pauline said, "we will all make mistakes. If this were easy, everyone in the world would do it. Anyway, a lifeline is created by weaving a contrasting color through every few rows so that if you find a mistake, you don't have to frog, only tink a limited number of stitches."

Frogging, from the terms "rip-it, rip-it" refers to ripping out rows of work to get back to the place where the stitch was dropped or another mistake was made. Tink, which is knit spelled backwards, refers to undoing one stitch at a time for the same purpose. Needless to say, tinking takes much longer than frogging. And, luckily, everyone in the circle already knew the terms.

"Tink and frog," Mrs. Sorensen said. "I wonder what an alien would think if he could drop in on our knitting circle."

"I imagine she would be interested in learning heirloom lace knitting," Aunt Ianthe said. "Pauline, you are doing a wonderful job."

Tears appeared in Pauline Maki's eyes and I realized she was using the knitting circle, and her role as instructor, to hold off the pain of her recent loss. I realized, too, that the knitters, church basement ladies, all, were consciously helping in the effort. Even Ronja Laplander.

"Next we will do the fan and feather."

"Oh, that sounds so romantic. Like something from a fairytale," Diane Hakala said. "I hope these shawls will bring good luck to the brides who receive them." I knew she was thinking of Barb and wondered whether that marriage would be successful. Probably. They were so young. Matti would forget his mad passion for Liisa Pelonen and he and Barb would forge a family unit as they matured together. Hopefully.

We worked for another half hour with Pauline calling out the direction like a coxswain in a rowing crew. Finally, we each had what looked like a crumpled bird's nest dangling from our needles.

"Speaking of fairytales," Mrs. Moilanen said, holding hers out, "this swatch reminds me of the *Ugly Duckling*."

"Ah," Pauline said. "Just wait until we pin and dress it. It will burst forth into a beautiful swan."

"I look forward to that," Mrs. Sorensen said, politely, but she, like everyone else, didn't seem convinced.

No one seemed ready to go home, so Sofi and Elli and I got out the desserts and made more coffee, while Aunt Ianthe played, *Deck the Halls, It Came Upon a Midnight Clear* and *Silent Night*, after which Miss Irene launched into *Kaksi kysttilaa*, a Finnish favorite about an old lady spending Christmas Day visiting the grave of her beloved.

We were on the second verse when Arvo's cell phone rang. The music stopped as he answered it. And we all froze as the color drained out of his face. When he'd finished, murmuring only, "Thank you," he stood motionless in the room until his wife gently touched his arm.

"Who was it, dear?" Pauline asked, moving to his side. He took one of her hands in both of his and began to knead it, restlessly.

"Doc," he said, finally. Harsh lines created parentheses around his mouth. "He's done the autopsy, twice. He's convinced Liisa died because her heart stopped."

"We knew that already, dearest," Pauline said, gently. "The blow to the head caused a shock to her system. We know she had a weak heart, that she was subject to arrhythmia."

Arvo gazed at his wife.

"Of course. I'd forgotten." He sighed. "Our poor, darling, angel."

"She was a gift from heaven," Aunt Ianthe said.

"Every good gift and every perfect gift is from above," Miss Irene put in. "The Book of James."

"So there is no doubt it was murder?" Max's question brought us back to harsh reality. Everyone in the room stiffened as my thoughts flew to the two young men, Matti Murso and Reid.

"But not," the Reverend Sorensen said, "necessarily intended murder. The assailant could not know about her heart condition."

I glanced at his kindly face and wondered if he could find a way to exonerate the perp on the topic of slamming a rock into her skull. It must be wonderful to possess that capacity for forgiveness.

"O death," Miss Irene said, on a roll, now, "where is thy sting? O grave, where is thy victory?"

The deep, grave lines on Arvo's face told me that, for once, he disagreed with First Corinthians. The sting was real, death's victory, complete. I could see him looking bleakly into the empty future that he had pictured as father and grandfather. His heart was broken. Pauline moved away from him as if his grief were wearing her down.

I turned the information over in my mind in the next few minutes. It seemed to me it was important to find out more about Liisa's heart condition and the only person left who could tell us was Jalmer Pelonen. It was while I was putting away my mom's punch bowl that I remembered Einar's message that Lars had called. Before I could call him back, though, the doorbell rang and I hurried out to the foyer to see Max opening the door. I watched his shoulders tense as Sonya Stillwater, snow twinkling on her lovely, long eyelashes and hair, stepped into the room followed by a darkly handsome man who was smiling at something she'd said, and helping her off with her parka. My husband.

"My goodness," Mrs. Sorensen said, driving a dagger into my heart. "Don't they make an enchanting couple?"

# TWENTY-THREE

"Forgive me for being so late," Sonya said, after a minute. "We were tied up with a new baby."

"For unto us a child is born," Miss Irene said, only this time she sang the words to Handel's Messiah.

Sonya smiled at Miss Irene. "It was almost as much of a miracle as the one in the manger and Jace, here, was a knight in shining armor." She flashed him a brilliant smile. I could feel the two halves of my heart withering inside me.

"Rusty armor," he murmured, modestly. "It was all accidental."

"Don't be modest," Sonya said, giving him a playful dig in the ribs with her elbow, as if they'd known one another for decades. "You were a grade A hero."

She went on to tell the story of Cindy Gray Squirrel, a young, first-time mom on the rez, who, when labor started, had no way to get to the hospital in Hancock.

"Jace happened to be with me when I got the call. He offered to pick Cindy up at her home and drive both of us—through a snowstorm, mind you—down to Hancock. And then," she said, with emphasis, "he stayed with us all through an emergency C-section. I mean, in the operating room."

As Sonya talked, Elli made sure that the newcomers got out of their outdoor clothing, were settled in comfortable chairs in the parlor and served with fresh coffee. Food and drink mysteriously appeared in their hands as Sonya continued the story with the other guests who had crowded around them. All except me. I didn't help or crowd. I just stood in a corner with my fists clenched at my side, wishing I had never met Jace Night Wind, but since I had, wishing he would disappear in a puff of smoke and give me back my life. Bits of the story drifted into my consciousness.

"Cindy trusted Jace because he is Chief Joseph's grandson," she said. As usual, her basic goodness glowed from within and seemed to be reflected on all the other faces. All, except mine. And one other. There was no enchantment in Max Guthrie's expression. I was heartened to see no hero worship there.

"I think she would have known instinctively to trust him, anyway," Sonya said. "And you'll never guess. She named her new baby Jason Night Wind Gray Squirrel. Jace gave him an Ojibwe blessing."

"Full disclosure," Jace said, "Sonya fed me the lines. I'd never heard of it before."

"You made a good team," Arvo said, leaning over to clap my husband on the back. "And here on the Keweenaw, teamwork is everything."

While the ladies asked questions about the baby and offered to help the family, and Sonya answered them from her position on the Victorian loveseat next to Jace, I fought the green-eyed monster. To tell the truth, I was shocked at the depth and breadth of my feelings. Sonya Stillwater, I reminded myself, was one of my best, most trusted friends. She and Jace had joined forces to take care of a young mother. It was something typical for her and, in his own way, typical for Jace. But, now, with my marriage all but over, I watched the easy companionship between the two and I felt such a surge of anger that it scared me.

It was the first time I really understood the elemental strength of jealousy; the first time I recognized the hateful emotion as a valid motive for murder.

The doorbell rang again and this time, Charlie answered it with a joyful shout.

"Daddy!"

My niece wrapped her beanpole body around Lars's lean frame. She looked like a tightly wound tetherball, and my eyes flew to Sofi's face. It had turned to stone.

"Hello, Snork Maiden," he said, using a nickname based on her favorite character in *The Moomins.* "Been up to mischief?"

"His mischief shall return upon his own head, and his violent dealing shall come down upon his own pate," Miss Irene said. "Psalms, of course."

"Very apt, dear," Aunt Ianthe said, after a respectful pause. "Lars, dearie, it is so nice to see you."

"Look at the tree," Charlie chattered. "Isn't it awesome? Max and me decorated it."

"I," Lars corrected. "Max and I decorated it."

"And Larry," Charlie told him, with an impish grin. He grinned back at her and set her on her feet. "Come into the kitchen with me," she said, pulling on his hand. "You look like you're starving."

Lars cast a quick glance at Sofi, but she was deliberately ignoring him and had turned to say something to Sonya, so his eyes moved to me and I thought I read a summons there. I followed father and daughter out to the kitchen figuring he must have found Jalmer Pelonen.

Lars accepted a cup of coffee then told his daughter he wasn't hungry and that he needed to talk to me alone.

"I'm not a little kid," she told him. "I'm helping Hatti with the investigation, you know."

"Investigation?" Lars looked at me.

"Charlie went to school with Liisa Pelonen and she's been helping me build a profile on her. And you might be interested in this. Doc Laiti-maki just called Arvo to tell him she most likely died of syncope which is when the heart slows down so much that the brain doesn't get enough blood. Apparently Liisa had a heart condition."

Lars frowned. "Was the heart condition listed in her medical records?"

"I don't know. I think it was just generally known and it makes sense if you consider that the blow to the head caused enough shock to trigger the arrhythmia. At least we'll have some cause of death to tell her father when he gets home."

"He won't be getting home," Lars said, with a quick glance at his daughter. "I finally tracked him down to the Ontonagon County morgue. They've had the body for a week but there was no I.D."

"Jalmer's dead?" I could barely wrap my head around it. "Did he fall through the ice?" Ice fishing wasn't considered dangerous except if a fisherman decided to try his luck in deep waters. With the sub-zero temperatures of our lakes, a person could die of hypothermia before he drowned.

"Car accident. His truck went off the cliff road and incinerated. He was on his way to Lake Gogebic and I found it odd that he carried no I.D. Not even a driver's license."

"Maybe his wallet burned in the fire."

He shook his head. "The wreck is still down in the ravine. I hiked down to check it out and found a couple of interesting things, including his wallet, which had fallen clear and a blown-off fender with a piece of wood wired to it. I think it was the remains of a homemade sticky bomb."

"You think he was murdered," I squeaked.

"What's a sticky bomb?" Charlie asked. I wondered whether she was just curious or whether she'd seized on that question to avoid having to come to grips with the awful loss of sudden death. In any case, Lars had no chance to answer as the door from the butler's pantry opened and Pauline, Arvo and Jace entered the room.

"I'm afraid we have to leave," Pauline said to me. "Thank you for having us tonight, Hatti."

"Wait," her husband said, looking from me to Lars and back again. "You look like *pulla* dough, Hatti-girl. Something's happened, hasn't it, eh?"

There seemed to be no legitimate reason not to tell him. I nodded at Lars who repeated what he'd discovered.

"A bomb?" Arvo repeated the word in a bewildered tone. "A bomb was planted on Jalmer's truck?"

"Looks like it," Lars said.

Arvo looked at his wife whose face was whiter than squeaky cheese.

"This changes everything," Pauline said. "This means that it was about money."

I stared at Arvo.

"You knew about her trust fund?"

"Of course we knew. We were her legal guardians for the past year. We never met Jalmer Pelonen but he sent us a packet of material that included her financial information and her vaccination records. We knew all about her background, including the heart condition," Pauline said. "In fact, we were given temporary power of attorney. What is a sticky bomb?"

Arvo's eyelids flickered but he kept his gaze on Lars.

"Tell me what you know," he said and Lars went through the story again while Arvo pressed his thumb and forefinger against the bridge of his nose. When my brother-in-law finished, Arvo said, "Pauline is right. These terrible deaths must be because of the trust fund. It was quite a lot of money, wasn't it, Pauly?"

"Two million," Pauline said, slipping her hand through his arm. "Sometimes wealth can be a curse."

There was nothing but sympathy for the Pelonens in her voice but I couldn't help thinking about the fact that the money she and Arvo used so generously in Red Jacket had come from her family.

"A sticky bomb," Jace explained, "is a homemade explosive used most often by terrorists targeting a single vehicle. You can get the ingredients—bits of glass and metal, compound, and accelerant—at any hardware store, and instructions are available on the Internet. The bombs are usually detonated with a cell phone."

"A robot bomb," Charlie said.

"Geez Louise," I whispered, appalled that someone I knew would assemble and detonate a bomb meant to kill an innocent person like Jalmer Pelonen and equally horrified that the finger of guilt was now aimed directly and solely at Reid Night Wind. The death of Jalmer Pelonen appeared to lock down the case for Sheriff Clump. There was no other relative to inherit Liisa Pelonen's trust fund. My heart ached, again, and this time it was for Jace.

Sonya Stillwater opened the door from the butler's pantry, her face composed but grave.

"I hate to interrupt," she said, "but I just got an emergency call from the rez and I don't have a car here."

"I'll drive you," Jace said, promptly. He followed her out the door and back through the house without a glance at me. Soon everyone was leaving, which was just as well. The grapevine would pick up the information about Jalmer soon enough. I, for one, had no energy to handle any questions about it tonight.

Lars was the last to leave and I walked him to the door. He asked all the salient questions about Liisa and I told him what I knew.

"I'm sorry, Squirt. This now appears to be a double-homicide, most likely for mercenary reasons, and that means a criminal who will stop at nothing. It's time for you to hand this thing over to the sheriff's office."

"He'll bury Reid Night Wind," I said, without thinking.

"He'll probably try," Lars agreed. Lars, himself, was no fan of our sheriff. "Certainly he will if Reid did the two murders."

"He didn't, Lars. I spoke with him last night. He's full of piss and bravado, like anyone would be at twenty-one, but he said he didn't do it and I believed him."

Lars had never been one to rush to judgment, except, maybe, in his marriage.

"The guy should get the benefit of the doubt," he agreed, "but that doesn't mean you need to stay involved. It's too dangerous and you can't help him, anyway."

But I had to help him. I had to help Jace, too. It would be my last official act of my marriage but I vowed to make sure Reid Night Wind was not unfairly convicted.

"I can see by the tilt of your chin that you're going to ignore me. That's my Squirt. Loyal to a fault." He gave me a quick hug and sighed. "I'll be back later tonight. Get me a blanket and a pillow, will you? I'll bunk out on the sofa."

"There's no need."

"There's every need. It's snowing like the Dickens out there and I don't want to drive back to the lake."

It wasn't until I was tucked under my quilt, with Larry warming my feet, that I thought about how calculated these crimes seemed to be. Jalmer had been killed well before Liisa, so that he could not possibly inherit the trust fund. It also meant there was no chance that Liisa's marriage to Reid could be annulled. The two deaths, and their sequence, pretty much ensured that Reid Night Wind would be the prime suspect.

My mind trailed back a little further. Did all this mean that Pops' hit-and-run "accident" had been deliberate? Had someone known that Carl Lehtinen would be scrupulously fair in an investigation? Had that same someone suspected that I, Hatti, would have been named temporary police chief and that, what with my estrangement from Jace, I would be less likely to try to protect his brother? But if all that were true, it meant someone very close to me had wanted two people dead and was willing to risk Pops' death, too. It didn't seem possible. Not for a two-million-dollar trust fund. And, anyway, the only known beneficiary was Reid.

There was no comfort in that thought. Reid, if he was not guilty, had been set up and if convicted of two murders, he would be unable to inherit anything. So who did that leave?

Just before I fell asleep, a memory drifted through my mind. It was Pauline Maki's voice saying that she and Arvo had all of Liisa's documents and been granted temporary power of attorney. Arvo Maki. All roads seemed to lead back to him. He lived in the house with Liisa, knew her schedule and, just as importantly, knew Jalmer's schedule. He could have called Pops out on the snowy November night knowing the chief would take a snowmobile to a rescue and deliberately running him down with a car. But that was ridiculous. I'd known Arvo all my life. He was kind and jolly and full of grandiose ambitions for the people of Red Jacket. For us.

And then I recalled a distant memory. Mom, telling me she felt sorry for Pauline and not just because the marriage was childless. "Arvo is a good and faithful husband, *tytar* (daughter) but when all is said and done, he married her for her money."

Marrying for money, I told myself, sleepily, is not the same as killing for it. But I couldn't seem to get warm enough under the comforter. Not even with Larry's help.

# TWENTY-FOUR

I never did hear Lars return to the house, nor did I hear him leave, but he left his cosmic footprint in the form of the perfectly folded Hudson Bay army blanket on the sofa and the note in Larry's dish that read: I-8.

I munched on a chunk of Trenary toast and stared out the kitchen window at the snowflakes dancing and twirling in the pale morning light. I hadn't forgotten my thoughts of the previous night but I tried not to focus on them or anything else but to let the flotsam and jetsam of information drift and swirl in my head in the hope that they would lead me to the bigger picture.

On the surface, it seemed as if these crimes had been committed for money. But, somehow, it felt like more. It felt personal. There was deep emotion involved in all this. Deep, strong emotion. And, the deepest, strongest emotion was that of family. For some reason, I just kept thinking about parenthood and about how the greatest gift of all was so often a mixed blessing.

My parents wanted the best for me but my mother had fought a persistent, lifelong battle to try to keep me from moving away from the Keweenaw.

Jace's father had abandoned his mother, virtually causing her early death and Jace's hell-on-earth of a childhood.

Pauline and Arvo Maki had suffered the heartbreak of infertility for a quarter of a century and when, at long last, they became surrogate parents, the event ended in murder.

"You wonder why anybody decides to enter the sweepstakes at all," I said to Larry. "We should all just have puppies."

He wagged the white flag on the end of his tail once then nudged his bowl.

"Forget it," I told him. "I happen to know you've already eaten. See that note?"

I stared out the window again. The snowflakes were the large, lacy, drifting kind that permitted the observer to see some of their detail. I couldn't tell whether each was unique, only that each was beautiful.

Beauty, especially beauty like Liisa's, must have made life more challenging. You couldn't go unnoticed. People wanted to get near you or, in some cases, wanted to stay away just because of your looks. Matti Murso had fallen under the spell of that beauty and he'd disappointed the others in his life.

What about the other side of it? What was it like to be worshipped because of the way you looked and not because of your essential self? I wondered how Liisa Pelonen had viewed her own physical attractions and suspected she'd have traded the adulation for some real friendship. Maybe that oasis was what she'd found in Reid, why she'd trusted him and married him.

But Reid hadn't been able to keep her safe any more than Jalmer Pelonen had or Arvo. Instead of studying music in Marquette, Liisa would spend the winter in the holding facility at the Old Finnish Cemetery, waiting until the spring thaw would allow her to be buried.

I finally poured myself a second cup of coffee then wandered down the corridor to Pops's study which still smelled faintly of pipe tobacco although he'd given up smoking several years earlier. I felt the familiar warmth of being in his place and the added little thrill of seeing my own books on his shelves. He had introduced me to the Golden Age mystery detectives including Agatha Christie's Hercule Poirot and Miss Marple, Margery Allingham's Albert Campion, Patricia Wentworth's

Miss Silver, Ngaio Marsh's Roderick Alleyn and, of course, Lord Peter Wimsey, the creation of Dorothy L. Sayers.

I flopped in Pops's cracked leather chair, closed my eyes and wished I had the necessary little gray cells to figure out who was behind our murders. When I heard the door open, I expected to see Scotland Yard's Inspector Alan Grant but I would have been just as happy with Ellery Queen. I opened my eyes to see my cousin. She looked different.

"What's up, buttercup?"

"I cannot believe you are lounging around in a pair of bluejeans and that ancient old shirt," she said, pointing to the raggedy garment with the outline of the UP and the words, "Will UP Mine?"

"Don't you remember? You asked me to take you to see Mr. Jussi."

Geez Louise. I'd completely forgotten.

"I made an appointment with him. We're due there in two hours and it's snowing. You've got negative fifteen minutes to get cleaned up."

The best I could do, considering the laundry situation, was a pair of green corduroy jeans and a butter-yellow sweater. At least it was a step up from a sweatshirt. I raked a comb through the haystack on top of my head and swiped my lips with gloss then raced out the back door to join Elli in the aging, oversized SUV she bought used for the Leaping Deer and that Lars always referred to as the Queen Mary.

She pulled out of the alley onto Tamarack Road then headed south on M-26.

"I'm a little worried about your memory," she said, as she sped down the highway. "You forgot to pick up the yellow roses for Pauline and Sofi asked me to do it."

"Why didn't she just call me?"

"I don't know. Maybe it had something to do with the fact that Lars was staying at your house."

"On the sofa," I said. "What is all this?"

"Oh, just a short fuse because people all around us keep dying."

"It's nothing to do with us, El," I said, patting her arm even though I knew it was a lie. "A girl staying at the funeral home and her father."

"What about Pops?" Elli and I had grown up as close as twins and had, more than once, noticed that our minds operated the same way. Here it was again.

"What if the snowmobile crash wasn't an accident? What if somebody deliberately hurt him?" Her voice was getting louder and higher. "What if this is some kind of conspiracy?"

"I know," I said, deliberately calm. "I thought of that, too. It seems to me that we're doing everything we can do. We're going to see Mr. Jussi to find out who will inherit the trust fund."

Elli was silent for a moment.

"Do you think that's who it is? That Mr. Jussi will just hand us the answer?"

I thought about my earlier swirling thoughts and my sense that there was more to these murders than money.

"It's possible," I said, trying to stay upbeat.

"Hatti," she said, taking her eyes off the road and gazing at me for longer than was healthy. "What if it's Arvo?"

# TWENTY-FIVE

E lli shifted and navigated through the thickening snowfall with the ease of someone who has been driving in difficult conditions all her life. We can all drive in snow because we have to. Elli enjoys it.

"It's not Arvo," I said, unconvincingly. "It can't be Arvo. You know that as well as I do. Geez Louise, Elli. Arvo is our *Joulupukki.* There's no way he's a killer. But, listen. Before you came over I was thinking about Lord Peter Wimsey and that case where the killer used a syringe to get arsenic into an egg."

"But Liisa wasn't poisoned."

"Wasn't she?"

"No! You know as well as I that she was hit on the head and fainted from the shock and then her heartbeats spaced out so far that she died."

"That's one possible explanation. But this killer seems too organized for that. I mean, would he—or she—leave it to chance that the heart problem would kick in? I don't think so. I think he would make sure."

"By poisoning her? But didn't Doc do a tox screen?"

I smiled, despite the grisly topic. I loved it that Elli used a term she'd heard on *Law and Order: Special Victims Unit.*

"There are lots of kinds of poison and Doc wouldn't have known to run any that were out of the ordinary. The trouble is, I wouldn't know which poison to suggest. It's probably something arcane."

"Speaking of arcane," Elli said, "what was going on at your house last night?"

"What do you mean?"

"Jace. I spotted him letting Larry out this morning and I thought maybe the two of you had reconciled."

My heart beat a little faster.

"That wasn't Jace. It was Lars. He needed to talk to Sofi about something and then he was going to come back and sleep on the sofa."

"You sure he came back?"

"I didn't see him," I admitted, "but somebody slept down there. The blanket was neatly folded. And whoever it was fed Larry. It had to be Lars."

She shook her head.

"I'll admit those guys you married have some superficial likenesses to each other but you'd better check your guest register. You may have spent the night in the same house alone with—gasp—your husband!"

"Very funny," I said, but secretly, I was pleased. If true, it meant that Jace had not stayed out all night with Sonya.

"And, if that weren't enough," Elli continued, "I saw Lars outside the duplex at zero dark hundred."

"Geez Louise."

"It would be weird if a murder was the catalyst to restoring both of these marriages," Elli said, thoughtfully. "Weird, but good."

The offices of Jussi & Jussi were nestled into a two-story house-turned-office on Quincy Street in Hancock.

Except for the discreet sign, the Jussi office house was indistinguishable from all the other homes on the street with their steeply pitched rooflines, their covered front porches and, as always, the bump in the back that was, or had been, a sauna.

Hancock was constructed on a hill so the houses on the east side (like the Jussis') were fronted by terraced front yards while those on the west hunkered close to the earth. As Elli and I climbed the concrete steps that constituted a front walk, I wondered why the attorneys didn't have a ramp. Or an escalator.

"What do they do about their elderly clients?" I asked, trying not to huff and puff.

"They make house calls, of course."

I laughed. "This is probably the last place in the civilized world where lawyers provide that kind of service," I said, thinking of the high-powered, charge-by-the-minute lawyers I'd met in D.C. Elli paused and looked at me.

"At least you're calling us 'civilized.' Remember how badly you wanted to get away from here and, I quote, have an adventure?"

Though spoken in a spirit of lightness, Elli's comment reminded me (as if I needed reminding) that my time away from home had created a string of problems I had yet to solve.

The office reception area had obviously started life as someone's parlor. There was an arched brick fireplace behind the solid, walnut desk and imposing, leather-covered desk chair, and frilly curtains framed the windows. The room was unoccupied, but, almost as soon as we arrived, a dapper elderly man opened the glass doors that led to the rest of the house. He was small and wiry with a full head of wavy white hair. He wore a forest-green plaid shirt, a barn-red tie, a chocolate corduroy sports jacket and a pair of designer jeans. The blue eyes set in the wrinkled face revealed humor, intelligence and a touch of friskiness.

"Hatti, this is Jaakonpoika Jussi," Elli said, as he captured her hand, lifted it to his lips and kissed it. "Jake, this is Hatti Lehtinen." He turned to me and took my hand in his, pressing it, rather than kissing it. Very proper.

"The reigning Red Jacket police chief," he murmured, revealing that he knew the purpose of the visit. "I hope you don't mind walking to lunch."

The shoveled part of the sidewalk was a narrow path between three-foot piles of packed snow. Even so, Jake Jussi managed to keep us together by gripping Elli's arm with his left hand and mine with his right. I got the impression he'd had plenty of practice squiring ladies. We reached the Kalevala Café in about ten minutes.

"Jake's home away from home," Elli explained, as he deftly held the door for both of us.

"You eat at the same place every day?"

"Not only the same place, the same lunch," Elli said, with a laugh. "*Pannukkaku* with thimbleberry sauce. And coffee."

Jake Jussi winked at me. "Sometimes I order maple syrup just to shake things up."

We were warmly welcomed and assigned the pride of place, a square table near the front window from which we commanded an excellent view of the Christmas wreath on the front of the Miner's Bank across the street and of the business lunch crowd and Christmas shoppers on the sidewalk. Compared with Red Jacket, downtown Hancock was Times Square.

The pancakes were as good as Elli's and I found myself wolfing them down.

Elli smiled at Jake Jussi. "She skipped supper last night and, I suspect, breakfast this morning."

I realized to my astonishment that it was true. It was most unlike me to miss a meal. I was letting the murder case get to me. Or, maybe, I thought, being honest with myself, it had to do with the presence in town of my soon-to-be-ex. My heart sank a little as it occurred to me that Mr. Jake Jussi would be an excellent divorce lawyer. I told myself the timing was wrong. Murder, first, marriage, after.

"I imagine you want to know everything there is to know about Liisa Pelonen and her trust fund."

I nodded, grateful for his ready understanding.

"Liisa and her father were both clients and, naturally, whatever they told me was confidential while they were alive. Normally, I would be wary of revealing any of it to the police but Elli trusts you and that's good enough for me."

Tears pricked the backs of my eyes. It was just another example of the importance of being with your own tribe, the folks who will have your back.

"Liisa's mother came from Turko," he said, naming a Finnish city, "and a family with a lucrative furniture-making shop. The money in the trust fund comes from her. Liisa was still very young when Katia, her mother, died, and the family wanted to ensure the child would ultimately benefit from her inheritance. They didn't know Jalmer, you see. They didn't know he was a man of honor."

A slight wobble on the last word of the sentence reminded me that Jake Jussi had sustained the loss of two clients and, perhaps, an old friend.

"I'm sorry," I said and he nodded, seeming to understand.

"I worked with the family and their lawyer via telephone and interpreter," he went on. "They were willing to make Jalmer a trustee as long as I was one, too. And they wanted a provision stating that Liisa was to gain access to her inheritance when she turned twenty-one or when she married, whichever came first."

"So Jalmer Pelonen—and you—had access to the money, for what, fifteen years?"

"Fourteen. And, yes. Either of us could have withdrawn sums. There was no other oversight." He bent his head so his blue eyes stared very directly into mine. "I should probably point out, before you ask, that neither of us did. Withdraw any money, that is. Jalmer paid me for my services for him and his daughter out of his own fortune."

"Fortune?" Elli looked at the lawyer. "Jalmer Pelonen had a fortune?"

"A portfolio," Jussi amended. "Not as big as the trust fund but healthy enough to call him a millionaire."

"Mr. Pelonen was a millionaire?" The question came from Elli and I remembered she hadn't seen the high tech set up at his cabin.

"Oh, yes. He traded on the stock market. Not every day, just enough to keep solvent. His real interest was investigating conspiracy theories."

I stared at the man. "You mean like terrorism?"

Jake Jussi nodded. "And plots to overthrow the government."

"Did he find any?" Elli asked.

Jussi held his hands to the side, palms up, as if to say, he didn't know.

"I imagine he thought he did."

"Geez Louise," I said, as something struck me. "Is it possible that father and daughter were killed because of Jalmer's hobby?"

"He spent time in underground chatrooms and researching what he called the deep state. I suppose he could have uncovered secrets but I think it unlikely he ever blew the whistle on anybody. He didn't trust the government, you know. Not federal or state. He was one of those who wanted the UP to secede from Michigan and form a separate state called Superior."

"Hatti," Elli said, excitedly, "think how great it would be if some undercover revolutionary was responsible for both deaths!"

"It would be great," I said, without enthusiasm. "The sticky bomb points to a terrorist group and I can see some guy tracking Jalmer to Lake Gogebic but how would someone from outside the community know when Liisa would be home alone at the funeral home? And, we still don't even know how she died. Surely a terrorist would have used a bomb, or a gun or a knife."

"Jake," Elli said, "I hate to ask but I think we need to be clear. Can you think of anyone, including her father, who would have wanted to kill Liisa Pelonen?"

Jussi shook his head. "From what I heard, everybody considered her an angel."

We were all silent for a moment, until the waitress came to re-fill the coffee cups.

"I guess," I said, "the last question is the most important. Who benefits from Liisa's and Jalmer's estates now that they're both dead?"

"A very interesting point," Jussi said. "If Liisa had died first, her trust fund would have reverted to her father and, according to his will, the residual beneficiary was a loosely-organized group called the Minuteman Militia."

"Vigilantes," I said. Jussi nodded.

"Even with Liisa dying second, the Minutemen could have made a case for the whole kit and caboodle." He paused. "At least they could have except for one thing." He reached into the inside pocket of his jacket and pulled out a single piece of paper and unfolded it. I could see the state seal imprinted at the top of it.

"As you probably already know, Liisa Pelonen got married on December twelfth, the day she died. Her husband is now the sole beneficiary of her estate and that of her father, a total of some three million dollars."

It was what I'd been expecting, so I couldn't account for the pit in my stomach.

"I'd say," Jussi said, reading from the certificate, "Reid Night Wind is one very lucky young man."

"Unless," I said, "he's convicted of murder."

I stared out the passenger-side window of the vehicle as we retraced our steps to the interstate. The snowfall had stopped while we were in Hancock but now the skies opened up again. with a vengeance, and by the time we reached Chassell, golf-ball-sized pellets of hail were pounding the SUV. It felt like driving in a piñata.

"They say the first settlers of this area were the Paleo-Indians, who walked here from Northern Asia," Elli commented. "On days like this I wonder why they didn't just keep heading south."

"Want me to drive for awhile?"

She shook her head. We both knew our odds were better with her at the wheel.

"Thanks for setting up the meeting with Mr. Jussi."

She glanced at me. "Things look bad for Reid Night Wind."

"Yep, they do."

"Hatti, has it occurred to you he might have killed her?"

"No." I spoke in a low voice. "I've met him. I like him. I can't imagine he would ever kill a girl like that."

"You couldn't imagine that his brother would ever walk out on his marriage, though, could you?" I didn't answer. "You just never know what people will do when there's so much at stake. With three million dollars, Reid could go anywhere in the world to start his adult life. And then, there's the baby. Hatti, somebody fathered that child."

She was right, of course. Add to that the fact that Reid had no alibi at all for Liisa's murder and, in fact, he admitted to being at the murder scene within minutes of the attack.

"You're thinking he has no alibi," Elli said, reading my mind. "What about Arvo? He could have gone home to check on Liisa, found her waiting in the sauna, ready to run away, and struck her in a fit of rage."

"He could have," I said, "but I can't believe he did it anymore than I believe Reid Night Wind did it."

Elli was silent for a moment as she downshifted to gain better control of her vehicle.

"The trouble is," she said, "there isn't anyone else. It had to be Arvo or Reid. Unless it was Matti Murso."

I pictured the gangly youth with the engaging grin.

"It couldn't have been Matti, either," I protested.

"You know," my cousin said, throwing me a half-smile, "you are way too softhearted to be the police chief."

"Acting, temporary," I corrected her. "Thank goodness Pops will be home this week."

The SUV hit a patch of black ice. Elli gripped the steering wheel hard as we hydroplaned, and landed facing the wrong way. By the time Elli had steered us out of danger, we'd lost interest in discussing the cases. We were just glad to get back to Red Jacket alive.

Elli finally pulled into the old carriage house that served as her garage, and we both collapsed against the seats. After a while she spoke.

"You know, I kind of hate knitting lace. I've had to take out my swatch four or five times already. I can't get the stitch count straight."

"You know we have to go through with this. Pauline's counting on it."

"Did you hear that Pauline is going to place her Shetland shawl in Liisa's coffin? She'll have time to finish it since the ground is frozen now and burial will be in the spring."

"I guess that's sweet," Elli said. "But kinda wasteful."

My phone rang and Sofi's number popped up on the screen.

"Where the H-E- double hockey sticks are you? Arvo's making tomorrow's memorial service into a doubleheader for Liisa and her father, so I need to make twice the usual number of flower arrangements."

"You need help?"

"Dang right I do. Think you could find Elli?"

"You're in luck. I think I can."

Elli, who had heard the conversation, pulled the SUV back onto the street.

# TWENTY-SIX

Main Street Floral and Fudge reminded me of a beehive in full throttle. I didn't think I'd ever seen it as busy.

I waved at Charlie behind the counter as Elli and I wended our way through the throng of customers. Some were there to buy flowers for the funerals, some to order poinsettias for the holidays, some were there for fudge and all were there for gossip. And not just about the murders. I saw several pointed looks from the ladies of the church and I knew the stories of where Jace and probably, Lars, too, had spent the night were high on the charts.

We escaped, as quickly as possible, into the workroom where Elli slipped on one of Sofi's dark green aprons embellished with a single pink rosebud before beginning to stab stems of evergreen and holly into a Styrofoam form.

"This funeral comes at a most inconvenient time," Sofi complained, without even greeting us. She brushed the sweat off her forehead with the back of one gloved hand. "I wish we could just postpone Christmas."

She sounded just like Snow White's dwarf Grumpy which answered one question. Nothing good had happened last night between herself and her ex.

"What do you want me to do?" I asked, although I knew the answer. Sofi pointed to the completed arrangements of snapdragons, daisy poms, glads, greenbills, bachelor buttons, lilies, and several containers of yellow roses destined, no doubt, for the grave blanket.

"Take those up to Pauline, would you?"

I didn't really mind. I felt restless and anxious and as though the investigation was slipping through my fingers and I had no clue what to do next. As I was loading the delivery van, it struck me that at least one answer had been handed on a silver platter. I was about to head up to the Maki Funeral Home, scene of the murder. It could be the perfect chance to do a little more snooping.

The drops of hail had morphed into heavy, wet globs of snow. Despite the best efforts of the windshield wipers, I had zero visibility. Luckily, I'd driven the route so many times I could do it in my sleep.

I turned off Tamarack into the alley and pulled up next to the door in the Maki's covered carport, right behind the big, black hearse.

Arvo, who has always had the hearing of a bat, arrived, coatless, to help with the flowers.

"We'll take the arrangements straight to the chapel," he said, in a low voice. "You will be able to see how lifelike she is, eh?"

I'd always disliked that term. At every single open-coffin funeral, with the guest of honor primped to the gills as though for an appearance on Good Morning America, my impression was always the same. They did not look lifelike. They looked dead.

Liisa Pelonen was no different.

Don't get me wrong. She was laid out in a simple gown of white taffeta that could have been a wedding dress and a crown of tiny white rosebuds had been threaded into her blond hair. Long, darkened lashes brushed rouged cheekbones and pink gloss brightened her lips. She was still beautiful, I thought, but not lifelike. Death, as always, had stolen the animating spark that had defined her.

As I stared at her I felt a thunderbolt of rage. Someone had snuffed the girl's light when she was just about to start her life and I vowed to find that person and bring him to justice. Even if it was Arvo. Or Reid. Or Matti Murso.

"Horace Clump is looking for the Night Wind boy," Arvo told me, when we were back in the hall outside the chapel. "It won't surprise you to know he's calling this a slam-dunk."

"No. It doesn't surprise me. Arvo. The two deaths have to be connected, right? I've heard that Jalmer was involved in a vigilante group. Do you think that someone he was investigating decided to shut his mouth?"

Arvo's blue eyes looked puzzled.

"It's possible, eh? But then why kill Liisa?"

"For the money?"

"How would that get them the money? It's in a trust fund managed by a lawyer down in Hancock."

I nodded and felt a frisson of relief. I hadn't intended to test Arvo but I'd been curious to find out what he knew. It seemed like he was as bewildered as everyone else.

We had just picked up the two pails of roses when his office phone rang. He excused himself and I could tell from his side of the conversation that he was responding to one of the dozens of S.O.S. calls he gets every winter. The hearse, with its heavy body and snow chains, was the most reliable vehicle on the Keweenaw.

Anyway, Arvo was always willing to go and never let any stranded motorist pay for his help.

"I'll be back in a bit," Arvo said, shouldering into his heavy jacket. "Why don't you take the roses out to the greenhouse? Pauly is upstairs resting."

Perfect, I thought. That would give me a few minutes alone.

# TWENTY-SEVEN

The glass-sided room smelled earthy, damp, warm and welcoming. I felt more comfortable here than I had during my earlier visit and I felt a curious longing to sit down on a bench and close my eyes. I reminded myself that it was Pauline's sanctuary, not mine.

I deposited the buckets of roses on the worktable and gazed around the room, taking in specifics, the seedlings, the hybrids, and the succulents. The amazing spread of blue flowers including orchids, foxglove, iris, and belladonna, drew me. I wandered over to view them more closely and tripped on a clay pot that protruded from underneath the table. Pain lanced through my toe. I hopped around for a minute, seeing stars and trying not to curse. When the pain eased, I knelt to tuck the pot back in its place only to find that didn't fit. There was something in the way.

I dropped into doggie position, butt in the air, to identify and remove the obstruction, but it was too dark to see anything. So, I stretched out on my stomach and reached as far as I could. My fingers grasped some kind of webbing and I pulled.

It was the strap on a pink, rhinestone-studded, soft-sided suitcase.

For a moment I just stared, shocked that I'd found it, even more shocked at where I'd found it. Did this mean Arvo Maki was the killer? I refused to let my mind go there. I didn't know enough yet. I wanted to grab the bag and hightail it home but then I remembered Pauline was in the house and I thought about how awkward and embarrassing it would be if she caught me.

My heart was pounding ten to the dozen as Pops would say as I unzipped the item and searched through its contents, which included clean underwear, an orange turtleneck sweater, a pair of lime green corduroy jeans, a flannel nightshirt and a bag of cosmetics. There was a pink electronic notebook, too, and a wallet with a driver's license, a library card and money—a ten-dollar bill and two ones—and some coins.

There was also a photograph of a short, bearded man with a wealth of thick, dark hair, a stocky build and brilliant, intelligent-looking blue eyes. He had his arm around a sylph-like blond and they were both smiling. Liisa's father and mother.

I replaced the items as neatly as possible and shoved it back in place. The offending clay pot, I set on the tabletop. I was so enchanted by the photo that it took me a minute to realize that there was nothing in the suitcase that would, in any way, help with the investigation. Nothing, except where I'd found it. Did that mean Arvo was guilty?

The silence in the room felt eerie, all of a sudden, and I started to tiptoe toward the door, intent on getting out and getting home before somebody found me there. I was nearly there when a sudden clicking sound practically stopped my heart. An instant later the timed sprinkler system came to life, soaking me to the skin. Geez almighty Louise. I made it home in record time but it wasn't fast enough to keep my wet hair from freezing.

Moments later I stood in the shower, my thoughts caroming off each other like a mad version of a pinball machine. Had Arvo been the baby's father? Had he killed his surrogate daughter? But, if so, why had he kept the suitcase packed and hidden in the greenhouse? Why hadn't he just unpacked it and put it away? Or, better yet, have driven the fifteen miles to the shore of Lake Superior and flung it under the waves? Why leave it in his own house where it could be discovered during a search?

Maybe because he knew his house wouldn't be searched. Maybe, because he knew that Sheriff Clump would arrest Reid Night Wind for the crime without a second thought.

What if Reid had killed her? Would he have taken away the suitcase and risked having it found in his possession? Or would he have hidden it somewhere in the mortuary in the hope that cops would eventually find it and link the crime to the Makis?

The same scenario could apply to Matti Murso, although somehow I didn't think Matti would have had the presence of mind to frame someone else.

One thing I knew for certain, though, the killer wasn't Jalmer Pelonen. I was glad Liisa hadn't known about her dad's death. And then I was thunderstruck.

Maybe Liisa had known about Jalmer's accident. Maybe she had been contacted—and threatened—by the killer, someone from his dark world of conspiracy. Maybe it was the fear of that killer that had driven Liisa to run away with Reid Night Wind. I liked that last theory best, of course. The problem was, none of those possibilities accounted for the money. None, except the one involving Jace's little brother.

I threw on some old pink sweatpants and a taupe-colored, long-sleeved tee shirt and curled into Pops's leather chair with a fresh cup of coffee. A moment later my phone rang.

"*Hei*, Hatti. Jake Jussi here. Remember me?" He laughed at his own joke. "The darndest thing has happened. A pure fluke and I don't know what to make of it, but I thought you would want to know. I was cleaning out my files this afternoon and I found an unopened letter from Jalmer Pelonen. It was dated three weeks ago and, somehow, had gotten incorrectly slotted. This was the first I'd seen of it. Ya still with me?"

"Yes," I said, breathlessly. I couldn't imagine what was coming but I sensed it would be important.

"He wrote to ask me to add another name as an executor in his daughter's trust fund. Not to replace either of us, you understand. Just one more adult in her life to keep an eye on her and her holdings."

It had to be Arvo. I felt a little sick. Had Arvo convinced Jalmer to give him some status in Liisa's business? What did that mean? What could that mean?

"Will this person be in line to inherit?" I asked.

"Oh, no. This is strictly an advisory position. Like mine. At first I was taken aback, you know, but then I thought it through and it makes sense. The new trustee could keep an eye on both of them."

"Both of them?"

"Liisa and her young husband."

The sick feeling was getting stronger.

"You mean Jalmer didn't trust Reid Night Wind with Liisa or her money?"

"No, no, I don't think that was it. Jalmer knew they were both young, that's all."

"I don't understand."

"Of course not. What's wrong with me? The *pannukakku* must have gone straight to my head. The third trustee is an attorney and Reid's brother, Jason Night Wind."

If I suffered from syncope I would have fainted.

"What?"

"You know him?"

"Yes," I said, my brain scrambling to make sense of this. "When was the letter dated? Three weeks ago? That must mean that Liisa had been in contact with her father and that she'd shared her plans for marrying Reid Night Wind."

"I'd say so. Oh, and Night Wind, as trustee, will be able to facilitate the release of the trust fund to his brother. Hope this helps. Good-bye, Hatti."

I stared at the bookshelves but didn't see them. This was terrible news for Reid. One more nail in his coffin.

It was terrible news for me, too. It meant Jace had withheld vital information about the case. It meant we were not really partners trying to solve a crime. It meant we were two separate agents, each with our own agenda. It meant he hadn't trusted me enough to tell me the truth. A part of me realized I shouldn't have been surprised. After all, he hadn't told me the truth at the altar, either. A bigger part of me was shocked senseless. I'd trusted Jace at the beginning and, on some level, I'd trusted him even when he'd broken up with me. I'd trusted that he had an unshakeable reason.

The old anguish of rejection rolled through me again and I got to my feet and started to pace. Eventually, I made it to the kitchen where I couldn't help but notice covered dishes of brownies and casseroles and three-bean, potato and macaroni salad. I opened the refrigerator door and smelled Mrs. Moilanen's lamb stew and Miss Irene's potato soup. In the breadbox, there was a fresh *tiikerikakku,* or tiger cake from Aunt Ianthe. The marbled confection of orange and chocolate layers topped with a fudge frosting was my favorite. Well, to be honest, it was everybody's favorite.

The Ladies of the church basement had been busy and, I suspected, I was about to host another potluck.

The phone rang again. This time it was Pauline Maki.

"I am so upset," she said, disregarding my greeting. "I don't know when I've been more upset." I could hear the anger quivering in her voice and I knew she had discovered Liisa's suitcase.

"I can imagine," I said, inadequately. "I would be upset, too."

"I am glad you realize it," she said, "the consequences here could be catastrophic. Something will have to be done."

I was getting confused.

"About the suitcase?"

"Suitcase? What suitcase? I'm talking about Edna. She has gone completely off the deep end. I learned from a reliable source that she has abandoned her swatch and started off on her Shetland shawl. Even worse, she's doing some kind of fern design instead of the shells in my pattern. It's anarchy, Hatti, and I won't have it!"

"No, no, of course not," I said, half laughing at the irony of Pauline being as upset as Ronja Laplander had been. "Listen, there's lots of food here. Why don't we have a potluck and an impromptu knitting session tonight? We can iron it all out. Can you make the calls?"

"Yes, yes, of course." She paused. "What suitcase were you talking about?"

I started to brush her off but stopped. It was too late in the day to play games. Maybe, if Pauline knew about the suitcase she'd confront Arvo and he would either admit what he'd done or be able to clear his name.

"I found one under a table in the greenhouse. Pink and soft-sided with rhinestones on it. It looked like something that would have belonged to a teen-aged girl and I just wondered how it had gotten there."

The next few seconds felt awkward, almost as if Pauline were struggling with herself about something.

"I'm afraid I don't know," she said. "But you can be sure I will look into it."

All the ladies arrived at once so there was no chance to speak with Pauline, privately. The entire circle was there except for Sonya.

"She called to tell me she was going down to Hancock to pick up her patient," Elli said, with a concerned glance at me. "She intends to join us later."

None of the men showed up, not even the Reverend Sorensen who was usually attached at the hip to his wife or Arvo.

"Quite frankly," Pauline was saying to everyone in her vicinity, "I told them not to come. We have some things to settle." Her eyes narrowed on Edna Moilanen's plump face. "Either we are going to knit our shawls correctly or we are not going to knit them at all."

"But, Pauline," Mrs. M. said, "I don't see why we can't have a little variation, a little individuality."

"No more ferns. No cat's paws. No diamonds in the rough. It is shells or it is nothing."

I watched the hostility flash then disappear in the older woman's eyes. Each of the feminine pillars of Red Jacket society likes to have her own way but, fundamentally, they are kind. Edna Moilanen, I thought, had considered Pauline's terrible, horrible week and decided to cut her some slack.

"All right, Pauline," she said. "Shells, it is."

It was a perfect spot for a Bible verse and Miss Irene obliged.

"Then said Jesus unto him, put up again thy sword into his place: for all they that take the sword shall perish with the sword. The Gospel of Matthew."

In other words, I thought, live by the sword, die by the sword. Was Miss Irene referring to knitting patterns or was she referring to Arvo's unfortunate decision to make Liisa Pelonen this year's St. Lucy? I couldn't seem to stop thinking about that question. I couldn't seem to stop wondering whether, somehow, the St. Lucy debacle was at the heart of our murders.

An hour later, after we'd all fragmented our fragile yarn and had to splice it together numerous times I began to think that knitting lace was like trying to solve a murder. An exercise in endless frustration.

"You know," Sofi said, in an effort to pour oil on the troubled waters of the knitting circle, "lace is a kind of a metaphor for life. It isn't just a smooth ride. There are the spaces and the holes and the things seen and unseen. Shadows and mysteries. A challenge."

"We are troubled on every side, yet not distressed; perplexed but not in despair; persecuted but not forsaken; cast down, but not destroyed."

"Corinthians, again?" The mild complaint came from Mrs. Moilanen.

"It just goes to show, then," Aunt Ianthe said. "Lace is like the Bible."

# TWENTY-EIGHT

The ring of the doorbell, followed by the appearance of Sonya Stillwater, distracted us. The glow of her smile and the crystals of snow in her midnight hair made her look like a fairy queen. My first reaction was warmth and welcome. But those feelings froze in my chest when I became aware of her companions. I was upset and distracted at seeing a smiling Jace right behind her, but not so distracted I didn't notice Charlie's reaction to Jace's younger brother.

She looked, to paraphrase a line from *While You Were Sleeping*, 'Like she'd just seen her first Trans Am.' A quick glance at Sofi's expression confirmed this impression. It was as if Charlie's mother had gazed upon Medusa's face and been turned to stone. My niece had been hit with the love-at-first-sight stick and my heart went out to her and to Sofi, too.

"How is Cindy Gray Squirrel," Elli asked, apparently oblivious to the silent drama playing out in front of her.

"Healthy, happy and back home." Sonya touched Jace's shoulder. "Thanks, again, to Jace."

I looked away to avoid torturing myself by watching the affectionate look they exchanged, and, when I looked back, I found the gray eyes focused on me.

Elli and Charlie took the newcomers out to the kitchen while the rest of us resumed our struggles with the lace. Just when I thought I could not bear one more twisted yarn-over or the splitting of frail wool in a knit-two-together, Pauline called it quits.

"Nothing worth doing is ever easy," she reminded us, as we packed up our knitting bags. "You'll thank me when you've produced a beautiful wedding ring shawl."

Sofi was the first one out of the room. She dashed into the kitchen and emerged, seconds later, gripping the sleeve of Charlie's sweater. She reminded me of a mother cat with a kitten in her mouth.

"It's snowing hard out there," she said to me. "I'm heading home with Charlie."

"Aunt Elli was nice enough to invite Reid and his brother to stay at the Leaping Deer," Charlie told me, unfazed by a poisonous glance from her mother. "I thought you'd want to know."

"Thanks." I wanted to ask what about Sonya. Would the snow prevent her from traveling the three blocks to her apartment? And then I realized I had a solution to that. "I'll invite Sonya to stay here."

"No need," Jace said, as he came through the door. "I'll take her home."

Sofi took Aunt Ianthe and Miss Irene with her and I walked Mrs. Moilanen and Mrs. Sorensen down to their houses on the other end of Calumet Street. It did me (and Larry) good to get out in the cold. By the time I got home I was too cold and wet to think about Jace and Sonya. For the most part, anyway. I stripped off my parka and boots and turned the key in the lock before heading upstairs for a shower and bed. I was still inches away from the front door when something exploded against it. A fist.

"Open up," Jace growled. "I know you're in there. I can hear you breathing."

It never occurred to me to refuse but I could barely speak as I wrenched the door open. My heart pounded so hard my ribs hurt.

"What do you want?"

"To go to bed," he said. Jace, with his dark coloring, looked as magnificent as Sonya had with flecks of snow in his thick, dark hair and on his long lashes. His gray eyes gleamed in the porchlight.

"Why? Isn't Sonya expecting you?"

"What?"

"I mean Elli. She offered you a room, right?"

"You're my wife. I'm sleeping here."

I just stared at him.

"The sofa will do. It was fine last night."

So it had been Jace who'd left the note about Larry.

"Thanks for feeding the dog," I said, automatically.

"C'mon, Umlaut. Let me in. It's colder than Hades out here."

I couldn't think of any other good reason to keep him out so, with great reluctance, I stepped aside and let him in.

"What makes a couch better than a bed?" I asked.

"You," he said, making quick work of shedding his wet outer clothes. "You're a little pig in a house of straw and there's a big bad wolf somewhere out there. I figure the least I can do is intercept him when he tries to blow your house down. Okay? Questions answered? Just leave me a pillow and blanket and I'll see you in the morning."

"I suppose you could sleep in Sofi's old room," I said, feeling a rush of guilt.

"Nah, I'm fine here. Goodnight sweetheart."

I didn't think I'd be able to fall asleep knowing Jace was downstairs but I was wrong. The only difference was that, when I awoke, it was not to the voice of Betty Ann Pritula. The room was dark except for the glowing stars on the ceiling and it was silent, too, except for the sound of a distant coyote. I checked the clock and found it was only three a.m. I lay back against the pillows and tried to relax. That's when I heard the coyote again. Only it wasn't a coyote.

It was Larry.

# TWENTY-NINE

I thrust my feet into the bunnies I'd had since freshman year, searched for a bathrobe, abandoned the effort and flung myself down the stairs. What, as Pops would say, by Jupiter, was Larry doing out in the middle of the night in a snowstorm? It is worth noting that a basset hound is not your attention deficit disorder type of dog. Larry, at ten years old, had developed into the embodiment of the term "chill." He would never have gone out at night alone. Even if it had been an option. I felt like Miss Clavell in the book, *Madeline.*

Something was terribly wrong.

I twitched my still-wet parka off the hook in the foyer and sprinted through the house, pausing only to grab Pops's LED Maglite out of one drawer and a steak knife out of another. I'd nearly reached the back door when I slammed into something large and warm. It—that is, he—smelled achingly familiar as he bound his arms around me. I could feel the timpani of his heart. Oh, no. Another catastrophe. I pulled back, desperate to get away from him; desperate to find Larry.

"I could have killed you," I said. He responded by pressing his mouth against mine just long enough to rocket me into a state of shock, then he pulled back.

"Hush. There's someone in the backyard."

"I know. My dog."

"Larry," Jace said, "does not have opposable thumbs and thus he did not let himself out."

"Nonsense." I backed away and tried to go around him.

"We'll go together," he said, in a crisp whisper. "Me first. Get your boots."

"Why you first? It's my dog."

"Exactly. Use your head. He's been locked out on purpose to lure you into danger."

Danger? "You exaggerate."

"You have two choices. You can come with me to the pickup or you can stay here."

Another mournful baying sound reached my ears and I ran back to the foyer for my boots.

"Give me the flashlight," he said, when I returned. "And, for god's sake, stay behind me."

We were, I thought, going to have a little talk about this dictatorial attitude just as soon as Larry was back, safe and sound. I was, after all, the acting, temporary police chief.

As we stepped onto the back porch, the first thing I noticed was that the snowstorm had ended. A full moon peeped between drifting clouds casting the backyard into a black-and-white moonscape.

The second thing I noticed was the back gate. It was open.

Jace must have noticed, too, because he suddenly grabbed my hand and started to run toward the pickup truck parallel-parked in the alley. He ran to the passenger's side door, opened it and shoved me inside.

"C'mon, Umlaut," he ordered, tersely. "Buckle up."

And then he disappeared and I heard him unlatch the driver's side door but instead of jumping in, he let out a horrified shout.

"Hatti! Get the hell out of the truck!"

I responded to the urgency in his voice and lurched for the door, the buckled seatbelt forgotten. Fear threatened to strangle me as I clawed at the clasp. And then he was there, ripping the metal apart, lifting me by the shoulder and hip and hurling me facedown into a snow bank. A ton of male dropped onto my back and I could feel myself diving into the white stuff. It was like being buried alive. Especially when I tried to inhale air and got only snow.

The impressions must have happened in seconds because I hadn't even panicked when the world exploded around me and Jace's curse echoed in my ear.

---

I pulled the oxygen mask off my face and rejoiced at the ability to take an independent breath. How much, I thought, we take for granted. I spotted Jace on the other side of my mom's kitchen table. A guy was dabbing ointment onto the red, puckered splotches on his torso and the back of his neck and I focused on the pain rather than the fact that he was half-naked.

"That looks like it hurts," I said to Arne Wierikko, who is both Red Jacket's sole paramedic and my onetime senior prom date.

Arne, in true Finnish male tradition, kept his reply short as he continued to apply salve to the blisters. "Dude's got balls."

"Thank the Lord he was wearing a thick, leather jacket," said another voice. I turned to see Pauline Maki. She was wearing a long, chenille bathrobe under her wool coat and the small spit curls on the sides of her long face were secured by crisscrossed bobby pins. Otherwise, she looked as calm as ever. She was carrying a cup of tea and she handed it to me. "We're relieved to have you back in the land of the living," she said.

"Jace probably saved her life when he jumped on her," said Elli, who materialized out of the kitchen, carrying a plate of sandwiches. "Or, at least her skin."

Arne nodded. "She'd of been toast."

Speaking of toast made me question the food.

"Why are you making sandwiches?"

"For the firefighters, dear," Pauline explained. "The explosion burned up the truck and it caught the Ikolas sauna, too. Pops always said that sauna was too close to the roadway."

"There was an explosion." It wasn't really a question because, even as I spoke, I remembered. "A bomb?"

"Got it in one," Jace said. "I told you someone was after you, Hatti."

"After me? Oh, no! What about Larry?"

"He's here," Jace said, shifting slightly, so I could see the basset hound dozing as my husband's fingers stroked the soft skin behind his ears. "He's fine. He wasn't affected by the blast."

"He was in our yard," Pauline explained. "Heaven knows how he got there. I heard him barking and went downstairs to see what was what and I found him on our back porch. I knew you would be concerned, Hatti, if you woke up and found him missing, so I intended to use the key in the milk chute to let him back in the house. But before I could leave my yard, the truck exploded."

"Thank goodness for the timing," Elli said. "You and Larry could have been seriously hurt."

I thanked Pauline for taking care of the dog then turned back to Jace.

"What do we know?"

"Max Guthrie found a bomb under the fender," he said, telegraphing me a message with his gray eyes. Unfortunately, I couldn't interpret it and said exactly the wrong thing.

"A sticky bomb?"

It was too specific. It immediately connected the perpetrator of this incident to Jalmer Pelonen's accident and, by extension to Liisa Pelonen's death. It was one more arrow in the quiver of ammunition targeted at Reid Night Wind. Now, thanks to my question, everyone in the room was silent, watching. *Damn.* I searched for a subtle way to change the subject.

"How did you know about the bomb?" I asked Jace. "You yelled at me to get out of the truck well ahead of the explosion."

"It was a combination of things. I was already suspicious because of the dog being out, and then we were sitting ducks in the back yard, but no one attacked. As soon as you strapped into the truck, a kind of sixth sense kicked in and I knew that the attacker had wanted you alone in the truck."

"But why?" The question came from Elli and it was more of a cry. "why would someone want to kill Hatti?"

Jace shook his head then winced as the skin pulled tight against his burns.

"I think it was meant as a warning to her to back off the investigation of Liisa Pelonen's death."

"Oh my god," Pauline's face, moist but extremely pale with night-cream, looked hollow. "I had no idea you were in danger, dear. It's time to turn the whole thing over to Sheriff Clump. And I want you, and, uh, Larry, to come stay with us until this is over. You can have Liisa's room."

"Thank you," I said, flashing her a grateful glance, although I had no intention of taking her up on the offer. I couldn't imagine any place less comforting than a funeral home. "The sheriff is in charge and I imagine we'll hear from him, shortly. He usually takes his time."

"I can take care of Hatti and Larry," Elli said. She knows me so well. "They'll be safe at my place. In the meantime, someone should light a fire under the sheriff's butt." Jace glanced at her and she giggled. "Whoops! Bad turn of phrase."

"Actually," I said, "this latest attack is different from the others. Both Liisa and Jalmer's deaths were carefully planned, so carefully they might have been ruled accidental. This time the killer panicked and was clumsy. That means he's getting rattled."

"I hope you're right, dear," Pauline said. "I can't help but worry about you."

The back door opened and then Max Guthrie, who, I remembered, belatedly, is our volunteer fire chief, stepped onto the mat just inside the door.

"I won't come any farther," he said. "I'm a human ashtray. I just wanted to make sure you were all right, Umlaut. You didn't look so hot when Arne and Lars carried you in here on a stretcher." He looked at Jace. "Neither did you, Sir Lancelot." Max turned back to me. "This guy's been in town for what, twenty-four hours, and he's already saved your life and delivered a baby. Hats off to him."

I felt a surge of pride in my husband.

"F.Y.I.," Max said, looking at Jace. "You were right about the bomb. It was taped inside the pickup's wheel arch. Just like the one in Pelonen's truck."

The two men exchanged a long look. It seemed to suggest a bond between them and I felt, curiously, left out.

"I'm going home to get cleaned up," Max said, "but I have one thing to say to you, Hatti Lehtinen. Someone's got it in for you. You need to back off this case."

"So I've been told," I said.

# THIRTY

I stood in the shower for a long time. I had some decisions to make, not including whether or not to continue with the investigation.

The attack on Jace was a turning point. I no longer felt any reluctance to nail someone from our community. In injuring my husband, the killer had stepped over my personal line of loyalty. I pictured the wounds on Jace's bare back and clenched my fists. No more mercy. I intended to pursue this person—whether it was Arvo, or Matti, or even Reid Night Wind—with everything in me.

By the time my skin had pruned up (and I'd used up all the hot water), I decided it was time to join forces with Sheriff Clump. I might not trust him, entirely, but he was a law enforcement officer with decades of experience and, for all that people considered him lazy, they did not consider him stupid. He could help identify the perp.

The other decision on my plate—whether to declare my marriage D.O.A. and file for divorce—could wait until everyone in Red Jacket was safe again. And, by everyone, I meant Jace.

I dried off and rubbed a towel through my hair then remembered the neglected laundry. Not that it mattered, I told myself. Clothes, and how I looked in them, should be the last item on my agenda. I pulled on a pair of rhinestone-studded bluejeans I vaguely remembered from the eighth grade and a white blouse with a peter pan collar from the same era. It, like the jeans, was too small and I decided to camouflage that fact by adding a black, boiled wool vest with embroidered hearts and frog closures. It was my outfit of last resort. Sofi called it my lonely goatherd costume.

Just as I was slapping on some lipgloss and wondering who was still in the house, my bedroom door opened and Jace stepped in. His hair was wet, as if he'd just showered, and his eyes were bloodshot from the smoke but he still strode across the room as if he owned the place.

I swallowed hard and resolved to act nonchalant.

"You borrow that red flannel shirt from Max?"

He grinned. It was the grin I remembered, quick, rare and without sarcasm or underlying anger. My heart puddled.

"I think I did better than you. You look like you're preparing to cross the Alps to freedom."

He dropped onto my bed, winced as his back came to rest against a bolster pillow and patted the mattress next to himself.

"Take a load off," he said, with a noticeable lack of romance. "We've got to figure out some strategy here." He glanced upwards. "What's up with the ceiling?"

I explained about the glow-in-the-dark stars.

"I suppose your stepdad put them up for you."

"Yes," I said, gazing into his brooding gray eyes. All at once, I had an epiphany, of sorts, about something I should have noticed long ago.

"Why do you always refer to Pops like that?"

"Because he is your stepdad."

"No, I don't mean that. With that ironic twist in your tone of voice. You've never met the man but you neither like nor trust him. What gives on that?"

He shrugged and winced, again, which threw me off.

"You're right. I don't know him. I just don't have a high opinion of fathers in general."

"That's very inclusive of you," I said. "Now all you have to do is get an attitude about mothers and you'll have covered most of the adults on the earth."

He managed to refrain from another shrug because it hurt, but the impulse was written on his face.

"My folks are coming home today and I'd like you to meet them."

"You sound more like a girl bringing home her boyfriend for the first time than someone on the cusp of divorce."

I tried to absorb the shot without a visible reaction. I had, after all, asked for it. I went back to my epiphany.

"This isn't really about my dad, is it? It's about yours. The man who abandoned Miriam Night Wind all those years ago. Jace, don't you think it's time to find some closure on that? You're in danger of letting it taint your entire life."

He held my gaze for what must have been about thirty seconds and then he patted the bed again and I sat down.

"I wish," he said, wincing a bit as he turned toward me, "things were different, Umlaut. But they aren't."

I sensed we were finally getting close to the reason for the separation and I was frantic to learn more but I was aware than when the gray eyes turned to slate, it meant the Gone Fishin' sign was up.

"Let's go over the suspect list," he suggested.

I sucked in a breath and started.

"I've got three; Arvo, Reid and Matti Murso."

He flinched a little at the second name but stayed calm.

"Motives?"

"Arvo and Matti Murso loved her and Reid married her. One of them had to be the father of her baby and if it was Arvo, that fact coming out would have ended his marriage. Matti, I think would have married her but she wanted someone more mature so she married Reid. Reid may or may not have loved her and claims he married her for the money." I looked at the face only inches away from mine and yelped. "OMG!"

"What? Do I have butter on my nose?"

"I forgot about you!"

"Probably not a bad move under the circumstances."

"No, I mean, Mr. Jussi, down in Hancock, told Elli and me that Jalmer Pelonen wanted you to be a third trustee on Liisa's trust fund."

"What the hell?"

"You didn't know?" He shook his head, his burns forgotten.

"Jalmer Pelonen wrote to Mr. Jussi asking him to add you to the portfolio. The letter got misfiled and Mr. Jussi never acted on it. It doesn't directly implicate you but it is one more box checked against Reid because it means he knew about the trust fund at least three or four weeks ago."

Jace's curse was less politically correct than mine.

"I wonder if Reid knew about the request. Or Liisa."

"What about Jussi himself? He could have dipped into the trust fund intending to pay it back and then he discovered the girl was getting married and he would be called to account much sooner than expected."

"It's a possibility," I admitted, wondering why I hadn't thought of that myself. And then I realized why. "Jake Jussi could have installed a bomb on Jalmer's truck or yours but I don't see how he could have known Liisa would be home alone at the funeral home on Friday night after the parade. Or that she would be planning to run away with Reid that night. Oh, something else I forgot to tell you. I found her suitcase. It was hidden behind a pot in Pauline Maki's greenhouse."

"So the arrow points to Arvo?"

"Not necessarily. Anybody could have hidden it there."

"God," he said, running his fingers through his hair. "What a frickin' mess," he muttered, only he used a different word.

"Jace," I said, apropos of nothing, "why did you cut your hair?"

He countered instead of answering.

"Why did you cut yours?"

"More efficient," I said, knowing that he knew it was a lie. We had, during our brief time together, talked about cultural traditions, including the custom of cutting long hair as an expression of grief.

"Same here. More efficient." He quickly returned to the subject.

"What about women? Weren't there a couple of mothers who resented Liisa because of her beauty?"

There it was again, the implied indictment of a girl who happened to be pretty.

"Ronja Laplander was mostly angry at Arvo as he was the one who line-jumped Liisa ahead of Astrid for the part of St. Lucy. Diane

Hakala was pretty disappointed when Matti abandoned her daughter, Barb, and, yes, I think she did blame Liisa more than the faithless suitor. All's forgiven now, of course. Barb and Matti are going to get married as planned, and during spring break so they can attend a cheese festival."

"Sounds like the Hakala woman had the stronger motive."

"Yes, but she doesn't have a killer personality. Ronja, on the other hand, would go to the mat for any advantage for her kids."

We pursued our own thoughts, silently, for a moment and I'll admit I was distracted by the warmth I could feel from him even though we weren't touching.

"Doc Laitimaki said Liisa could have been poisoned but that nothing turned up in the tox results." I was aware of a slight tremor in my voice. "He said he'd need to know what to look for."

"Maki has access to all kinds of chemicals in his embalming room," Jace pointed out. All at once a memory jumped into my head. It was the vision of a deep blue flower with petals shaped like the bell of a saxophone.

"Look, Hatti," he said, interrupting my thoughts. "I've got to get off this bed. And fast."

"Or what?"

"Or this." He leaned across the inches that separated us and kissed me. It was a soft, lingering kiss without any sexual intent behind it and when it was over, I felt that it had been a good-bye.

An instant after Jace vaulted off the bed the door burst open and Charlie catapulted into the room. She raced across it to grab my arm, heedless of the fact that I was not alone, and I realized she was sobbing.

"The sheriff's here. He's come to arrest Reid. Aunt Hatti, you've got to do something!"

Jace removed himself from the bed and glared at me.

"You called him, didn't you? Judge, jury, and executioner. I should have known where your loyalty lay. You talk a good game but when push comes to shove, you're going to back your Grand Pooh-Bah, every time."

I felt sick and sad and helpless in the face of his anger. I hadn't called the sheriff but I'd intended to. And, anyway, the flare-up was just one more sign that all hope was gone. My marriage was over.

# THIRTY-ONE

Horace Clump had been sheriff of Copper County for as long as anyone could remember, certainly long enough to have earned the sobriquet "valued institution" or "favorite son." As it happened, he was called neither.

Clump's body type had always been egg-shaped, his gourd-shaped head joined to a barrel-shaped body without benefit of a neck. Many hours devoted to doughnuts and pancakes had expanded his girth enough that, by age fifty, he resembled no one so much as Humpty-Dumpty. It was an image reinforced by his waddle-like walk and the suspenders that had long since replaced a belt at his middle.

But neither that nor his bald pate, too-close eyes and loose, liver-colored lips, had impaired his personal life. Clump's wife RaeAnne and his three surprisingly attractive daughters appeared to be devoted to him.

And, as Pops had pointed out, Clump was no fool. He was physically lazy and penurious but ambitious enough to consolidate his power by pressuring small communities in Copper County to sign contracts with him for law enforcement services. Thus far, Red Jacket had resisted but I knew, and everyone knew, that these murder cases would tip the balance. I knew Pops would be disappointed if that happened on my watch and I sighed. Just one more thing to worry about.

I attempted to be polite to the oval male sprawled in a chair in my kitchen even though he didn't bother to stand up when I entered the room. Neither did he remove his wide-brimmed sheriff's hat.

"Good morning, sheriff. Would you like some coffee?"

"Yer sister's takin' care of that, Ms. Lehtinen."

I nodded. I hadn't really expected him to call me (acting, temporary) chief.

"This here's Elwood Snow," he said, jerking his thumb, hitchhiker-like, at the tall, thin individual who had risen from the table. "Elwood's my deputy." He pronounced it "depooty." Elwood was apparently the latest in a revolving door of deputies, a position Lars had once held. Like I said, few people can tolerate Clump for very long.

I glanced at Sofi, who was filling mugs with fresh, fragrant coffee. It was business as usual. A Finnish-American hostess always provided fresh coffee. My mother would have offered coffee to a burglar.

"I'm here to collect Reid Night Wind. I'd 'ppreciate it if you'd call 'im."

I glanced back at Jace who had followed me into the room.

"Sheriff, have you met Reid's brother, Jace Night Wind, attorney at law? Jace, this is our sheriff, Horace Clump."

Clump nodded but stayed sprawled in his seat, his belly mounded, his thumbs twanging his suspenders.

"Night Wind," he said to Jace, then he turned his gaze to me, a not inconsiderable feat for an individual with no neck. "We've had some doings before over this boy." I remembered Reid's earlier brushes with the law and tried not to wince.

"I imagine you know that my father thinks a lot of Reid Night Wind," I said. "And his brother."

In fact, Pops had never met Jace but I ignored that in order to build a respectable connection for Reid.

"Shoot-a-mile," Clump said. "Boy met the dead girl at your house, ain't that right?"

I felt Jace's long fingers on the back of my neck and figured he wanted me to stop before the hole I was digging for his brother went all the way to China.

"How-do, sheriff," Jace said. "You got a warrant?"

"Don't need no warrant for a little chat."

His laid-back hillbilly act was so good I halfway expected him to produce a stalk of alfalfa and stick it in his mouth.

"Ain't got a warrant for you, either, Ms. Lehtinen, but I think we need a little pow-wow. How's come you didn't give me a buzz as soon as the corpse turned up?"

I couldn't answer that without implicating Arvo, who was already in this up to the top of his fishing waders. And, anyway, I was in full sympathy with the funeral director and with Jace. Clump clearly intended to nail the low-hanging fruit in this case, i.e. one Reid Night Wind.

As if he'd read my mind, Clump produced a fake smile and said, "This here's gonna be a slam dunk."

"He didn't do it," Charlie sobbed. "There's no proof he did."

Jace didn't even twitch at the ill-advised comment, but his fingers dug into my shoulder. Clump signaled to Elwood who dug into the back pocket of his brown uniform trousers to pull out a much-folded sheet of paper. The sheriff scowled at him.

"Dad gummit, boy, why'd you have to wrinkle it up?"

The deputy was too new at the job to realize he'd be better off not answering the rhetorical question.

"Had to make it fit in my pocket," he mumbled.

"Damn fool." Clump unfolded the paper and held it out to Jace, who stepped forward to take it. "Proof positive yer brother's a murderer."

Fear gripped my heart. "What is it?"

Jace, not surprisingly, didn't answer me. He didn't hand over the paper, either.

"Marriage license," Clump said, triumph in his voice and in his piggy eyes. "Shows that Night Wind married the Pelonen girl on December twelfth, the day she was to inherit her money. With her old man dead, he gets the whole enchilada. We'll be lookin' at him for that death, too."

How had Clump found out about the clandestine elopement? Did it matter? How could we save the young man? Then I remembered that it was either him or Arvo and I simply didn't believe that the man who had been a loving, if eccentric surrogate uncle all my life, could have killed the girl and anguish filled my soul.

Maybe Reid was guilty, after all.

With perfect dramatic timing, Elli arrived trailed by Reid, whose raven hair was still wet from a shower. This time I ignored his devastating good looks and focused only on his youth. His dark eyes looked scared.

It was too much for Charlie. She made a strangled sound and buried her face in her hands.

Reid straightened his shoulders and assumed a bravado I was sure he didn't feel.

"Lookin' for me, sheriff?"

The fat man heaved himself up from the chair. "I come to offer you some hospitality at the county's expense. You'd best bring a toothbrush. You may be with us for some time."

"He doesn't have to go," I said, helplessly.

Clump's expression revealed an unctuous, faux sympathy.

"I got me a eyewitness."

Jace, Reid and I all stared at the lawman and my heart sank. Of course, he had an eyewitness. Reid had been at the sauna within minutes of when Liisa Pelonen had died.

"So what if he was there," I said, semi-hysterically. "He was her husband and she had planned to meet him but she was dead when he got there."

This time Jace's gimlet stare was trained on me and I knew why. I'd just handed Clump another three yards toward the first and ten he needed to convict Reid.

"Neighbor lady named Ikola. Got a signed statement from her. She says he shot out of the mortuary like his tail-end was on fire and he was carrying a pink suitcase."

I felt sick as I contemplated the statement. The Ikolas were our back door neighbors on the other side of the alley. If Grace had been in the upstairs back bedroom tending to her invalid mother-in-law, she could easily have seen the Reid in the Makis's backyard.

Reid smiled at me.

"I never had the suitcase. Don't worry, sis. I'll go along with him and we'll get this straightened out. I didn't kill Liisa and no one can prove I did."

That might have been true in *Law and Order* or *Murder, She Wrote*, but in real-life, the prisons were filled with innocent people. If this was a frame-up, someone had done a bang-up job with it.

I tried a last Hail Mary.

"Sheriff, you know the autopsy report concludes that Liisa Pelonen died of heart failure. I fail to see how you can charge anyone with murder when the coroner's verdict is natural causes."

No shadow of doubt crossed the sheriff's jowly face. "Heart failure after a faint due to the shock of bein' hit on the noggin," he said. "That still adds up to murder." He struggled to his feet then spoke to his deputy without bothering to look at him.

"Cuff 'im, Elwood."

"I'll be right behind you," Jace told his brother, then he made a face as if remembering he no longer had a vehicle. I grabbed the keys to the Jeep off the pegboard by the door and threw them to him.

"Thanks," he said. For some reason, my eyes filled.

After they'd left Elli sized up the despair I was feeling and suggested that she and I and Sonya and Sofi should meet for lunch.

"Let's pool our mental resources," she said. I agreed because I didn't know what else to do and because I wanted to be left alone. I felt utterly helpless in the face of the heartbreak threatening the Night Wind brothers and I just needed to regroup. After everyone had gone, I poured a fresh cup of coffee and, with Larry curled at my feet, I planted myself in pop's leather chair and promptly went to sleep.

The doorbell woke me an hour later and, thinking it was Jace, I flew to answer it then banished the flicker of disappointment when I found Max Guthrie on the doorstep, his rugged features reflecting an ill-concealed concern.

"Hey," he said. "I found myself with some time on my hands."

I wasn't fooled. His concern touched me.

"Max, you were up all night."

"Sleep can wait. I understand we have a real crisis on our hands. What can I do for you, Hatti?"

The offered support, along with the power nap, combined to give me an idea.

"Jace took my Jeep to the jail. How would you like to drive me over to Frog Creek? I want to talk to Doc."

The gentle snowflakes that kissed our faces as we walked to Max's truck thickened as he navigated the five miles to Frog Creek. Doc Laitimaki was finished with the official autopsy and I knew Arvo wanted to hold a funeral service this afternoon. Some might have said it was too soon but I thought I understood. Arvo was looking for closure for himself and Pauline.

I just hoped he wouldn't have to cancel because of the weather.

"Looks like we're in for a blizzard," Max said, peering through the frantic windshield wipers. "Visibility is already practically nil."

We passed my Jeep, parked in front of the sheriff's office on Main Street.

"Looks like Night Wind is still there with his brother."

"Is that a good or a bad sign?" I asked, really wanting to know.

"Good. It means Clump can't string the guy up by the thumbs or try any other questionable interrogation methods. The case against Reid is fairly conclusive, from what you've told me."

"Yep," I said, my heart sinking. "It seems to me the only way to clear him is going to be finding out who really did it."

Max's eyes left the road to glance at me.

"You really think he's innocent? Or is it just wishful thinking?"

"He shouldn't have married her for the money but I don't believe he killed her," I said, a little surprised that it was true.

But then, I didn't think Arvo was a killer, either.

Max heard my heartfelt sigh and patted my hand.

# THIRTY-TWO

Doc's office, three blocks south of the sheriff's department and on the same side of the street, is actually his home. The depression-era bungalow always reminded me of Hansel and Gretel, with its white stone exterior set off by red bric-a-brac trim around the arched front door and along the steep roofline. It was cute, quaint and tiny, with low ceilings and small, cozy rooms, perfectly calibrated for Mrs. Doc, a miniature version of Mrs. Santa.

Doc himself was a tall, robustly built man with thick white hair and a beard and the slightly hunched posture of someone who spent most of his day ducking to move through his home.

He answered the door to my knock. "*Hei*, Henrikki," he said, gathering me into a hug. "This your young man?"

I didn't know what to say, but Max did. He chuckled.

"Been a long time since I was called a young man."

Doc nodded and seemed to study him while I introduced the two men. Without further comment, the physician led us into his office and invited us to sit down. A moment later, Flossie Laitimaki arrived with coffee and *Joulutorttu* and I introduced Max again.

Doc asked the inevitable question about why Max had decided to move to the Keweenaw and buy an old fishing camp and Max answered with his usual combination of courtesy, humor, and evasion. Then Doc turned to me.

"And you, Hatti? How is your family?"

I told him what there was to know about my folks (he already knew), and Sofi and Elli (he knew that, too) and I realized how much I had missed that kind of connection when I'd lived in D.C. It wasn't that people weren't pleasant or even friendly in some cases. It was that they didn't know me and that it would take a lifetime for them to know me and my family the way Doc did.

"All right, *tytar*," he said, using the word for daughter, "you came because you want to know more about Liisa Pelonen, eh? Well, I'm sorry to say, it isn't much."

"You can't find any indication she was murdered?"

He shook his head. "She was hit on the head, a blow that would not have killed her, and then she died. My best guess is that she had an arrhythmia and the shock from the blow caused her heart to stutter and slow so that her blood pressure dropped and she fainted."

"Are you certain about that?"

"As I say, it is a guess based on the lack of other indicators and the knowledge that the girl was prone to vasovagal syncope." I nodded. And then he threw me a curve. "I must say, between you, me and the lamp-post, I didn't see any evidence of heart problems."

"You didn't?"

"No. Not everything shows up, of course. More likely the girl fainted once and a doctor spoke to her parents about syncope and it became part of family lore."

"You mean she didn't have the condition?"

He shrugged. "Like I said, I didn't see any evidence of it. But I'm hardly an expert."

A thought had been playing in my brain and I voiced it.

"Doc, is it possible Liisa's heart was slowed by drugs?"

He didn't respond right away and I got the impression he had already considered that possibility.

"I found no drugs in her system."

"But you didn't check for every kind of drug, right?"

"That's right. There's a standard tox screen for an autopsy."

"So what if someone had introduced a more arcane substance into her system?"

"Like what?"

I spread my hands to the side, frustrated.

"I don't know. I thought you could help me figure it out."

"Are you asking me what I would have used if I'd wanted to kill someone and make it look like an accident?"

The idea of Doc, who had brought hundreds if not thousands of babies into the world, including me, deliberately killing someone was ludicrous but that was exactly what I meant and he knew it. I nodded, again.

"It would have to be some kind of poison, right?" The suggestion came from Max. "Something that wouldn't show up on a tox screen, or else something that would masquerade as something more innocuous. Maybe something herbal."

Thoughts and images exploded in my head like a child's piñata. *Something herbal.* Something like the aconite in the monkshood flower in the Makis's greenhouse.

"I still have the specimens and could run more tests," Doc said, "but I'd have to be looking for something in particular."

I knew I needed to tell him but it would be tantamount to a death knell for Arvo. For a moment, I couldn't bring myself to do it.

"If anything occurs," Doc started to say. I stopped him by putting my hand on his arm.

"Aconite," I said.

Doc eyed me, curiously.

"That's from a flower, isn't it? Wolfsbane or some such?"

"Wolfsbane or Monkshood it's called," I agreed. "Pauline Maki has some in her greenhouse."

"Surely you don't suspect Pauline," Doc said, shocked.

"No. Oh, no. I don't suspect Arvo, either. I just know about the poisonous flower."

My mind was racing but I must have been quiet during the drive back to Red Jacket.

"A penny for your thoughts, Umlaut," Max said, his tone light.

"I'm feeling a little guilty. I just kind of threw Arvo under the bus."

"No, you didn't. You did the right thing. Your job is to gather as much information as possible and to make connections. We were talking with Doc about poisons and you recalled a poison you'd just seen in the home of one of those involved in the case. It was right to tell Doc about the monkshood. It was your duty."

"But what if there is no connection between the flower and Liisa's death? What if I cast an aspersion on the Makis for no good reason at all?"

"You've got to look at everything objectively," he said, basically repeating the point. "Just remember, when you've eliminated the possible, what remains, however improbable, is the truth." Max said

"Sherlock Holmes?"

"Yep. He also said follow the money."

"He did not."

"Well, he should have."

I was quiet the rest of the way to Main Street and Patty's Pasties. If Doc confirmed the presence of aconite in Liisa's body, the finger of guilt would point squarely at Arvo, which would clear Reid Night Wind. I was ashamed at how badly I wanted that to be true.

"Follow the money," Max repeated, "and the emotional impact." It was as if he'd read my mind. "Reid Night Wind, if he's telling the truth, felt sorry for the girl. Arvo Maki loved her and, at least to my mind, that level of attachment seemed a bit unnatural."

"What are you saying?"

He held up his hands. "Nothing kinky, Babe. It's just that if the Makis had wanted a child, they should have had one of their own. You can't just annex a kid at age eighteen, you know. She's not a business or a piece of property."

"Are you saying you think Arvo killed her?"

He shook his head. "I'm just pointing out that love and hate are two sides of the same coin."

"Whatever that means," I muttered. "Let me buy you lunch?"

He wasn't listening to me. The smile had dropped off his face as he gazed through the plate-glass window to see Sofi, Elli and Sonya gathered at a table.

"No thanks," he said. "I'm not hungry. Raincheck?"

"Of course." I didn't understand it but I felt his pain and there was a gentleness in my voice. He leaned over and kissed me on the cheek.

"You're a nice person, Hatti."

# THIRTY-THREE

The pasty, legend has it, was invented by a Cornish miner's wife so that her husband, deep underground at mid-day, could enjoy a hot meal. The original pasty was a pastry-enclosed meat pie that included vegetables and gravy.

The concept crossed the Atlantic with the immigrants coming to work in the copper and iron mines in the UP, and the pasty had become iconic on the Keweenaw. Nowadays, though, there are pasties for every taste including vegetarian pasties, salad pasties, tuna, chipotle, Asian pasties, Italian pasties with pasta and, for the fast-food lover, the bacon-cheeseburger pasty.

Just for the record, all of Patty's pasties are all delicious.

I found my buddies sitting at a corner table. They'd already put in their orders—and mine—so all we had to do was wait. It was a perfect time to catch them up on developments and to pick their brains.

"I'm concerned about Reid Night Wind," Sonya said, her brow furrowed. "The case is starting to look watertight. There's the money he will inherit and the eyewitness account of Friday night behind the sauna. He has means, motive, and opportunity and Jace thinks Sheriff Clump is hesitating only because he's waiting for a confession which would make everything much simpler and result in less paperwork for him."

"You talked to Jace?"

The words came from Sofi but I was silently screaming the same question.

"He called to ask me to pick up some clothes and things from the rez in case Reid has to spend a night or two in jail. Chief Joseph packed a little bag."

*A little bag.*

"Omigosh," I said. "I forgot to tell you about the suitcase I found in Pauline's greenhouse. It was hidden under one of the tables and I found it when I stubbed my toe on a pot." They all leaned forward.

"Anything in it?"

"Just the stuff you'd expect. Clothing. Nothing nefarious. There's something else, too. I just talked to Doc about what could have caused the syncope."

"You mean something other than the shock of getting hit on the head?" Sonya asked.

I nodded. "Right from the first it seemed like that blow to the head was just a diversion. I mean, you determined that it couldn't have killed Liisa and Doc agreed with that. And, it seems kind of risky to have depended upon shock killing her."

"Not so risky," Sonya said, "since she was known to have a heart problem."

"About that. Doc said he saw no evidence of heart disease or dysfunction. There's no way of knowing whether Liisa really believed she had a heart condition or whether it was made up, but the fact is, her heart was healthy, then."

After a long silence, Elli spoke.

"So what do you think killed her?"

"Poison. Maybe aconite, which comes from the monkshood flower and is strong enough to stop the heart."

"From a flower? One of those blue ones in Pauline's greenhouse?"

I looked admiringly at my sister. "Yep."

"Then that means it was Arvo," Elli said, with a little cry. "It just couldn't be Arvo."

"I know," I said. "But I guess we'll find out. Doc is going to test for the poison."

"What about Grace Ikola," Elli asked. "She claimed to have seen Reid Night Wind running away from the sauna, carrying a suitcase."

"About that," Sonya said, apologetically. "Jace talked with the Ikolas. Grace did see Reid in the yard by the sauna but she didn't see a suitcase. Who said she did?"

"Sheriff Clump," I said. "He was so proud of his eye-witness but he didn't tell us how he'd come by that report." I paused. "I feel like we're getting closer to the answer."

"I feel like that, too," Elli said. "Only I just wish it was not Arvo."

I walked back home through the pelting snow. As a kid, I'd pretended to be a Siberian husky mushing against the weather. Today I was barely aware of it. My mind was in a whirl. It felt like the lottery wheel on a game show, spinning, spinning and slowing. And just like on TV, I didn't know where it would stop.

I let Larry out (but kept an eye on him because it is not great to be a short dog in a deep snow.) Then I made some coffee, poured a cup and headed for the study and my neglected laptop. I normally kept it at work as it contained all my records, invoices and spreadsheets, but since I had been focused on the murder I'd kept it at home and now I was glad of it. There was something niggling at the back of my mind and I thought if I could get lost in one of those mindless computer searches for shoes or purses, I might be able to sweep enough cobwebs away to get at the nugget of information.

But, for once, shoes didn't hold my attention and I found myself looking up aconite. The juice of the plant or its roots was so powerful that the Nazis had used it as an ingredient in poison bullets. If swallowed, it could bring on vomiting and death but even contact with the skin could cause numbness and cardiac symptoms.

*Contact with the skin.*

I scrolled down until I found a knitting reference. Intrigued, I read the story out of Tasmania, headlined "Wedding Shawl Turns to Shroud."

"When Charlotte Lambie of Binalong Bay told her mother she was engaged to be married, Mary Binalong,

219

a master knitter, decided to make a very special gift, a Shetland wedding ring shawl. Composed of nearly one hundred thousand stitches of decreases, increases, knit two together through the back and yarn-overs, this shell-white masterpiece took two years to create.

(There was a picture of the bride wearing a wispy shawl knitted in the shell pattern.)

Mary Lambie told this reporter that, despite her many years of knitting, this heirloom project had been unbelievably difficult, composed as it was of a fine mohair yarn whose strands tended to stick together.

"I had to go back and undo," Mary said. "Oh, so many times. I dropped out of church choir to find more time and I developed a squint. My dear husband, Declan, learned to cook and to clean to support me in this effort. It was worth it. The shawl won the blue ribbon at the Australian National Knitting Expo in Melbourne."

Editor's note: After this interview was published, there was an incident involving the shawl and we contacted Mary for a follow up.

"I left the shawl spread out on my white bedspread," she said, from her cell at the Binalong Jail. "While I was out, my so-called husband dumped out the laundry basket on that bed then he scooped everything into the washing machine. I got home to find my shawl shrunk into a diaper."

When asked what she did next, Mary Lambie replied, "oh, there was nothing to be done about the shawl. I went to work on Declan. I make my own soap, you see, and I made up a new batch, substituting the leaves of the monkshood flower for lavender. Then I offered to scrub his back in the bath. I will say he died a happy man."

I sat in a kitchen chair staring at the computer screen for a long time and remembered a conversation from the Moomins.

"Moominpappa: Tell us all that's happening in the world!
Snufkin: Fuss and Misery."

# THIRTY-FOUR

The only black dress I could find was a tunic that I paired with black tights and knee-high fashion boots. I borrowed a seventy-year-old mink jacket that had belonged to my *mummi* and the socially-inappropriate, dominiatrix look was complete.

It didn't matter. Practicality was the name of the game on this, the day of Liisa Pelonen's funeral. The fur jacket had pockets deep enough to carry what I needed, too.

Just as I was about to tuck my cellphone into one of the deep pockets, I decided it was foolish not to call for backup. Or, at the least, to let someone know where I was.

I punched in a number and realized, with some surprise, that I'd called my husband. Naturally, he did not answer. Jace always had bigger fish to fry than me. I left a message telling him where I was going but not what I intended to do there. I didn't want him to be disappointed if it didn't work or if I was wrong—a very real possibility.

Pauline's evergreen wreaths on the double-front doors looked as fresh and unrevealing as ever and it occurred to me, inconsequentially, how something as innocuous as a door decoration can provide an observer with information. And then I second-guessed myself. What was I thinking? Arvo and Pauline were running a business here. The undecorated wreaths were not a personal statement. They were part of the job.

Arvo never locked the door on funeral service days so I didn't bother to knock. I let myself into the shadowy foyer and glanced at my watch. It was three p.m. and the service was at four-thirty. I was surprised to find the lights off and the entry way deserted but there was a majestic arrangement of yellow lilies, roses and delphiniums in a copper container on the pedestal in the corridor and a stack of freshly printed programs on the desk. The profile of Liisa Pelonen, on the front, was artistic and lovely but didn't do justice to her ethereal smile. I figured it had come from Arvo's camera.

I had shaken off my umbrella on the doorstep and set it in a brass holder by the door, despite my desire to keep it in my hand as a kind of impromptu weapon. The silence felt eerie. There was always soft, classical music (mostly Sibelius) playing on funeral days. Where was the music? Where were the lights? Where was Arvo? I forced myself to tiptoe down the main corridor.

The chapel was wide open and empty except for the white coffin spotlighted up near the altar. I felt an unreasoning sense of relief as I realized I wasn't alone. I didn't feel my usual aversion to gazing at a corpse, either. Instead, I experienced a stinging anger. How dared someone deprive this young woman of her future? How dared he?

I slipped my hand into one pocket and pulled out the bracelet from Matti and the dreamcatcher from Reid. I tucked both items under the counterpane pulled up to her waist.

"You should have these gifts," I said, "to remind you of how much you were loved." The sentiment brought me back to Arvo. He had loved Liisa Pelonen like a daughter. Had he found out about quickie marriage to Reid Night Wind and her plan to escape Red Jacket? Had it broken his heart? I realized I had felt all along that this murder wasn't about money but about emotion. Someone had loved Liisa Pelonen too much.

There was still no sign of the Makis or anyone else when I re-emerged from the chapel, but I knew folks would start to arrive soon. I strode down the corridor through the darkened kitchen and into the greenhouse. Sleet and hail and the occasional roll of thunder made a cacophony of noises that did nothing for my nerves, but the windowed conservatory was brighter than the rest of the gloomy house, and the scents of loam and fertilizer and earth were somehow reassuring. The greenhouse, I thought, not for the first time, with its aura of new life was the perfect antidote to death.

I knew now what Pauline had suspected all along, what she'd tried to convey to me without using words. I'd finally figured it out and had come back for the proof. I crossed my fingers, hoping I'd be able to just stroll in and grab it without interference

My breath was coming hard and fast, my heart beating crazily in my chest as I made my way past the rows of plants and flowers toward the workbench.

"Looking for something, Hatti?"

Pauline stepped into the narrow aisle, blocking my view of the work table. I hadn't heard her come in and figured she'd been in here all the time, a deduction that only made sense. It was, after all, her answer to the crack in the teacup.

"Hello," I said, immediately aware that something wasn't right. "Why aren't you dressed for the funeral?" She had on a plain shirt, loose sweatpants and gardening gloves.

There was an unfamiliar glint in her normally kind eyes and I wondered if she had been drinking.

"Haven't you heard? The funeral's been postponed because of weather. Everybody else knows it, even Betty Ann Pritula. You should turn on your radio, Hatti."

There was something in her voice that matched the weird glitter in her eye and, with a shock, it came to me; malice.

A shiver wriggled its way down my spine.

"Where's Arvo, then?"

"Out on a stranded motorist call. It's just you and me, Hatti. And all these lovely plants." She swept her arm to include them but did not take her eyes off me. "May I ask why you're snooping around my greenhouse?"

"I'm not snooping," I said, beginning to feel distinctly uneasy. "I came back here to check on something."

"Mmm? And what was that? Evidence? You think you've solved the mystery? I thought you would. People underestimate you, Hatti. I know I did."

I finally got it. Too late, of course. I wanted to say she'd estimated me exactly right but it wasn't a moment for humor. The someone who had loved too much was Pauline.

"You killed Liisa and Jalmer," I said. "You wired a sticky bomb under the fender of Jace's truck and then you set off the bomb with a cellphone. You could have killed five people, Pauline. It was the baby, wasn't it? When you found out Liisa was pregnant you knew she'd get married and get out of town and you'd never see her again and you just couldn't bear it."

The woman before me, a woman I'd known all my life, started to laugh.

"I take back what I said about underestimating you, Hatti. You've got it exactly backwards. Liisa might have left town, but she'd never ever have left my life. I overheard her talking to Arvo one night. She'd planned to get rid of the baby but when she saw how heartbroken he was, she relented. That girl and her child had made a mockery of my life. I couldn't allow her to go on."

My mind scrambled with what she was saying.

"This is about Arvo, isn't it? Arvo invited Liisa here. The love he'd saved up for his own children went to Liisa and then her baby. He told me you felt the same way."

"Did he? But then men are stupid creatures. They see what they want to see. And when life disappoints, they cling to the concept of duty. I have spent twenty-five years knowing that he married me for my family's money. I thought it would change when we had a family but that little miracle was denied us."

"You're saying Arvo doesn't love you?" I was aghast. "You know that isn't true. He's always talking about you, about what will make you happy."

"Duty," she said. "And duty is cold comfort. You will find out if you reconcile with your husband. Marriage, without love, is anguish."

I was shaken to the core.

"You can't account for why one person is drawn to another. This might have happened with a child of your own. The bond he or she had with Arvo might have been closer than the one with you."

"We'll never know now, will we?"

I stared at her tall, gaunt form and thought of all the hot dishes she'd brought to church potlucks and smorgasbords, and all the charity work she'd done in the local thrift store. I thought about her passion for lace knitting.

"Oh, Pauline," I said. "What about the shawls?"

"Not your problem, anymore, Henrikki." I realized she'd slowly closed the distance between us.

I might have been slow to figure out the motive and the killer in this case but now that I was alone in the greenhouse—her turf—with a killer, I was well aware that she intended to kill me, too. Panic exploded inside me and I tried to control my breathing. There was a chance, a slight chance, that either Jace would get my message and come to find me or Arvo would get back from his rescue mission. In any case, my best bet was to keep Pauline talking.

"You've told me why," I said, fighting to keep my voice steady. "Will you tell me how?"

"Are you telling me you don't know? I thought you were here to pick up the evidence."

"I've got a theory," I said, stalling. "I think you ground up the poisonous leaves of the Monkshood and mixed them into the jar of Vicks Vaporub that you used to soothe Liisa's cough and sore throat."

"You came up with that by yourself?" She sounded surprised, as if a sluggish student had suddenly come up with a perceptive answer.

"Not really. You showed me the monkshood and it reminded me of an incident in a Father Cadfael mystery."

"Ah," she said. "A murder solution with footnotes."

"How did you know Liisa was planning to meet Reid Night Wind in the sauna?"

"Foolish question," she said, disappointment evident in her voice. "This is my home, remember? I know about everything that goes on here."

"The baby?"

"I have installed listening devices in most of the rooms so I overheard it the night Liisa told Arvo while they were in the embalming room. But I'd known before that."

"Was Arvo the father?"

She made a derisive sound.

"No. It wasn't like that between them. He actually loved her like a daughter."

Maybe that was even harder to accept than a mistress. I wondered.

"Do you know who the father was?"

"Of course I know. That idiot who's going to marry the Hakala girl. It happened after the homecoming dance in the backseat of his rattletrap."

"If you knew, why didn't you stop it?"

"Why should I? I misjudged my husband. I thought he'd be disgusted with her feet of clay but he just became besotted with the idea of becoming a grandfather."

A thought occurred to me.

"Was Liisa dead when you left for the smorgasbord?"

"In a coma. She was dead by the time I came back for the jam. That's when I carried her down to the sauna. I figured the Night Wind boy would panic when he found her and he'd leave a trail of evidence right back to himself."

"So why'd you hit her with a sauna rock?"

"Justice. She had delivered the death blow to my marriage."

"Justice," I repeated. "And closure?"

"I suppose."

"And you kept the pink suitcase as what, a trophy?" She shook her head.

"A reminder that all of this happened because a man could not see beneath the surface glitter."

My eyes flickered to the jar of Vicks on the work table. Unfortunately, Pauline and I both had the same thought and we moved toward it at the same time. She was closer but I am younger and we got there together. I snatched the jar and dumped it in my pocket. Pauline opened the cupboard and grabbed another jar of Vicks. This one was open and, with one swift motion, she dipped her fingers into it. Her gloved fingers.

Geez Almighty Louise.

"What," I asked, my voice hoarse, "will Arvo think if you kill me?"

She was so close I could inhale her breath. It smelled like raw fury.

She grinned and her long, narrow face suddenly reminded me of a vicious jack o' lantern.

"It will hurt him and he will find out, once again, how I've felt all these years."

She started to move toward me and I fought down a surge of panic. I kept contact with her eyes and slid my right hand into the pocket of the fur jacket. I curled my fingers around my weapon and slid it out of the pocket, ripping the ancient lining. Luckily, the timing was perfect. Just as Pauline lunged for my face with the Vicks, I aimed at her eyes with my canister of artificial snow.

She shrieked and scrubbed her own face, heedless of the tainted ointment on her hands. She'd collapsed on the floor when, a moment later, thunder exploded overhead and, in what can only be described as a suitably Biblical touch, a plague of frogs, in the form of splintered glass, rained down upon us.

I ignored the intrusion and wrenched off my jacket, trying to get close enough to Pauline Maki to wipe the poison off her face.

And then three things happened almost simultaneously. I became aware of Arvo on his knees next to me, holding Pauline's hand. Sheriff Clump lurched through the door and hollered at Elwood, "Cut her, deputy!"

And a pair of strong arms airlifted me and a hand pressed me against a leather-covered shoulder and I could hear Jace Night Wind's voice in my ear.

"Geez Louise. Geez Almighty Louise, Umlaut."

# THIRTY-FIVE

"Tell me again how Aunt Hatti flocked Mrs. Maki," Charlie begged my husband.

My niece sat cross-legged on the floor next to Reid Night Wind, who was rubbing Larry's tummy. Reid seemed to be amused rather than annoyed by Charlie's hero worship and Larry, upside down, his stubby legs in the air, was ecstatic with the whole business.

Jace was next to me on the love-seat in mom's parlor. He looked somewhat the worse for wear, as added to the blisters and burns from the explosion were scrapes and abrasions from his free-fall through the glass ceiling of Pauline's greenhouse. Sonya had made him a makeshift sling to ease the pressure on his dislocated shoulder.

He'd staged the rescue for me which, in the end, hadn't been necessary, but still I cherished the moment.

Miss Irene chose to celebrate the occasion with a Psalm.

"The pastures are clothed with flocks, the valleys also are covered over with corn; they shout for joy, they also sing."

"Your aunt was very brave," Reid said, with a wink at his big brother. "In a mano-a-mano war of controlled substances, she picked the right weapon."

"Shouldn't it be womano-a-womano," Sonya asked, playfully. "And the best womano won."

"Hatti took an unnecessary risk," Jace said. "She should have waited for backup before going into the lion's den to confront a killer."

"I didn't know she was the killer," I said, simply. "I thought it was Arvo. I hadn't figured it out even though the clues were there. It was never about money, except for Pauline's conviction that Arvo had married her for her family's fortune. She had spent twenty-five years trying to earn his love by being the perfect helpmate. They'd developed a rhythm, a comfort level with one another and she told herself she was satisfied with that."

"And then disaster struck, in the form of a lovely young girl who gave Arvo what Pauline hadn't been able to give him: a chance to be a father."

"I don't get it," Reid said. "Arvo Maki wasn't interested in Liisa romantically. There was still room for Pauline in that family picture." I nodded.

"Theoretically. But, for whatever reason, Liisa didn't warm to her. Pauline felt excluded. The coming baby, with its promise of another generation for Arvo to love, was the final straw."

"So she was behind all of it," Elli said. "The attack on Pops, the sticky bombs on the vehicles, the aconite poisoning in the Vicks."

"That's right," I said. "She told me all of it. I should have hit the record button on my phone but I never even thought of it."

"But Arvo did," Sonya said, somberly. "He must have suspected Pauline from the first and, even though he wouldn't turn her in, he rigged up a recording device in the greenhouse so that if anyone," she looked at me,—"got into a confrontation with her, there would be a record."

"The recording may not hold up in court," Jace said, "but it, along with Hatti's statement, was enough to get her arrested without bail."

"Poor Arvo," Charlie said.

"I guess," Sofi said, "but it all goes back to him. He was an excellent husband all except for the most important thing. He just couldn't love her."

"Jace," Charlie said, as if she'd known him for years instead of hours, "tell us again how Hatti saved herself with the artificial snow. And then tell us how you dropped through the roof."

"A bumbling batman," he said, with a rueful smile. "Too little, too late. Hatti had saved herself. She didn't really need me at all."

I wanted to tell him that I had needed him, that I'd always needed him, but things were still unresolved between us.

"In the end," I said, "Jace saved Pauline by wiping the Vicks off her face."

"I'll tell you the whole story," Reid said, turning to the girl next to him. Charlie's eyes lit up and her face turned bright pink. "Jace and I were in Frog Creek. The sheriff had decided to release me for the moment due to lack of evidence and we got in Hatti's Jeep. The snow was falling hard and fast and there must have been ice underneath because we cruised into a snowbank. Jace got out his phone, listened to the message from Hatti, and first thing he did was to call 911."

Everyone in the room leaned forward as if with baited breath, even though we'd already heard the story several times.

"The 911 call was forwarded to Red Jacket's Mobile One. The call was answered and we gave our location and twenty minutes later, Arvo Maki showed up in his hearse. We both wondered if it was a trap. After all, we still thought Maki was the murderer. But then I remembered Liisa telling me about how the hearse was the heaviest vehicle in town and therefore the safest in snow. She said he got called out on a daily basis during the winter months but that he never complained. So we got in. He paused and smiled at Charlie, whose face grew even redder.

"Arvo told us that the service for Liisa Pelonen and her father had been postponed until tomorrow because of the weather and Jace said something about Hatti having missed the memo because she'd left a message that she was heading over to the funeral home this afternoon."

"What did Arvo say to that?" Charlie asked.

"He said, Holy Wha! And all the color drained out of his face and then he pumped the gas."

I noticed Reid had embellished the story since the previous telling by incorporating a description of Arvo's complexion.

"We were on Tamarack Street when Arvo told us he was afraid

Hatti was in trouble. It seems he has known all along that his wife killed Liisa."

"Poor man," Sonya said. "He must have been torn between the desire to do the right thing and his sense of loyalty to his wife."

I was aware of the tension in Jace's upper arm and along his thigh, the points where our bodies touched.

"Tell us what happened when you got back to the funeral home," Elli said, although, she, too, had already heard the story.

"We cased the joint," Reid said to Charlie, twirling a fake mustache. She giggled. "We discovered they were in the greenhouse and we split up. Maki took the door from the kitchen, I took the one near the sauna and Jace, well, he took the roof."

"Why the roof?" Sonya asked.

"We didn't know what kind of weapon Mrs. Maki had and we figured we had the best chance of saving Hatti if we converged from all angles." He grinned at me. "Little did we know she was armed with her trusty canister of snow."

"Believe me, the help was needed," I said. "I'd surprised Pauline and stopped her for a minute but she would have recovered and come after me again. There was no way she could let it go, not after what she'd told me."

"Poor Pauline," Aunt Ianthe said. "She'd wanted a child for so many years and then, when she finally got one, it all backfired on her."

I hated to publicly disagree with my aunt but I'd thought a lot about what had happened.

"You know, I think it was Arvo who longed for a child. Pauline wanted one because she thought it would make him happy and, more than that, that it would make him love her."

Aunt Ianthe nodded but repeated her first remark.

"Poor Pauline."

"Love suffers long and is kind; love does not envy; love does not parade itself," Miss Irene said, quoting First Corinthians thirteen.

"Quite right, Irene," Aunt Ianthe said. "Quite right."

On those words, the front door opened and Pops and Mom entered the parlor.

"You all came over to welcome us," Pops said, with a big smile and lots of hugs.

"No, Carl," Aunt Ianthe said, giving her nephew a kiss on the cheek. "We are here because of our heroine, Henrikki."

Pops's blue eyes rested on me and I felt the comfort and warmth that had supported me all my life.

"Well, then, Hatti-girl," he said. "I think you have a story to tell us, eh?"

When I'd finished and my parents had had a chance to react to the story, the room was silent for a moment. Miss Irene filled in the blank.

"And that is not the only news," she said. "We are knitting heirloom lace."

"Yes," Aunt Ianthe chimed in. "My shawl will be for Liisa so that she will know she was loved."

I blinked hard at the kind sentiment. And because I could not help noticing that the warm arm and thigh next to me had moved away. I felt abandoned. Again. This time, though, I did not intend to take it lying down.

"I'm going to take Larry for a walk," I said, turning to Jace, "would you like to come with me?"

# THIRTY-SIX

The storm had finally blown itself out. The air was fresh and clear, the stars visible in the night sky. The plowed snow, mounded in piles along Calumet Street, obliterated the curbs and sidewalks and forced us to walk in the middle of the road.

Since there was literally no traffic at all, it wasn't a problem.

"Do you want to tell me what's wrong?"

He glanced down at me.

"You mean aside from the fact that you were nearly poisoned by a murderer?"

I ignored that.

"Everything changed when my folks arrived home."

"Sure. The focus was off you."

I ignored that, too.

"You don't like my folks and there's no reason for it. You met them for the first time half an hour ago. What gives?"

"Your mother is very nice. Your sister looks just like her. I wonder if you take after your father."

"My father?" I studied him. "Is this about my birth father?"

"Of course not. It's nothing. Listen, I'm going to take Reid back to D.C. with me. He needs something to do and he's expressed an interest in working for the law firm. If he decides to go to law school, I'll help him out."

"You won't force him to take the hard road you did by enlisting in the marines first?"

Jace shrugged. "I want him to have a chance."

The old, familiar feeling of helplessness burned inside me and I gathered my *Sisu*. Whatever he said would hurt me less than another year or more of silence and wondering.

"You want a chance for Reid. What about a chance for us?"

An obstinate look appeared on his face and his lips pressed into a straight line.

I grabbed his arm and stopped in the middle of the street and we faced each other in the moonlight.

"No more stonewalling. If you want a divorce, I'll give you a divorce. Heck, I may even initiate a divorce. But first I want to know what this big issue is. I want to know why you appear to be fond of me but are bound and determined to break up this marriage."

"Don't ask me, Hatti."

"Why not?"

"Because I have found myself to be very weak around you. If we were to get back together, we would both come to grief."

Jace was and is an excellent orator and I'd heard him speak passionately about a number of things, including the rights of Native Americans. I'd never heard him speak with this kind of hopelessness.

"Tell me."

He looked down at me for a long minute and then, suddenly, he put his arms around me and pulled me against him and then he kissed me. I should have broken it off right away but by the time I'd figured that out, I was going down for the third time. When it was over he put his hands on my shoulders and held my gaze.

"I can't ask you to choose between your family and me."

"Why would you have to?"

He sighed and dropped his hands.

"Last year, when I stopped off at the reservation on my way back from South Dakota, I found a box of my mother's papers. They included my real birth certificate. The one I'd used before, provided by my mom, had been a false one. This was the first time I'd seen the name of my natural father."

"Wow," I said, but there was a cold sensation behind my nose and I sensed a mountain of pain around the next corner. "Are you going to tell me who it was?"

"It was Carl Lehtinen."

"Pops?"

"Pops to you. The devil incarnate to me."

I understood. Without any further explanation, I understood why Jace had felt so gobsmacked by the name on the birth certificate. I understood why he wanted to sever all ties with me. The man who had made my childhood enchanting had made Jace's life, and Reid's and even Miriam's a soulless misery.

Just for a second, my heart felt like a boulder and then I looked up at the stark grief in his face.

"It's not true."

He shook his head, slightly. "Denial won't help."

"He isn't your father, Jace. He couldn't be. There's no way Pops could skip out on a teenaged girl and gone off to marry another woman and become a father to her children."

"He undoubtedly didn't know my mother was pregnant."

I shook my head. "He's not like that. Careless, I mean. He doesn't leave loose ends, especially not with people. Look at the way he befriended your brother instead of arresting him. There are certain things a person can do and certain things he can't do. Pops would never have abandoned you. But don't take my word for it. Let's go talk to him."

# THIRTY-SEVEN

My folks were just hanging out in the kitchen, enjoying being home for the first time in a month. Pops was on the mend but he was changed. The man who had always seemed larger than life to me had lost weight during his six weeks in traction. There were more lines in his face and even his shock of white hair seemed duller. The blue eyes, though, still twinkled and he still radiated the calm strength and the deep kindness that I'd always known.

I felt Jace's hand jerk in mine when I asked if we could talk to him in the study.

Pops had a knack of finding the right thing to say in any situation and I half expected him to welcome Jace into the family but he remained silent, a thoughtful look on his wrinkled face.

When Jace got up from the old sofa where he and I were seated and started to pace the room, the tension ratcheted up.

"Hatti," Pops said, softly. "What is this then, eh?"

"Jace believes you are his natural father," I said, unable to come up with a more subtle way of introducing the topic. "Your name is on the birth certificate he found among Miriam Night Wind's possessions."

"Ah," Pops said. "I see."

I looked at this man who had reared me and felt all the impossibility of the charge.

"It isn't true, is it? You wouldn't have abandoned a teen-aged girl."

My stepfather passed a hand over his face, as if to shake off memory or fatigue, and he sighed.

"I will tell you what I think and what I know," he said. "It is many years now and time for the truth." He looked directly at Jace, his eyes filled with compassion. "I knew your mama, for sure. The summer after college, I was one of those hired through a federal grant to work on the reservation to put in sewer and water lines. We had only three months to do the work and it was decided that, in order to make the most of the daylight hours, we would stay with families on the rez rather than drive back and forth to our homes in Red Jacket and Hancock and down in Gogebic County."

Jace had stopped pacing but the deep furrow between his eyebrows revealed his reluctance to take Pops at his word. Pops didn't respond to the anger.

"We worked all the time, but on Saturday nights there was always a bonfire and picnic and the workers mixed with the teenagers and young adults on the rez. It was summer and we were young and, naturally, some of us fell in love. Or, at least," he added, "thought we did. Your mama, Miriam, was the prettiest, liveliest girl on the rez. All the boys liked her and, forgive me for saying this, Jace, she was a bit wild."

That wasn't news. Jace had told me, back in the early days of our acquaintance, that his grandparents hadn't known what to do with their willful, impulsive daughter.

Jace had propped himself against Pops's desk. Now his lip curled and he spoke for the first time.

"So you decided to take advantage of her."

Pops didn't take offense.

"She picked me out, probably because I was the oldest in the group, probably seven or eight years older than she was. We would talk at the bonfires and sometimes she stopped by to see me at work during the daytime. Then one time she kissed me and said she loved me."

"He kissed her," Jace said, looking at me. "You, of all people, know where that leads."

Pops smiled at me.

"In this case, Miriam and me, it led nowhere. I explained that I was too old for her, that we must be friends only."

I heard a low moan and knew it had come from me. If I knew anything about teen-age girls, the "friends-only" talk would have just made Miriam more determined.

"She asked me more times to talk but I was careful not to be alone with her." He threw an apologetic look at Jace. "I'm sorry to speak like that of your mama."

"Never mind that," Jace said, anger in his voice, "how do you explain the pregnancy?"

Pops hesitated.

"What did not work with me, was successful with someone else. As far as I know, it was just the one time and the other man, who was only seventeen at the time, was very repentant. I believe it did not occur to him that there might be a baby. At least, not then. I don't think he knows, even now. We have never spoken of it in thirty years."

My jaw dropped. I'd expected Pops to say he knew nothing about Miriam Night Wind.

"You know Jace's father?"

"*Joo.* " Yes.

My husband wasn't ready for that information. He had been nursing his grudge against Pops for a long time.

"Why is your name on my birth certificate?"

"That I can only guess," Pops said. "I left the Keweenaw in the autumn of that year, to work as an engineer in the copper mines in Minnesota and I didn't have any family, except Aunt Ianthe, left in this area. Perhaps Miriam reasoned that she would get less hassle from her family if she named someone who was out of reach. She may have wanted to protect the man in question or," again he looked apologetic, "she may have wanted some revenge on me for the rejection. I'm sorry, Jace. I did not know I was on your birth certificate. For the record, I would be proud to be your papa."

Anger still smoldered in Jace's silver eyes but it was damped down, like a dying campfire.

"Pops?"

He nodded to me as if acknowledging the unspoken question. Then he turned back to Jace.

"I hope you can find it in your heart to forgive him."

Suddenly I knew who it was. I think I had known during the entire story. I felt a tidal wave of sympathy for the man who never knew he was a father and for the son who had never known any father at all.

"It's Arvo, isn't it?"

Pops nodded.

"He is my oldest friend," he said. "And I know him well enough to know he will be overjoyed if he finds out about this. Overjoyed and full of guilt."

"Will you tell him?" I asked. Pops shook his head.

"That is for his son to decide."

It wasn't until Pops had left us and we'd been alone, without words, for some time, that either of us spoke.

"Do you believe him?"

He nodded. "There's no reason to lie at this point."

"The birth certificate is why you broke up with me, isn't it? You believed that the man who had abandoned you and your mom was the stepdad I kept raving about."

"That's probably part of it. My memories of my mother, drunk, sick, prostituted, derided, have made it difficult for me to forgive. I didn't think I could bear to be near the man who had destroyed my mother's life and I did not want to make you choose between your family and me."

"Do you still think that? That Arvo destroyed Miriam Night Wind's life?"

He got a funny look on his face.

"Not entirely. She was in a tough situation but she could have gotten help from her own parents if she'd stayed on the Copper Eagle." He stared out the window at the snow. "I should have helped her more when I was old enough. I should have stuck around here while Reid was growing up. I don't know that I can be a good husband to you, Hatti."

The highs and lows of the last few days, including the relief at discovering the reason for the break-up, and the regret that I wasn't going to get the fairytale ending, after all, converged on me. I excused myself and shot up to my room where I buried my face in my pillow and cried.

# THIRTY-EIGHT

With the case solved and Reid out of danger, Jace said he had to get back to D.C. to catch up with his own work. I accepted that along with the long, passionless kiss as the grand finale and with every mail delivery, I expected to receive divorce papers as my Christmas present.

It hadn't happened. At least, not yet.

In fact, he'd called a few times and we'd talked. Not about anything significant. Fishing. Hockey. What was happening in town, including and especially, with Pauline Maki.

For whatever reason, I began to feel better about things. Don't get me wrong. I had no idea what he was thinking, but, for the first time, in a very long time, I felt as if we were friends. He said he'd call on New Year's Eve to talk about where we stood, to settle our future. I wasn't sure what he would say or even what I would say. The year apart had changed things between us. I'd come back to the Keweenaw in an emotional body bag but I'd come to realize that it was my home. I was beginning to realize that, even though I still loved Jace, I was reluctant to return to D.C.

The prospect of that fateful call was in the back of my mind while we made molasses popcorn balls and drank wine, while we gossiped and worked on our heirloom lace while we watched *An Affair to Remember.*

By eleven o'clock we were all weeping and Sofi said she was ready to call it a night.

"You can't," I said, scandalized. "It isn't midnight yet. And, besides, we still have to cast tin."

"And, don't forget," Elli added, "we agreed to ring in the new year with a sauna followed by a roll in the snow."

My sister made a face.

"We're not six, you guys. We don't need to tell fortunes and make snow angels."

I wondered at the edge in her voice. Something had been bothering Sofi for the last few days. Now Charlie was down in Lake Worth, Florida with our folks and Sofi was alone. I was worried about her. That is, I was worried about her in between being worried about myself. Why hadn't Jace called? It was almost midnight.

"Sofi, are you okay?"

She turned on me. "I'm fine. You're the one waiting for a call."

They all knew about the proposed call, of course. I began to wish I'd kept my big mouth shut.

"Do you know what you're going to say to him, Hatti?" Sonya asked.

"I guess it depends on what he says to me."

"You can't expect him to come live in Red Jacket, you know," Sofi said. "His career is in D.C. Besides, the Keweenaw must remind him of his mother and the trauma of his entire childhood. If you want him, H, you're going to have to go back East."

I'd never thought of it that way. Of course he wouldn't want to come back here. So there would be no compromise. Then I realized I was getting ahead of myself. He might very well call and tell me the whole thing was over. He'd done it before.

"Have you ever noticed," Sonya said, trying to lighten the mood, "that nothing about men is easy?"

"You wonder why God invented them," Elli said.

"Probably part of the portfolio of punishment for Eve biting that apple," I said. "Let's cast some tin."

Sofi mentioned a headache and we let her go. Then the rest of us gathered in Elli's kitchen around our grandmother's tin basin filled with icy-cold water. There was a pan of boiling water on the burner and the three of us shifted between the two pots as if we were McBeth's weird sisters whipping up a brew.

When all was ready, Elli threw a horseshoe-shaped metal charm into the hot water. A moment later she lifted it out with a long-handled spoon and transferred it to the cold water. We had already explained the odd custom to Sonya.

"This first one is for Sofi," Elli said, as she turned off the overhead light and left the room in semi-darkness. "The metal melts and forms a shape and we interpret the shadow of that shape to predict what will happen during the next year."

I lit a bayberry candle and positioned it to cast a shadow.

We all stared down at the concoction until finally, Sonya yelped.

"It's a rabbit! As clear as day. See the long ears and the little cottontail?"

"A rabbit? Her future is Easter?"

"Well," Sonya said, "in Native American mythology the rabbit can be a trickster."

"That's all my sister needs," I said, "more tricks."

"Isn't the Easter Bunny a harbinger of spring and new life?" Elli asked.

Sonya and I shared a look.

"New life. Fertility," I said. "How can that affect Sofi?"

We all knew that Sofi and Lars barely spoke to one another and that, even if they ever reconciled, they were unlikely to have another child. They'd spent more than ten years grappling with what's called secondary infertility.

"I don't think the tin is working tonight," I said, finally.

"Let's keep going," Elli said. "This one's for me." After a moment she shuddered. "It's a parallelogram. Just what I needed, a reminder of my disastrous year in geometry."

Geometry had been the tenth grade and, coincidentally, the year she and Grant Aaltonen had decided to marry. The decision had stood for almost three years until he, abruptly, married someone else.

"A parallelogram could also be a diamond," Sonya said. "Maybe you're going to be rich. Or married." She smiled.

"You try it," Elli said so Sonya cast her own horseshoe charm.

"It looks like a steak knife," I said. "And that's odd because you're a vegetarian."

"A knife can also symbolize cutting," Elli piped up. "Separating things or pruning. Like clearing away the dead wood. Do you have dead wood in your life, Sonya?"

Sonya's smile, for once, didn't reach her eyes.

"Don't we all," I said, hastily. "Everyone can use a thorough house-cleaning and a fresh start. Let me try."

I knew perfectly well it was just a superstition, a parlor game for a cold, snowy New Year's Eve, but still, I hoped I'd get something encouraging. Something like a heart or an XO for kisses and hugs. Heck, I'd settle for the shape of a telephone. It seemed to take my metal blob a long time to morph and settle. I wondered if it was because my life was moving in slow motion but figured it was more likely that the ice had melted and the hot water was cooling.

And then a shadow picture emerged that was so clear, so unmistakable, that we all gasped in shock.

"A skull-and-crossbones," Elli said. Her voice shook.

"Hey," I said, bracingly. "It probably means I'm going to be kidnapped by pirates."

"You know what I think?" Sonya said, half-kidding, "I think it means you've found your calling. You're destined to investigate another murder."

There was no time to contemplate her words because finally, at long last, well after midnight, my phone rang. I just stared at it, aware of an immense fatigue. Was this it then? Was I about to learn—or seal—my marital fate? I sucked in a deep breath and answered, using the traditional greeting.

"*Onnellista Uutta Vuotta!*" Happy New Year!

There was a pause and then a deep, masculine voice. The wrong voice.

"*Hei*, Squirt. I hope your year is starting out better than mine."

"For a moment I was so disappointed I couldn't breathe. Then I forced out some words. "Lars. What's up? Where are you?"

"Jail."

I closed my eyes. After three years of abstinence, he'd been drinking.

"I'll come and get you. What's the bail?"

"This isn't a DUI, Hatti. I'm here for the duration."

I didn't understand. "Duration of what?"

"Until Clump finds enough evidence to formally arrest me."

"I don't understand."

"It's simple enough." I pictured his loose-limbed shrug. "When I got home tonight, I found a girl in my bed. A dead girl."

"What? How? Who?"

He answered on the last of my questions.

"She is—or was—a waitress at the Black Fly in Chassell. Her name's Cricket Koski."

Cricket Koski. The woman my sister had nicknamed the insect.

Three years earlier Lars had indulged in a one-night stand with her, the confession of which led to his divorce. I sent up a prayer of thanks that Sofi had gone home early tonight and wasn't here for this call.

"I didn't kill her," he said.

"I know," I replied, meaning it. "How did she get there?"

"Beats me. The thing is, I need to find out and I can't do it from Frog Creek's finest accommodation. I need your help, Squirt."

"You've got it."

"Thanks, Hatti. Come by in the morning. Early. Before Clump gets in. Okay?"

I disconnected.

"You were right," I said to Sonya Stillwater. "There's been another murder." I paused, then told them what Lars had told me.

"Holy wha," Elli said. She and Sonya looked at each other, nodded and then back at me.

"All right, Sherlock," Sonya said. "Just tell us how we can help."

# A DOUBLE-POINTED MURDER

## THE BAIT & STITCH COZY MYSTERY SERIES, BOOK 3

The girl with the hole in her chest was no Jane Doe. She was not only known to me, she was a relation.

If you count adultery as one of the ties that bind.

Cricket Koski, a barmaid from the Black Fly Roadhouse down in Chassell, had been the catalyst in my sister's divorce three years earlier, a breach that was only now beginning to heal. I shook my head. I was pretty sure, like ninety-nine-point-nine percent sure, that the reconciliation between my sister Sofi and her ex, Lars, would not survive the discovery of the 'Insect' in Lars's bed. The fact that Cricket was dead would not make much difference to my sister.

I should probably point out that I'm not a cop or even a private detective, but I've had a year of law school, and even more importantly, I'm available. Up here on the remote witch's finger of land called the Keweenaw Peninsula, that's a big deal. So when Lars called me from his jail cell, of course I came.

The barmaid was about my age (twenty-eight) and, as far as I knew, had lived as innocuous a life as my own. Although, in my own defense, my professional life had experienced a slight uptick recently when I took over the operation of Pops's bait shop and added knitting supplies. My personal life was, of course, a more dismal story. But the point was, that I could think of no reason for anyone wanting to turn Cricket Koski into a shish kebab. Anyone other than my sister.

"Weird wound."

I jumped. I'd completely forgotten my presence at the Frog Creek morgue at zero-dark-hundred was thanks to Waino Aho, the sheriff's deputy with whom I'd experienced my first kiss fifteen years earlier during Vacation Bible School at St. Heikki's. I gazed up at the handsome, if vacant, Nordic features then back at the perfect shape of the aperture underneath the victim's perky left breast. The surrounding skin was smooth and the wound was bloodless.

"A wormhole," Waino said.

I knew he wasn't referring to the hypothetical, topological feature that would be (if it exists) a shortcut through time and space. When Waino said "wormhole" he was referring to the orifice in a piece of fruit created by a burrowing maggot.

"A nail-gun coulda did it."

"Maybe. Or a skewer."

His eyes widened. "A what?"

"One of those long, metal things people roast marshmallows on."

"I use a birch stick."

I nodded. A stick of birch is used to fashion a *vihta*, a whisk used to bring the blood to the surface in a sauna.

"Something long and thin," I said, following my own train of thought. The truth slammed into me with the force of a felled tree. Triumph at my extraordinary deductive powers caused my voice to shake. "A tool with a long shaft, tapered at the end, and made out of the same carbon fiber composite used in stealth fighter jets and formula one racing cars."

Waino stared at me, uncomprehendingly, as I paused for dramatic effect.

"A knitting needle," I said. "A size-five, double-pointed knitting needle like the ones we use on mittens and socks."

His blue eyes met mine and my childhood buddy's sudden mental leap made my heart plummet.

"If she was kilt with a knittin' needle, Hatti," he said, "your sister musta did it, then."

---

**Available in Paperback and eBook from Your Favorite Bookstore or Online Retailer**

# ALSO BY ANN YOST

A Pattern For Murder

A Yarn Over Murder

A Double Pointed Murder

A Fair Isle Murder

# ABOUT THE AUTHOR

Ann Yost comes from Ann Arbor, Michigan and a writing family whose single greatest accomplishment is excellent spelling.

After six years at the University of Michigan she completed her degree in English literature and spent ten years working as a reporter, copy editor and humor columnist for three daily newspapers. Her most notable story at the Ypsilanti Press involved the tarring and feathering of a high school principal.

When she moved with her Associated Press reporter husband to the Washington D.C. area, she did freelance work for the Washington Post, including first-person humor stories on substitute teaching and little league umpiring.

She did feature writing for the Charles Stewart Mott Foundation on building community in low-income neighborhoods and after-school programs throughout the country.

While her three children were in high school, Ann began to write romantic suspense novels. Later, she turned to the Finnish-American community in Michigan's remote Upper Peninsula for her Hatti Lehtinen mystery series.

She lives in Northern Virginia with her husband and her enterprising mini-goldendoodle, Toby.

**www.annyost.com**

 facebook.com/Ann-Yost-Author-Page-766297356800373